WISHING
FOR
Christmas

CAROLINE STOWE

WISHING FOR *Christmas*

HARPETH ROAD
PRESS
Nashville

HARPETH ROAD PRESS

Published by Harpeth Road Press (USA)
P.O. Box 158184
Nashville, TN 37215

Paperback: 978-1-963483-29-1
eBook: 978-1-963483-30-7
Library of Congress Control Number: 2025947609

Wishing for Christmas: A Wonderfully Magical Holiday Romance

Copyright © Caroline Stowe, 2025

Cover Design by Vanessa Mendozzi
Cover Images © Shutterstock

Harpeth Road Press, October 2025

For military spouses, my cherished community for so many years

CHAPTER ONE

CLARA

The urgent clack of high heels against a marble floor sent an echo throughout the corridor of the Darlington Hotel. Clara Jenkins glanced at her watch. It was already past five o'clock, and she now felt slightly ridiculous for having spent the entire day hiding in her office. She slowed her steps and drew in a breath. She couldn't avoid this conversation any longer.

Clara rounded the corner into the lobby and let out a gasp. The Darlington was always warm, inviting, and full of elegance. Tonight, though, it was also perfectly decorated for Christmas. An eighteen-foot evergreen radiated with the bright glow of thousands of tiny white lights; the crystal chandeliers glimmered in the fading light of an early December evening; and fluffy garlands of wintery frost were draped across the length of the front desk.

Clara inhaled a deep breath of fresh pine and noticed the tension lift from her shoulders. The lobby felt both luxurious and delightfully cozy, like a beautiful fur coat. She hurried over to the tree, reaching out to touch one of the perfectly placed ornaments glittering with gold. Underneath it, packages wrapped in glossy red paper sat atop a plush ivory blanket of synthetic snow. A fire crackled, and the soft jingle of a holiday tune played overhead. Like a layer of freshly fallen snow glistening under the moonlight, tonight, the Darlington was sparkling.

Clara gave herself a mental pat on the back for hiring a professional decorator this year. It was exactly what she needed to impress Mr. Spencer at their meeting next week.

As the sales manager of the hotel, Clara brought in the accounts that kept the property thriving. Her top clients provided consistent guests and meetings, ensuring the Darlington remained the leading luxury hotel in the area. And keeping the place looking impressive, especially at Christmas, was a big part of that job.

Clara gazed at the glow of candlelight that sent a shimmer across the polished floors and let out a quiet sigh of delight.

With perfect timing, the opening notes of "Jingle Bells" sounded from her pocket.

As she checked her phone, she couldn't help but smile at her background picture. A recent photo of Brent beamed back at her. With his soft brown eyes and deep dimples, just a picture of him gave her stomach a flutter of excitement, even after two months of dating. An Air Force flight suit adorned his tall, muscular frame as he posed in front of a military jet.

She noticed the incoming text was from him, and it felt like an early Christmas present.

Can't wait for our date tomorrow night!

Clara immediately typed a response, her fingers flying with giddiness.

I'll be there!

She added a heart emoji—then quickly deleted it. She didn't want to get ahead of herself. Eight weeks of dating was certainly not long enough to discuss *love* yet. Still, heart emojis were certainly flying around in her head as she thought about Brent.

She sent the message sans emoji and then typed another right afterward.

Have a good flight tonight!

Clara felt as if she was sparkling, just like the hotel, as she thought about Brent. What better time than Christmas to really get to know each other? It's what she loved most about this time of year—the possibilities, especially for romance. And *this* Christmas was full of promise.

"Clara, do you have a minute to talk?" Her boss's deep voice sliced through the moment.

She squeezed her eyes shut and tried to hide the obvious wince on her face. She forced herself to turn toward Matthew Edmunds, the general manager, with a smile. Here it was, the moment she'd been dreading all day.

"Sure." The high-pitched discomfort in her voice was clear, and she hoped he didn't notice. She walked toward him, her overwhelming desire to suddenly vanish hidden behind the professional square of her shoulders.

Matthew stood with his feet apart, chin raised, and arms folded across his chest. His striking good looks, combined with a hint of swagger, gave him a more distinguished look than most other thirty-five-year-old men.

"The decorator you hired sure did a great job." He tossed a nod of approval at the tree. "I know I give you leeway over the lobby at Christmastime, but I'm curious to know why you didn't decorate it this year like you normally do."

Clara considered telling him the truth—that she had simply been too overwhelmed with her accounts this year to think about decorating. She'd been spending late hours in her office, poring over sales reports and budgets to uncover as much potential business for the hotel as possible, and she was on pace to finish out the year with record-breaking revenues. Still, with her sights set higher than the sales department, the last thing she needed was for Matthew to think she couldn't manage her current responsibilities.

Besides, it wasn't that she *didn't* have the time. She could have committed a couple of days to it like she always had in the past. Last year, she and the staff had done it themselves using the Darlington's own decorations. The lounge sat in chaos for days, with the hotel's expensive decor strewn all over the place, and Clara had to manage it all between her client visits. It was fun decorating with the staff, but it was complicated too. She supposed the honest answer was that she'd wanted it done quickly and easily this time. With this critical meeting looming, she wanted to get straight to the beautiful result—without all the hassle. Mission accomplished.

She shrugged. "It's important it looks perfect this year. If I can impress Mr. Spencer during next week's meeting and finally land that account in the new year, well . . ." She ran a finger down the newly decorated table and admired the shimmering garland. "Well, it couldn't hurt."

Matthew's smile held a hint of intrigue. "It sounds like my sales manager has some big plans."

Clara gave a nervous laugh in reply. "So, what was it you wanted to talk to me about?" She tried to sound casual as if she hadn't given him a single thought all day when, really, it was *all* she had been able to think about. Ever since he had approached her that morning, wanting to discuss something *rather important*, she'd made painstaking efforts to avoid him. She braced herself now for what she knew was coming.

Clara liked him enough—as a boss. He was dependable and familiar after all the years they'd worked together. It was their personal relationship that was messy. After nearly eight years of on-again, off-again dating, things between her and Matthew were never simple. The last time he'd wanted to discuss something *rather important*, it had been to break up with her. She'd been crushed, but had quietly agreed to a mature and professional working relationship. What choice did she have? She loved her job and couldn't imagine working anywhere else.

She supposed that as another year had gone by, he was due for *another* change of heart—an idea she had no intention of indulging this time. She smiled to herself as she thought again about Brent. No chance whatsoever.

Clara took a deep breath, mentally preparing the firm but gentle rejection she'd been rehearsing all day. Sure, some feelings would always be there between them, it was only natural. But it was best they closed the door on that part of their relationship for good. As rational as it sounded in her head, she knew putting it into practice was another thing entirely.

Matthew said nothing, just motioned her over to the seating area in the center of the lobby. Clara blew a puff of air out the side of her mouth. She sat on the leather sofa, resigning herself to the painfully awkward conversation she knew was in store for her. She crossed her ankles and wished she was wearing pants instead of an unforgiving pencil skirt. She placed her hands in her lap and waited as Matthew poured himself a cup of coffee from the silver carafe on the end table.

He threw her a glance to offer her one.

She shook her head, just wanting to get it all over with.

He sat across from her, casually crossing one leg over the other. Matthew Edmunds, never Matt, was the ideal representative of the Darlington brand—impressive, beautiful—but at a high price. His dark hair was always perfectly styled, and his eyes were a piercing shade of green that still managed to tantalize Clara whenever he held her gaze.

He leaned forward in his chair. "I'll go ahead and cut to the chase, Clara."

Her stomach knotted.

"I'm leaving the Darlington," he said.

Her eyes popped open in surprise. "What?"

"I've been given an incredible opportunity. I've accepted an offer to manage the new hotel on Fifth Street."

Clara could tell he expected her to be impressed. She stared at him, her brain slightly disoriented as it tried to quickly process this unexpected information. "What?" she repeated.

"I know, you probably weren't expecting this."

No, she certainly was not expecting *this*. "You're leaving?"

He nodded.

She immediately exhaled with relief. An undeniable grin spread across her face before she could even stop it. She forced herself to temper her reaction and cleared her throat. "That's great, Matthew. Congratulations," she said.

An intense wave of relief washed over her at the realization that this wasn't an attempt to rekindle their romance at all. Instead, this was the best news possible. With Matthew leaving, she could finally rid herself of the constant stress that came along with working so closely beside him every day. The blurry lines between their personal and professional relationship would no longer exist. Her ex-boyfriend and his fickle heart would no longer matter to her. She could finally close that door and move forward with her new relationship without that additional baggage.

That was all she wanted at this point in her life—a simple, uncomplicated relationship with Brent. She felt herself fall into a daze of solace as Brent's dimpled smile appeared in her mind.

She shook her head quickly, her thoughts returning to the reality of the present conversation. It took a moment for her brain to catch up with what Matthew had been telling her. She held up her hands to slow things down a bit. Something still felt off, and she was beginning to realize what it was. There wasn't actually a new hotel on Fifth Street. At least, not yet.

"Didn't they just start construction on that hotel? It must be months away from opening."

"A year, actually—at least. But that's what I wanted to talk to you about."

"Okay."

"I've been meeting with corporate about plans for the Darlington's future after I leave." He paused to take a sip of his coffee, probably guessing that the suspense was killing her.

Clara held her breath. The news she had been longing for—although she would never admit it—was just within reach.

After the world's longest drink, he looked at her with a cocked eyebrow. "And we all agreed that *you* should be the next general manager of the Darlington."

"Really?" She let out a tiny gasp as if she hadn't been imagining this moment for years. She'd always hoped he would advocate for her when the time came. Their relationship had always remained positive—when it came to work, anyway. Clara hadn't expected it to happen so soon, though.

"Well, you earned it," said Matthew. "Your performance reports have been impressing corporate for some time now. It's apparent to everyone how hard you've been working." He gave her one of his flirty winks. "Including me."

A tingle of excitement surged through her, and she felt her cheeks grow warm. She forced herself to remain immune to his charm. "I would love—"

Matthew held up his hand, suddenly cutting her off. "That is after you get some additional experience under your belt."

She stared at him, having absolutely no idea where this conversation was about to go.

He set down his coffee mug in front of him and leaned forward, resting his elbows on his knees. "Look, Clara, corporate feels your experience in sales would make you a great manager for the hotel."

She nodded, urging him to continue.

"*But* they think you need to learn more first."

"Learn more?"

"About the operations side of running the hotel. They want you to get more experience with that."

She narrowed her eyes. "And how am I supposed to do that?"

"Well, they want you to shadow me throughout the hotel for the time I have remaining here. You'll help me in the day-to-day operations and management."

"So, I'd be your . . . assistant? For a year?"

"Think of it as an internship."

"What about the sales office?"

"You'll still manage it, for now. But you'll also learn everything you need to know to run the hotel on your own. You should probably move your desk to my office too, now that I'm thinking of it."

Her eyes widened.

"And then—when the new hotel is ready—I'll move on, and this one will be yours."

Clara tried to hide the sudden collision of thoughts going on inside her head. Becoming general manager of the hotel she'd loved for so long was a dream come true. And at her age? But to spend every day of the next twelve months, if not more, alongside her ex? At least in the sales office, she had some degree of separation from him. This arrangement sounded as if they would be attached at the hip for the next year.

Typical Matthew. Wasn't it just like him to turn something as simple as a well-earned promotion into something so drawn out and tangled? She shouldn't be surprised. The whole conversation was a perfect illustration of their relationship. Here he was, building up her hopes again, only to throw some curveball in at the last second.

It didn't matter whether it was personal or business. With Matthew, things were always complicated. He was her ex-boyfriend, her current boss, and the key to her future career. He was like her ghost of Christmas past, present, and future all rolled into one hovering spirit that never seemed to stop haunting her.

On the other hand, she couldn't imagine where she'd even be in her career without him. She'd been a front-desk agent working summers during college when he'd taken a liking to her, both personally and professionally. He'd mentored her through the ranks and supported her promotion to the sales department. Sure, she had worked hard to get to where she was in her career and, deep down, Clara knew she had earned it all on her own merit. Still, she couldn't help but wonder if she would have had as much success at another hotel, or career for that matter, without him helping her along.

There was nothing she wanted more than to finally prove herself instead of always riding on Matthew's coattails. It was why she'd been spending so much extra time at work lately, building these potential client portfolios. She knew she was capable of being successful without him.

Her feelings for him weren't only about work, though. Despite *his* ever-changing feelings, he'd always been a stable presence over the years—showing up for her, making her feel taken care of. She thought about his romantic side and the way he had been able to make her heart skip a beat with one look. Perhaps he still could.

She only wished he would stop stringing her along. Clara wasn't sure why she hadn't cut that tie already, but there was something about him she couldn't seem to shake. No matter how long she'd known him, she still felt like the same smitten twenty-two-year-old she'd been when they'd met. She supposed eight years was a long time to have feelings for somebody, and they wouldn't go away overnight. She'd known for some time she needed to move on from him. It had always just been so much easier to stay.

But what else could she do now—start a new career? No, moving through the ranks somewhere else would take more time than she was willing to put in. This opportunity was simply too good to pass up. Sure, she would have to endure an uncomfortable year, but after that she would be the general manager of the Darlington Hotel.

With new resolve, Clara stuck out her hand toward him and took on the most confident posture she could manage to drive home her unwavering determination. "Okay, I accept."

His perfect white teeth gleamed back at her.

"And thank you," she added. "Really, Matthew, I appreciate what you're doing for me." As much as she hated the situation she was in, an attachment to her ex was the price she'd have to pay to reach her career goals. She only hoped this continued relationship wouldn't come at the expense of her new one. Clara gritted her teeth and promised herself this would be the last time she would need Matthew Edmunds for anything.

"But remember," she said, with a look of warning, "our relationship will *only* be professional. Understand?"

Matthew smiled back at her from underneath a raised eyebrow and shook her hand. He placed his other hand on top of hers and gave it a warm squeeze. His green eyes held her gaze.

She hated that she felt her heart quicken.

"Of course," he said as if it was the most obvious statement in the world.

She only wished it could be that simple.

CHAPTER TWO

BRENT

Major Brent McNally watched through the windscreen of the airplane as heavy snowflakes fell to the ground. He kept a watchful eye on the night sky, his mind on the weather—for the most part. He stared ahead, his attention drifting to thoughts of his new girlfriend, Clara. He wondered whether she'd made it home from work before the snow started. The snowfall could be dangerous for travel, after all.

He snapped open his lovesick eyes at the reminder and shook the dreamy grin off his face. He forced himself to focus on the mission in front of him and frowned, assessing the worsening weather. The pavement around the aircraft was covered in a slippery blanket of white—more than he would like for an impending takeoff.

He prepared himself for the disappointment. It was only a training mission to keep him current on his flying hours. A two-hour flight in the KC-46 Brent flew for the United States Air Force. Still, it annoyed him when a mission was canceled. Especially one where the plane was already on the tarmac, waiting to take off, and the pilots were antsy to get going. Hours of preparation went into planning a flight, and Brent hated it when all that work went to waste.

He looked at the pilot next to him. Major Dave Cunningham, his closest friend in the squadron, was also the aircraft commander of the flight. With his dark hair and focused eyes, Dave had the serious expression of a pilot trying to make a tough decision. As they watched the snow fall around them, they both knew what this weather meant. They probably wouldn't be flying tonight.

"Man, it's really coming down out there. We're going to be tight on our holdover time. What's the radar showing?" Brent asked, remaining hopeful. Maybe it wouldn't be as bad as they thought.

Before Dave could answer, air traffic control came over the intercom and confirmed the bad news. "Extender two niner, the group commander called, and he's closing the airfield due to heavy snowfall."

Brent pushed the button on his headset to respond. "Roger. Extender two niner copies all. Requesting a taxi to spot two thirteen." He let out a sigh and immediately pulled out his after-landing checklist to begin working on the first item. "All that work. We got the plane de-iced and anti-iced, and now we're canceled." He ran a hand through his light-brown hair, freshly cut in the military style by the barber on base.

He was dressed identically to Dave, both in their olive-green flight suits. The bag, as they called it—the one-piece uniform that zipped up the front, with the patch displaying the logo of their current command over the right breast.

Brent had excelled in pilot training, allowing him his first pick of assignments after graduation. He had always wanted to fly this amazing tanker airplane after once seeing a video of a fighter jet being refueled over the ocean. Even in his third year at this assignment, he never tired of being at the controls of this plane.

"Sorry, man, I know how much you hate it when this happens." Dave began the process of returning the aircraft's systems to their original positions.

"What, and you don't?" Brent flipped a switch on the panel above him.

"Well, yeah, it's a pain." Dave looked out the window as a childlike grin spread across his face. "But look. It's snowing."

Brent shook his head, though he couldn't help but smile too. "Guess you were stationed in California too long if a few flurries get you excited."

"These aren't a few flurries, dude. The visibility is well below half a mile." Dave began a slow taxi of the aircraft, turning the nose back toward the direction where they started. "You know, something about a good snowfall always gets me excited." He looked over at Brent with a teasing smirk. "Maybe it's the element of surprise."

"Well, I'd rather stick to the flight plan, thank you." Brent's focus remained on the list in front of him as he continued to run through his post-flight check items.

"Yeah, I know," Dave said. "You are who you are, even after all the years I've known you. You've been the same way since training. Stick to the plan, no surprises, right?"

"It's how missions are successful," he said, not looking up. Brent was slow and careful as he continued to run through each item so as not to make any mistakes. He found comfort in a good checklist, ticking things off one by one in proper order so nothing was left to chance. "Besides, not all of us get the sweet deals you do when it comes to a change in the itinerary," he said, his eyes still glued to the paperwork.

Dave's nickname in the squadron was "Good Deal Dave," for his ability to find himself stranded with maintenance problems in the most desirable locations. In fact, Dave and his crew had recently been stuck in Hawaii for a week thanks to an unexpected landing gear issue.

Dave laughed. "Yeah, I suppose surprises do tend to work out in my favor."

Brent shook his head. "This paperwork won't take much time at all. It's not like we accomplished anything on the flight plan anyway."

"Speaking of plans, did you get approved for leave?" Dave asked.

Brent put down his pencil and finally looked up from his list, his shoulders slowly rolling back. "I sure did. I'll have the whole week off for Christmas this year." He looked out the window at the falling snow. "Okay, I'll admit, snow at Christmas is pretty . . ." He considered his next word.

"Romantic?" Dave supplied.

Brent smiled. "Yeah, I suppose it is." His thoughts went back to Clara. And to Christmas. Maybe he wouldn't be flying tonight as planned. But that also meant he could spend more time on his holiday preparations. Maybe Dave was right; unpredictability could have its merits too.

"Well, this girlfriend of yours must be something else to make you smile like that during a canceled flight."

Brent shrugged, trying to play it cool. Inside, he got a shiver of excitement as thoughts of Christmas filled his mind—Clara and his first one together. Clara had been able to take some vacation days from the hotel for the same week he'd be on leave, and he was looking forward to having the time together. He'd been planning the whole week the same way he planned his flights—with confidence that all would be executed accordingly.

"Always putting in the work," Dave said, seeming to read his thoughts. "Even for your romantic Christmas."

Brent thought about his own nickname within the squadron, "Rand." It started, as most nicknames do, with an embarrassing story from pilot training. He had made some navigational errors in an early check ride that nearly resulted in him landing the plane, with his instructor on board, at the wrong airport. It took him a while to live that one down. With the last name McNally, the name "Rand" —like the company that made maps—provided the perfect opportunity for his squadron buddies to christen him.

They all laughed about it now, but that check ride had truly affected him. He vowed to never let a dumb oversight like that ever happen again. Ever since, he'd been meticulous about his planning and checklists. His success was a direct result of that extra work. Now that he thought about it, that botched check ride was probably the best thing that had ever happened to his flying career.

"Well, I hope it's everything you've imagined," Dave said. He concentrated on bringing the airplane in toward the apron, where it would remain parked for the night. The plane came to a full stop. Dave set the parking brake and shut down the engines. He looked outside at the falling snow, still in awe. "Who knows, Rand, maybe you'll even get hit with a surprise or two yourself."

Brent frowned. He wasn't a big fan of surprises. Although, meeting Clara had been a surprise, nothing he could have possibly planned for. Maybe love was like an unexpected snowfall—unpredictable and exciting.

It was a nice thought, but he knew better. Like anything else, relationships took work. They took commitment. They required planning. He'd learned this truth firsthand by watching his parents' marriage over the years. His dad, a retired military officer, had always shown him the amount of work that went into maintaining a relationship, especially over long distances. There were times when it didn't look easy for either of his parents, but they'd always assured him it was worth it.

Clara was worth it. At least, he thought she could be. He sensed there was something different about her. Perhaps it was that they seemed to click together so easily. Maybe it was just that the timing was right. All he knew was that this relationship had a potential he'd never felt before. But maybe it was too early to know. It was possible he was simply getting caught up in the excitement of it all.

He'd had a few girlfriends in the past, but no one who had made him want to make a commitment. His focus had always been on his flying and making sure he was successful in his missions. It had worked well for him so far. Still, Brent wondered if he would ever be as devoted to a relationship as he was to his job. Sometimes, he worried his complete focus on his Air Force career would inevitably come at the expense of ever finding real love.

Brent shook off any thoughts of romance. He glanced at the engine shutdown checklist one last time to ensure everything had been completed. With the aircraft secure, he and Dave still needed to stop into the squadron for some quick post-flight paperwork.

He stepped outside the plane onto the attached stairs. Stopping at the top of the staircase, he took a moment to look around. The night sky was dark, and the air was frigid. The lights from the runway shined brightly, like red and white Christmas lights. The sound of jet engines hummed in the background, and snow swirled wildly around him.

He felt as if he was in a snow globe—only one that included airplanes. How he would have loved one of those as a kid. As he stood underneath the falling snow, his eyes widened with a sense of wonder.

He turned back to look at Dave. "You're right, man. This *is* pretty exciting." He laughed. "It's Christmastime."

The sudden bout of enthusiasm took him by surprise. He couldn't remember when he'd been so excited for Christmas, at least not as an adult. Maybe Clara *was* someone who would be worth the effort needed for a serious relationship. Maybe, with the squadron off his mind for the holidays, it was time to focus on a different mission— executing the perfect Christmas with Clara.

Somehow, he knew this Christmas was going to be different. Timing was finally on his side.

CHAPTER THREE
CLARA

Clara stepped out of the hotel as the Christmas lights began to glow throughout downtown Cranberry Pines. She beamed as she took it in, admiring the beauty of the scenic street. Her feelings about the promotion and Matthew were complicated —but Christmas was not. Christmas was simply perfect. The snow was just beginning to fall, and she felt a welcome shiver as the air grew colder.

Like nearly everyone in her small New Hampshire town, Clara loved being surrounded by the anticipation of the season. There was a certain magic about Cranberry Pines this time of year, the streets overflowing with both New England charm and fresh snow. The Darlington glowed from its position in the heart of downtown. She never tired of going to work there every day. The gleaming clapboard siding and the brassy gaslight lanterns had greeted guests there for over a hundred years.

Recently renovated and all brightened up for Christmas, she still couldn't believe *she* was going to be the general manager. Well, someday. Eventually. A sudden gratitude for Matthew and everything he'd done for her overwhelmed her.

Clara pulled her coat tighter and sped up her walk. The pub was only two blocks from the hotel, but she knew her best friend would already be there. Lily was always on time for their monthly Friday-night meetups at Buddy's Tavern.

It would be a welcome distraction to catch up with her. They'd both been so busy recently—she in her new relationship with Brent, and Lily with her boyfriend, Kyle. With Brent flying, it was a perfect opportunity to have some long-needed girl time.

Clara walked into the pub and was immediately welcomed by the warmth of a wood-burning fire. The paneled walls made it look like an old hunting lodge out of the northern woods. She squinted in the dim light. A candle at each table bathed the place in a soft haze. Her eyes landed on the fireplace, surrounded by a mantle of river rocks. It was framed by a brightly lit garland as Bing Crosby played softly in the background. She placed a hand over her heart and breathed in the smoky-scented air.

Lily waved from a tiny table in the corner. "Over here, Clar!"

As if anyone could miss Lily. With her dark hair full of thick curls and six-foot-tall frame, she was hard to miss. When it came to fashion, her style was constantly changing, but her brands were always from the hottest names. She loved anything flashy and bright, and her philosophy on color was that one simply couldn't get enough of it. Tonight, she wore a pair of sky-blue yoga pants and a hot pink sweatshirt that probably cost more than the professional attire Clara had on. It certainly didn't hurt that Lily naturally looked like a fitness model. Still, Clara never understood the idea of wearing workout gear as an outfit.

She and her best friend since kindergarten could hardly be more different, especially when it came to appearance. Clara was petite, or—put less eloquently—short. She had always dressed in simple, classic pieces and usually wore her thick blonde hair in a wavy—yet always polished—ponytail. When most friends were coordinating outfits for school dances, the two of them had never even tried to match up their styles.

"Have you been waiting long?" Clara asked with a look of apology when she reached the table.

Lily said nothing; just looked back at her with a huge smile plastered on her face. She held her left hand against her chest, a new diamond sparkling brightly.

Clara screamed. "No way! He proposed?"

"He proposed," Lily replied with a relaxed smile.

Several people turned their heads as Clara let out a high-pitched squeal and hugged her best friend, jumping up and down.

Lily pulled back. "Okay, enough of that. Everyone's looking at you."

Clara waved her off. She knew her best friend well enough to know she was squealing with excitement, on the inside. It was simply her uniquely reserved personality that allowed her to downplay the enthusiasm. Not one to wear her heart on her sleeve, Lily usually kept her biggest reactions to herself, although Clara was an expert at reading them by now.

She had always admired Lily's even-keeled and mild temperament, finding it ironic that her taste in style was the exact opposite. She'd always wondered if her tendency to lean toward all things loud and colorful was her way of expressing herself to the outside world. Either way, Clara knew the truth: Lily was thrilled. She had been dating her boyfriend, Kyle, for years now and had been eagerly antici-pating this.

"Well, tell me everything. How did he do it?" Clara grabbed her best friend's hand to get a closer look at the ring.

"Let's order our drinks first," Lily said with a sly tilt of her head. "I do believe this calls for a special treat."

"Yule log martinis," they said at the same time.

Buddy's yule log martinis were a holiday tradition. A martini glass full of vanilla-flavored vodka, chocolate ganache, rum, and espresso—topped off with a sprig of holly. Decadent and festive, they limited themselves to one per year. They learned the hard way a few years ago that, like many of the sugary-themed cocktails at Buddy's, they are best savored early, but not often.

"Well, I can't think of a more worthy occasion," Clara said, beaming with happiness for her best friend as they ordered their drinks. She took off her coat and settled in. "Okay, spill," she said with a little clap.

Lily's eyes were glued to her menu. "Well, he took me to a romantic dinner at our favorite restaurant and asked me to marry him. Should we order an appetizer?"

"Simple as that?" Clara asked, her eyebrows rising.

"Well, yeah." Lily looked up with a relaxed expression. "Clar, we've been together forever. We knew we'd eventu-ally get engaged—it was just a matter of time." She shrugged.

Clara thought about how long Lily and Kyle *had* been together. It had been a few years, at least. Unlike her and Matthew, though, those two had actually stayed together the entire time.

Why *had* it taken Kyle so long to propose? Did they

really need all that time to make sure they were right for each other?

She thought about Matthew and all the wasted time she'd spent with him over the years. Was that *him* trying to decide if they were right for each other, or had he only been prolonging the inevitable? Did a relationship really need to be so long and drawn out before making a commitment?

The waiter delivered their drinks, the glasses brimming with holiday goodness. He seemed to be in no hurry as he set each one down in a painstaking effort not to spill a single drop. Clara grew impatient, tapping her foot under the table. As soon as he left, she held her glass in the air. The martini immediately sloshed over the edge of the glass.

Lily laughed, shaking her head.

Clara ignored the spill and continued with her toast. "To my best friend and to helping her plan what's sure to be a spectacular wedding."

They clinked glasses, and took their first sip at the same time.

"So good," Lily said.

Clara nodded in agreement.

Lily looked happy, and Clara supposed she should be. She had certainly waited long enough for this. She had more patience than Clara could even comprehend. It was probably what made her such a great third-grade teacher.

"So, what about you and Brent?" Lily asked, eager to turn the attention away from herself. "How are things going with you two?"

"Oh, Brent is great. *We* are great." Clara felt a warmth crawl over her as her thoughts shifted to her boyfriend. "He's taking me out tomorrow night. And he'll be on leave for the entire week leading up to Christmas. I cannot wait to spend our first holiday together." She let out a delighted sigh as romantic thoughts of Christmas filled her mind. "Apparently, he's got loads of activities lined up for us."

"That sounds magical," Lily said.

Clara nodded as she took a sip of her drink.

"So, Clar, do you think Brent has the potential to be, you know, the one?"

"Oh, it's too early for that," Clara said, waving her off. She leaned back in her seat, her lips puckered. She considered what Lily had said. There was something about that word she'd used—*magical.*

Her thoughts shifted to her grandmother; her guiding star—her Grams. Grams had told Clara she'd immediately known Clara's grandfather was the one for her after spending their first Christmas together. That was it. No need for years of dating. No breaking up and getting back together. No complications. A little bit of Christmas magic, she had told Clara. That was all it took.

Clara sat up in her seat. *Of course! It could be so simple.*

She decided to amend her previous answer. "You know what?"

"Hm?" Lily's eyes were back on the menu.

"Maybe Brent could be the one. No, maybe he *is* the one, and maybe there's a way I can know it—quickly and easily this time."

Lily looked up. "How's that?"

"Christmas with Brent," she said, her hands held out wide as if it was the most obvious thing in the world. "Maybe that's all I'll need to figure out if he's the one for me."

"That simple?" Lily laughed.

"That simple." Clara folded her arms across her chest. She'd never been more serious or decisive in her life.

Lily stared at her, clearly not understanding.

Clara sighed and leaned in closer. "Look, I love that you and Kyle have been together forever and that you two took your time to make sure you were making the right decision."

"But . . .?"

"But it's not for me. Not anymore, anyway. It's too difficult, too time-consuming. I'm not the same girl who let Matthew pull me along for years. I'm thirty years old, and I'm not getting any younger. Besides, waiting certainly hasn't worked for me in the past."

Lily raised her eyebrows over her martini glass. "But don't you think that some things—usually the best things— are worth the wait?"

Clara pursed her lips and looked at her lap. "I used to believe that, but I don't know anymore."

It was true. As a child, Clara had always believed that the best part of Christmas was simply waiting for it. Before tearing into the wrapping paper, the anticipation that brought the day closer was the most exciting part of all. The entire season was like one of those advent calendars with a tiny chocolate behind each door. Every day would bring her closer to the approaching holiday, but not without its own delightful surprise waiting around each corner.

She wasn't sure she felt the same way anymore. Years of waiting around for Matthew to make decisions that affected *her* had evidently taken a toll. Clara shook her head as she replayed her earlier conversation with him—as she replayed everything. The truth was, she was tired of being forced to wait for things to happen in their own slow time. She was tired of everything being so complicated. For once, she just wanted things to happen. Now.

She drummed her fingers on the table as her theory

came together. She looked up at Lily with an assertive nod. "Maybe something as important as your first Christmas together really *can* tell you everything you need to know."

Lily shrugged. She didn't seem convinced.

"Too bad I didn't realize this sooner," Clara said, more to herself than to anyone else. "That first Christmas with him should have been my first clue."

"Who, Matthew? Yeah, I remember how that turned out." Lily made a face of sympathy.

"The first time he dumped me, but not the last." That should've been her first sign that they weren't right for each other. She wasn't going to make that mistake again. "I only need one simple thing this time: a magical Christmas."

Lily laughed. "Well, magical or not, Christmas is only a few weeks away. You think you can make a huge life decision like that in such a short amount of time?"

"I do," Clara said.

"Wow, so this Christmas is really important then," Lily said, her eyes wide.

"It's everything," Clara replied matter-of-factly.

"Well, okay then. I hope it all works out."

Clara nodded, biting her lower lip.

"I mean that." Lily paused, looking her in the eye. "But, Clar, what about all the other considerations? Have you ever thought about what it would mean to be married to someone, you know, with that kind of . . . job?"

Clara ignored that last question. She knew Brent's being in the military was something she would have to think about eventually. But not now. No, tonight was for celebrating and for talking about the fun stuff. Not any of those messy details.

She leaned back in her chair and glanced over Lily's

shoulder to the window. Fat snowflakes floated to the ground outside. She felt as if she were one of them, floating around on a holiday high. Yes, this Christmas *was* going to be magical. She needed it to be. She was done waiting.

CHAPTER FOUR
BRENT

With his flight canceled, Brent came home and changed out of his flight suit and into a pair of faded jeans and a flannel shirt. He couldn't wait to get downstairs to his woodworking shop. If he couldn't be in the air, it was the next best place.

He considered calling Clara to see if she wanted to get together, but it was the first Friday of the month. She would have plans with her friend, Lily. It was probably for the best, anyway. He couldn't just throw a date together at the last minute like that. A girl like her deserved a little preparation and planning—like what he had in store for their upcoming romantic dinner. As far as he was concerned, there were more important matters to attend to tonight.

His disappointment from the canceled flight was soon forgotten as he descended the creaky stairs into the damp basement. The smell of pine filled the air. There was nothing he loved more than that musty basement aroma, especially when he had one of his projects underway. His tools sat neatly organized on a sturdy workbench. A modest piece of eastern white pine lay on top. He took a slow inhale through his nose.

Brent had bought his house, a small 1970s fixer-upper on a great piece of land, when he first arrived in town a few years ago. Knowing the Air Force wouldn't keep him in any place too long, it didn't make a lot of sense for him to buy a property, especially one that needed extensive renovations. But there was something about this house he couldn't resist. He could tell it had potential, and all it needed was somebody who could put the time and effort into bringing it back to life.

After a year or so of planning, painting, and polishing, he had transformed the old house into a beautiful home. He planned to sell it for a sizable profit when it was time for him to move on from the area, a nice bonus. But, mostly, it was about the work he put into it and the pride he took in a successful outcome.

Brent turned toward his latest project and current source of happiness: a Christmas gift for Clara. He picked up his handsaw and began working away at the piece of wood, executing each move to perfection so it would turn out according to his plan.

That's what he loved most about woodworking, the skill involved. Dependent entirely on good planning and careful execution, nothing was left to luck. He blew the extra sawdust off the wood and stood back to take a look. Perfect. It looked exactly the way he'd anticipated. If all went according to plan, so would his Christmas with Clara.

Brent thought about the plans he'd made for the two of them. He flipped on the small radio he kept on the workbench. Michael Bublé was singing "I'll Be Home for Christmas," and Brent couldn't help but hum along as he carved. He already had several activities lined up for their week together, all laid out in a well-organized checklist. The first item on his list was to take her to Cranberry Pines

Christmas Tree Farm. He knew she'd been there before, but he—a relative newcomer to the area—had never visited. He hadn't even bought a tree last year, having spent the holidays at his parents' house. From his online research, Brent knew the farm could be the perfect spot for a romantic holiday outing. He would be able to show off his natural lumberjack skills by cutting down a fresh tree. He loved that idea.

Brent felt as if choosing their first tree together would finally solidify them as a real couple. It seemed like a rite of passage only a couple would do, as opposed to a date. He smiled to himself. He liked the idea of them choosing something together, syncing up their individual personalities to achieve a shared goal. Even if it was just a Christmas tree.

As he continued to carve away at the wood, Brent thought about the next item on his checklist: the squadron Christmas party. He hoped it would give Clara a positive impression of the squadron and not scare her away from Air Force life completely.

Although she had grown up in Cranberry Pines—only a couple dozen miles from the Air Force base—he didn't think she had ever dated anyone in the military before. Had she? She'd only mentioned having dated that sharply dressed boss of hers, Matthew. Brent rolled his eyes. That guy seemed to be about as different as one could get from most of the Air Force pilots he knew. If that's what she was used to, what was she going to think of his Air Force buddies?

He knew deep down she was going to love his friends. Still, Brent couldn't stop his mind from cycling through the worst-case scenarios. They had talked about his job quite a bit over the past couple of months, and she seemed to be supportive of what he did. Even so, he wasn't entirely sure yet what Clara thought about that part of his life or if she was interested in getting involved in it for the long term. How could anyone really know what they're getting into with this lifestyle?

He glanced over at his list to peek at the most significant item. He was planning to take Clara to his parents' house for their annual Christmas party. She would get to meet his parents for the first time, along with all their closest friends and neighbors.

Brent adored his family. They'd been his constant rock in a life that sometimes felt like sand that never stopped shifting. Living in the northeast, his parents had been thrilled when he got assigned to the base in New Hampshire. Their house was a short two-hour drive from his, and he loved to visit them as much as possible. He was ready for them to finally meet Clara.

There would be other holiday fun too, and it was all laid out in his list. They would bake cookies, they would explore the idyllic New England villages, they would drink cocoa, and they would exchange gifts.

On the surface, each item on his list appeared to be simple holiday fun. But he knew the truth. Each activity was well thought-out, with the specific intent of bringing them closer together as a couple. *It's how missions are successful.* If it all went according to plan, their relationship would take a huge step forward over the course of the holidays.

First things first, he was planning to take Clara out for a romantic candlelight dinner the next evening. Though December had just begun, this date would be the official kickoff to their romantic Christmas together. He thought about the upcoming weeks and imagined everything going perfectly as he continued to hum along with the music.

Deciding to remain optimistic, he made a last-minute

decision to add an additional detail to her gift. Taking his chisel, he inscribed the current year into the back of the wood. If things worked out between them—and he was beginning to think they might—they would always have this reminder of their first Christmas together.

Brent placed his safety goggles on top of his head to get a closer look at his work. A satisfied grin spread across his face. His phone rang, and he took off his gloves, hoping it would be Clara. Instead, the number for the squadron appeared, suddenly reminding him of the one thing he could never control.

The squadron rarely called. A simple issue like a schedule change or logistic update would usually be communicated through email. No, a phone call meant there was something urgent: a squadron recall, canceled leave—or something worse.

Brent's vision of his perfect Christmas plans came dangerously into view. Despite all his planning, there was one truth that always lingered in the back of his mind: Life in the military was completely unpredictable.

CHAPTER FIVE
CLARA

Saturday nights in Cranberry Pines bustled with activity, especially around Christmas. With tourists flocking to the area to soak up the small-town charm, a table at one of the downtown restaurants could be hard to come by this time of year. Clara wasn't worried, though. Knowing Brent, their reservation had been secured well in advance.

She'd spent the entire day at the hotel, prepping the conference rooms for a busy weekend of holiday parties. Brent had called her that morning to ask if he could stop by to talk. At the very least, he'd wanted to pick her up for the date. It was sweet of him, but she insisted on meeting him at the restaurant instead. Sure, there was a part of her that wanted Matthew to see her with her new boyfriend, but it was quickly overruled by the side that wanted to keep the peace. With this promotion hanging in the balance, the last thing she needed was any hard feelings, including jealousy.

Clara spotted him immediately as she entered the restaurant. Major Brent McNally was hard to miss, even when he wasn't in uniform. He sat at the table, his back to her. His tall head of perfectly trimmed hair stood out as a welcome preview to the handsome face she knew would greet her. Her eyelashes gave way to an involuntary flutter. She still couldn't quite believe he was *her* boyfriend.

She lingered back. Something was wrong. Brent seemed different, even from behind. He normally had a calm presence about him and a confident posture that seemed to be missing tonight.

She continued to watch him from across the restaurant. She could tell he was upset—or nervous maybe. His hands were in a pensive steeple on top of the table. His leg appeared to be in a rapid bounce underneath the tablecloth. An uneasy feeling crept over her. Clara watched his chin drop to his chest as if it were too heavy to hold up.

Her thoughts jumped to Matthew. They had been on dates that had this same eerie beginning to them. He had never *wanted* to hurt her when he broke up with her those times. It was hard for him too. It was simply that they needed time apart, or at least that's what he'd said.

"Can I come by the hotel so we can talk?" Brent had asked her that morning. The question now gave her an unsettling feeling that it hadn't then. He'd just been offering to visit her at work, right? She chewed on her lip. A queasy sensation formed in the pit of her stomach. Surely Brent wasn't going to break up with her already. Was he?

Clara was prepared for a romantic evening, not a breakup. She forced herself to remain calm and not jump to any conclusions, reminding herself that Brent was nothing like Matthew. That this relationship was nothing like theirs had been. She took the time to remove her coat and draped it over her arm. She wasn't sure she was ready to confront this yet—whatever *this* was. She smoothed out her new black dress and forced herself to take a deep breath, needing a moment to collect her thoughts. Grateful to have remained undetected, she continued to watch him from afar.

Her mind went back to the first time she had met Brent. He'd come into the hotel with a few other pilots to plan a retirement party for their squadron commander. Tall and impressive in his flight suit, Clara immediately took notice. He had a set of gorgeous dimples, the left one exaggerated whenever he smiled at her. After he had attempted a few jokes—that didn't land—she chalked him up to being a cocky flyboy, trying to show off.

She hadn't known much about the Air Force or about the military in general. Over the years she'd often seen airmen around town, but she'd never known any of them personally or even given them a second thought.

That all changed once Brent asked for her phone number. She couldn't resist the humble smile and the nervous tone of his voice. It was so different from Matthew's natural bravado.

Clara was intrigued by Brent. She wanted to know more about this guy who looked like an action hero yet seemed nervous around *her*. She'd suggested they have a drink right there in the hotel lounge after work that night, fearing he wouldn't call. She knew some women wouldn't condone her being the one to make the first move, but after all those years with Matthew, it was time she started going after what she wanted. She'd always let Matthew call the shots and lead the relationship. She was tired of being pulled along by a man. Besides, it wouldn't hurt for Matthew to see her with someone else—especially a good-looking military pilot.

Over a gin martini in the Darlington lounge, Clara discovered that Brent was not only handsome, but he was also incredibly interesting—and thoughtful too. To top it off, he *was* funny, in a dad-joke kind of way. They had shared their first kiss there, another departure from her usual "wait for the right time" mentality. Clara had felt an undeniable spark and, soon after, they'd shared their second. Matthew never crossed her mind again that night.

They hadn't been dating long now, but she was excited to see what would happen with their relationship. So why was she suddenly getting the ominous impression that something was wrong?

Clara decided to brush off the feeling and forced a smile as she approached the table with caution, hoping it was all in her imagination.

One thing she knew about Brent was that he always looked her right in the eye whenever he saw her. But not tonight. She couldn't help but notice that he avoided her gaze as he stood to pull out her chair. Still a gentleman, like always. He leaned down to kiss her on the head, a strange greeting for someone who always went in for the lips.

Her legs gave a slight wobble as she settled in. "What's wrong?" she asked immediately. Whatever the problem was, she wanted him to get to the point right away. He was clearly uncomfortable. She just didn't know him well enough yet to understand what it meant.

Brent sat down, and the leg bouncing resumed. He noticed and stilled it. He looked at her with a shake of his head. "Clara, I'm so sorry. You don't deserve this." He picked up the bottle of wine in front of him and poured some into her glass. His hand was shaking.

Clara pressed her lips together and closed her eyes. It felt as if her heart had plunged straight into the ground. So it *was* going to be that kind of talk. Years of experience with Matthew had conditioned her to anticipate what would be coming next. *It's not you, it's me. I need some space. We're moving too fast.* She had heard them all, always from him.

But for as little time as she'd known Brent, she certainly didn't expect to be hearing this from *him*. At least not so soon.

She pressed her hands against the sides of her head. She couldn't believe this was happening. They had been so happy up to this point. Hadn't they? She couldn't imagine what could have caused such a sudden change of heart.

She opened her eyes and began to speak. "Brent, I've really enjoyed our time—"

"Clara, I'm being deployed."

He'd blurted out the words so quickly she wasn't entirely sure she had heard them at all.

"Deployed?"

He nodded.

She allowed herself a deep release of breath as she felt the weight of an impending breakup lifted off her shoulders. Her entire body relaxed. She let out a slight laugh. It was just a deployment. Well, that wasn't so bad. It was a part of his job. Clara supposed a deployment every now and then was the price one paid to date someone in the military, right? It would probably be sometime in the new year, and she reasoned he'd be back in a few weeks or so.

She smiled at him, her jaw unclenching. Relief flooded through her body as she took a sip of her wine and leaned back in her chair. "Off to save the world, huh?" She gave him a playful wink.

Brent didn't smile back. He tried to pick up his wine glass, his hand still trembling. He set it back down. He looked her straight in the eye, his expression grave.

Her concern returned.

"I leave immediately," he said.

Clara blinked.

"And I'll be gone for a year."

Her eyes flew wide open. She wanted to draw in a breath but suddenly couldn't. The restaurant seemed to go silent. Everything faded into a black vignette around her. Had she heard him correctly? She couldn't be sure since the only sound was her own heartbeat pounding in her ears.

She leaned forward in her chair, set her elbows on the table, and pressed her palms over her eyes as she tried to get a hold of her bearings. A wave of dizziness flowed through her head. She drew in a breath slowly through her nose and tried to calm her racing heart. "A year—you'll be gone an entire year?" It wasn't exactly a question, more a statement of disbelief. Even so, she looked at him through desperate eyes, waiting for an answer.

He only nodded, a look of defeat on his face.

"Wow." Clara noticed her chin quiver and commanded it to stop. "And what do you mean by 'immediately'?"

He lowered his gaze to the table. "I leave tomorrow."

Her jaw dropped as she clapped a hand over her mouth. Any breath she had in her lungs seemed to rush right out of her.

Brent continued, fidgeting with his hands, as he spoke. "One of the pilots who was supposed to go on this deployment . . . well, he got injured pretty badly yesterday." His voice cracked. "And I have to fill in for him." He looked up at Clara to gauge her reaction so far, then shifted his eyes back down to the table again. "I won't return until this time next year."

She stared at him with horror-stricken confusion. She couldn't be sure she was hearing any of this correctly at all. Could they really do this? Could the Air Force just send him away like that, with no notice?

He raised his head and reached across the table to take her hand with an earnestness she had never seen before. "Clara, I'm so sorry."

She pulled her hand away, not ready to accept this news. "You mean we don't even get to spend Christmas together?"

"Not this Christmas." He bowed his head.

Clara looked at him, her eyes wide in disbelief. She still wasn't entirely sure she understood what was going on. Was this how deployments worked? Was this really happening, or was it all some kind of cruel joke? No, Brent could never be so mean. Looking at him, she could tell this was hurting him just as much as it was her.

"I'm really sorry, Clara," he repeated. "But it's my job. It's part of military life."

Clara pressed her tongue firmly against the inside of her cheek, desperate to prevent the tears that were beginning to form. She wanted to let them flow, to let them pour out. She wanted to sob into her hands over the injustice of it all.

But she knew she couldn't. She wasn't entitled to emotionally fall apart over this. She wasn't even entitled to feel inconvenienced by it, really. She was only a girlfriend— a new one at that. They hadn't been together that long, and he was right—it *was* his job. She hadn't earned the right to fight back against this.

Still, as much as she was beginning to understand the reality of the situation, her personal feelings on the matter were completely out of her control. Entitled to it or not, her heart had just been shattered into a million pieces.

Brent continued with a sympathetic look on his face. "The mission comes first, above our own plans sometimes. Military families all over the country face these challenges constantly."

She just nodded. Clara didn't care about the mission. She didn't care about all the other families facing canceled holiday plans either. All she cared about was Brent and what this would mean for their relationship—for their future. They'd never even had the chance to see where it would go. So much for her magical Christmas. She wasn't going to get Christmas at all with him, and most likely, no future either.

All of it, derailed by a dumb deployment.

"What's the purpose of it anyway?" The words left her mouth before she could stop them. She felt her face redden. The truth was, she was embarrassed she didn't know more about what he did. Sure, years ago troops were constantly deployed to the Middle East. But wasn't all that over? Wasn't his job now to refuel other airplanes? A flying gas station was what he'd always called it.

"It's a combat deployment, Clara. That's all I can tell you. I can't tell you where I'm going or even what conflict we're involved in. All I can say is that where the fighter jets and bombers go, my plane needs to go too. It's how they're able to have enough fuel to complete their missions."

She gave a slow nod and let out a long breath. She glanced at him through her prickling eyes. He no longer seemed nervous. In fact, he now had his confident demeanor back as he sat there quietly, watching her with his chin resting in his hands. How could he be so calm? Especially while she was trying her hardest to appear emotionally under control, a task that was becoming more difficult with each passing second. Her bright future with Brent— gone before it even got started.

Clara lowered her head, unable to hold back the tears any longer. She covered her face with her hands and broke down into them. She couldn't help it. The whole situation was awful.

She thought this relationship was going to be different. She thought Brent had the potential to be the one. Even though they hadn't been together long, she had connected with him in ways that made her confident it could actually go somewhere. The feelings she had for him were real, no matter how new this relationship was. She couldn't stand the thought of losing him so soon after meeting him—and to something like this? Something so outside of either of their control?

This was different from any breakup she'd had with Matthew. This seemed more hopeless. More unjust. More difficult than anything she'd ever endured before. Why did relationships always have to be so complicated?

Clara raised her head and wiped the mascara from around her eyes with a napkin. She looked at him and gave a resigned shrug. "Well, I guess there's nothing we can do about it then."

He gently took her hand in his. His warm smile was brightened by the soft candlelight. This time, she let him hold it.

"Well, that's not entirely true," he said.

"What do you mean?"

Brent leaned forward and looked at her under a brow of sincerity. "Clara, it's going to be hard—really hard." His voice was firm, but his thumb rubbed her hand with a tender touch.

She looked down at their intertwined hands, refusing to meet his gaze.

"A year is an incredibly long time," he added.

"Yeah, I know," she scoffed. She couldn't help the tone.

No matter how she looked at it, this wasn't fair. She was entitled to her sour attitude, if nothing else.

"But I am committed to putting in the effort to make our relationship work, even with the time and distance apart."

Clara looked up at him through her tears. His face softened, and he gave her a warm, close-mouthed smile.

"What?" She sniffed. "What are you saying?"

"I'm saying that we can make our relationship work, even with this deployment."

"You mean, you want to stay together? You want to have a long-distance relationship—for a year?"

"Yes."

"But why?"

"Because I think this relationship is worth it."

She stared at the table and shook her head. She wanted to believe everything could work out—that they could weather the storm of a yearlong deployment. But couples went through this all the time—strong couples that had been together for years—and *they* didn't always come out of it intact. As much as she liked Brent, the two of them hardly knew each other, really. Maybe it was too much for a new relationship to handle. Maybe a year was too long to be apart. Maybe this situation was just too complicated for her. Perhaps not getting to spend Christmas with him was the sign she needed to close the door on them entirely.

Clara didn't know what to say. She simply looked up at him with anguish.

He cocked his head to one side, watching her expression. "I know this is a lot to take in right now. You're going to need some time to think. I understand that."

She only nodded. What could she possibly say that would make any difference at all?

"Will you come to the base tomorrow to see me off?"

"What?"

"I can't imagine leaving without you there to kiss me goodbye and to tell me everything's going to be okay. That *we* are going to be okay."

She shook her head and pushed a stray hair off her face. "I don't know, Brent."

"Please? It's important to me that you're there." His eyes silently pleaded with her. There was a yearning beneath the surface of his expression, something urging her to trust in something she didn't fully understand. Perhaps it was simply a feeling of hope.

Clara thought more about their relationship. What chance did they have? The odds were definitely stacked against them.

Brent always seemed to work hard at everything, though. Maybe they *could* make it work. Deep down, she knew he was just as upset as she was about this. He was just willing to wait—and work—for them. But was she?

She looked up at her boyfriend with a sad attempt at a smile. Her perfect new boyfriend who was being ripped away from her right before Christmas. She studied his gorgeous brown eyes and, for the first time that night, suddenly thought about a future with him—a real future. It was certainly easy to imagine. But without Christmas to seal the deal, did they even stand a chance? Why couldn't they have their relationship-affirming magical Christmas as planned before he had to leave? That way, she would have at least known if they actually had a future together before making this type of commitment. Why did things always have to be so hard?

Clara felt the heavy weight of frustration press down on her chest. Before this dinner, she'd been floating on air, ready to celebrate a romantic Christmas. Ever since meeting

Brent, she felt as if she had a new appreciation for the world and everything in it. Now, in an instant, she was reminded just how unforgiving it could really be.

She wiped away her tears and sat up straighter in her chair. She raised her chin and, with the bravest voice she could muster, despite all her reservations, said, "Of course I will be there."

After all, what else could she say?

CHAPTER SIX

BRENT

Brent was exhausted when he got home from the restaurant. The heaviness of unloading that bomb had taken its toll. Neither of them had been able to work up an appetite, so they'd called it an early night. He needed to get ready to leave the next morning. Clara, she'd told him, needed to think.

He went down to his basement to decompress. He picked up the piece of wood he'd been working on and narrowed his eyes. It had come out exactly the way he'd wanted. Too bad he couldn't say the same for the relationship.

Brent replayed the entire evening in his mind. He hated to disappoint Clara like that. He knew it was asking a lot of her to even consider this type of long-distance relationship. It wasn't what she had signed on for when they began dating. But this deployment wasn't within his control, a fact that was becoming harder for him to accept by the minute.

He wished things were different. He knew that if he and Clara were to sustain their relationship, they would eventually have to face separations. If only they could have had more time together before having to endure one of this magnitude.

He knew he should spend the evening packing to get ready for the deployment. The only thing he cared about, though, was completing Clara's gift. He needed to get it right.

He held it up to the lightbulb that hung from the ceiling to inspect it. With the carving complete, Brent needed to start the process of sanding the wood in preparation for staining. He would finish it tonight. He would give it to Dave and ask him to deliver it to Clara's house on Christmas morning.

Thinking about Christmas, Brent started to grieve over all the canceled plans. His Christmas checklist was now obsolete. The entire mission aborted before it even began.

As he sanded the wood, he chewed over the possible outcomes. What were their chances, really? It was certainly possible that a deployment could bring them closer together, but more likely things could simply fizzle out between them the longer he was away.

He knew he could commit to making it work, but would Clara actually be willing to go through all of this? Or was this whole situation too much for her? He wouldn't blame her if it was.

Well, tomorrow would be his first clue. Clara had told him she would come to see him off. Though after an evening alone to think about things, she might not show up. The thought caused his entire body to deflate.

Clara was special. The feelings Brent had for her told him she was worth holding on to. A year away, and she'd surely be snatched up by someone else before he returned. Possibly even by that ex-boyfriend boss of hers. No, she was far too important to him. Maybe he couldn't change his circumstances, but unfortunate timing or not, he wasn't dumb enough to let her go already.

He thought back to that fateful autumn day two months ago when they had first met. Downtown Cranberry Pines had been filled with maple trees, brimming with orange leaves. He instantly understood why his squadron commander had loved the town. The guys were all excited to host his retirement party at the fancy hotel there. When the sales manager met them in the lobby, Brent's mood brightened even more. She had a unique bounce to her step, and her cheeks glowed. He never imagined that by the end of that day they'd be going on their first date.

Over cocktails that night, he'd been instantly smitten. He'd found himself losing a bit of that control he'd always held onto so tightly. Brent was far too level-headed to believe in love at first sight. Still, he knew there was something about Clara that caused him to throw out that mental checklist he'd carried around for years. That night, he scrapped it all down to one thing: He wanted someone just like her.

Brent looked down now at the gift he was holding. A perfectly formed star, carved out of wood by his own two hands. It was a homemade tree topper for her Christmas tree. Made from a single piece of wood and about the size of a dinner plate, it wasn't anything remarkable. He thought about the addition he'd added last night—carving in the year. It was a tiny gesture he thought might be a positive harbinger for them. But now he was forced to look at this gift—and their relationship—in a whole new light.

Perhaps a tiny gesture wasn't what he needed in this situation. Maybe he needed any omen to be as grand as the original Christmas star itself. Maybe, much like the magi, he needed to trust in the heavens to guide things where they should go—more than any of his navigational plans. During his many years flying over dark oceans, he had learned that a night sky full of stars can often lead a pilot better than any instrument could. In those moments, he often realized how insignificant his sense of control really was. There was always something so much bigger than himself that was truly guiding his route.

Brent picked up the can of stain he had planned to use on the star and turned it over in his hands, thinking about his next step. He walked over to the paint cans in the corner. Faced with the impossible situation before him, Brent had to dig deep into his heart to see what it was telling him. He closed his eyes. He could see Clara's blue eyes shining back at him as clearly as if she were standing in front of him.

At that moment, Brent accepted the simple truth: Sometimes life had other ideas. A resolve washed over him, and he gave himself a nod of encouragement. Sometimes his best-laid plans simply needed to change.

He set the can of stain aside and instead reached for the small can of blue paint. It was a gamble, but one he was willing to take. As much as he hated leaving things to chance, when it came to his heart, it seemed he had no other choice.

CHAPTER SEVEN
CLARA

Clara left the restaurant and drove straight to the only place she could think of to get a solid grasp on everything. She pulled up in front of her grandmother's house—her childhood home.

She turned off the car and popped down the mirror to steal a glance. Her face was red with tears, two streaks of black mascara running down her cheeks. Clara grabbed a wipe from her purse and cleaned her face before leaning back in her seat. She took a couple of deep breaths and turned to look out the window, allowing herself a second to enjoy the familiar sight of the house on a cold December night. It looked as it always did this time of year—perfect.

The large yellow farmhouse, with a sweeping wraparound porch, sat on four snow-covered acres. Sparkling lights and fluffy garlands were strung along the white picket fence. A bright, flickering candle sat in each window. The front porch was awash in light, with two oversized poinsettias and a fresh balsam wreath to accessorize the front door. Smoke rose from the chimney, and the scent of burning wood lingered in the crisp air. The whole scene felt like a warm blanket to Clara.

The memories of so many years of happy Christmases flooded her mind. Her heart filled with peace as she thought about the comforting smells, sounds, and sights of the holidays that she knew would always be waiting for her inside. The sweetness of freshly baked cookies. The fresh scent of a Christmas tree covered in clumps of tinsel and bright lights. The familiar Christmas songs pouring out from her grandmother's record player.

She and Grams had always loved "The Christmas Song" by Nat King Cole. She thought back to the time they had tried roasting chestnuts over their fireplace. It had been more work than either of them had anticipated, but it was fun. The entire house was filled with a cloud of warm, buttery sweetness. The bitter flavor took them by surprise, though, so much that they'd both spit them out immediately. She chuckled now at the memory. She always felt safe and loved there in that yellow house, especially at Christmas.

It was her mom and dad's house, really. They had recently begun a new phase of their lives—retirement. With her parents wanting to travel more, it had only made sense for Grams to move in to help care for the house while they were gone. Her grandmother had initially been reluctant to move away from the excitement of downtown, where she had lived on her own since Clara's grandpa had passed. It didn't take long, though, for her to realize that between the cozy house and the acres of land, this was where she was meant to be. She took up gardening and adopted a couple of dogs.

Now Clara's parents spent most of their time overseas, and this house felt more like Gram's than anyone else's.

Either way, it was home. Clara dropped by nearly every weekend when she wanted to leave the bustle that surrounded her townhome.

Every Christmas memory revolved around this house. Her parents had loved decorating it and throwing big parties every year, and Grams happily took over, continuing the family traditions while they were away.

Clara fanned a hand over her eyes to dry her tears. She got out of the car and turned in a slow semi-circle, taking in the view of the peaceful winter evening from all angles. Mrs. Roberts—Grams's neighbor and closest friend—sat on her front porch, watching the snow fall. Clara waved to her before a cold shiver ran through her as her thoughts quickly turned back to her current situation. As Clara approached the house—festive and warm—she was reminded again of the sad reality: This year would be different. There was no doubt in her mind that this was going to be a blue Christmas.

She used her key to let herself in. The house was toasty, as always. Grams's two beagles, Waylon and Willie, greeted her with wagging tails and wet kisses. Clara reached down to pet them. She could tell something had been baked recently—gingerbread cookies, probably. Her grandmother's favorite Christmas album was playing its instrumental version of "Silent Night." In the corner of the living room sat a freshly cut tree covered in lights and surrounded by overflowing boxes of tinsel, ornaments, and decorations. Clara managed a wry smile. Cozy, magical, beautiful Christmas. The sight of it all—as welcome as it was—also served as a cruel reminder of what she and Brent were being deprived of.

"Clara? Is that you?" Her grandmother's voice sounded from the kitchen.

Clara entered to find Grams sitting at the kitchen counter, addressing Christmas cards. Her thick red reading glasses were resting on the edge of her nose, her long silver hair pulled back loosely with a ribbon.

Grams looked up with a smile. "I'm glad you're here. I was going to finish decorating the tree tonight. So far, I've only managed to get the lights on."

Clara glanced over at the tree with a half-hearted grin.

"I spoke with your parents earlier." Her grandmother's eyes were focused on her cards. "They wanted to make sure you aren't upset about them missing Christmas this year. I told them to have a great time on their European cruise and not to worry one bit about us." She waved away the thought with her hand. "I said that between our annual festivities here and that new boyfriend of yours, you'll be busier than ever this Christmas."

Clara didn't say anything in response. She dropped her purse on the chair and her keys on the table.

"I've been thinking," her grandmother continued. "You and I should take a trip to join your folks in Europe sometime. Maybe we could go to Paris this summer. Or next Christmas, maybe? What do you think?"

What did she *think?* Clara couldn't think about summer. That was six months away. She certainly couldn't think about next Christmas; she was finding it hard enough to think about the next day. She didn't have space in her brain for anything beyond this current, confusing moment in time.

"Maybe," she said with a shrug.

Her grandmother looked up from her cards. "You okay?"

Clara's lip gave way to a forceful quiver as she tried to hold back the dam of tears. Eventually, she gave up. She couldn't wait another second to finally release her feelings. She needed to unburden herself to the person who, she knew wholeheartedly, could take it all on. Tears of disappointment came barreling out again.

Grams gasped and dropped her pen, standing up to take Clara into her arms. "What is it, honey? What happened?"

Clara said nothing, just continued to cry, her back shaking with each sob as she stood wrapped in those familiar arms.

Grams rubbed her back, the feeling both comforting and strong. "Problem at work?" she asked.

Clara clung to her, still unable to answer.

"The new boyfriend?"

She managed a nod and sniffed.

Grams let out a long sigh. "Well, I'm sure it's complicated. But whatever it is, we'll figure things out together." She pulled back from her and looked her in the eye. "It's going to be okay." She rubbed her thumb gently under Clara's eye to wipe away a tear. "Let's make some hot cocoa, and we'll talk all about it."

Clara nodded. Grams was exactly the person she needed right now. She longed for the comfort of her grandmother's assurance that nothing was hopeless and anything was possible. She needed to know there was a way to fix this, that there was a way to get out of this whole mess. She had no doubt that her Grams—the woman who could handle anything—would be the one to help her do it.

She watched as her grandmother pulled things out of the cabinet one by one. There was baking chocolate, peppermint extract, condensed milk, and cinnamon. Grams lined them all up neatly, pointing to each one as if she were taking attendance to make sure she had everything she needed. The peculiar act reminded Clara of something Brent would do.

Clara was dying to tell her what happened. She needed to unload everything, and quick. But she could tell her grandmother's focus was on the hot chocolate masterpiece she was trying to conjure up. It was typical of Grams. No crisis could be discussed without a comforting side of sugar to help ease the pain. She watched as her grandmother scooped and measured, slowly adding each ingredient into a pot. Grams hummed along with the Christmas album, now playing "God Rest You Merry Gentlemen," while she leisurely stirred. The scent of melting chocolate quickly filled the air. The record's tidings of comfort and joy only seemed to taunt Clara further.

Ever since she was a child, her grandmother had been the one to fix all her problems. When she had been picked on by another kid in kindergarten, Grams was the one who taught her how to stand up for herself. When she didn't make the basketball team in middle school, Grams helped her figure out what sport to try next. When Matthew had broken up with her, Grams convinced her she was better off without him. Clara hadn't always taken her grandmother's advice over the years. But looking back on it all now, she realized Grams had *always* been right. She had the solution to every problem.

Clara glanced at her watch. She wondered how long this cocoa was going to take. She was tempted to start talking about everything, but she knew that she was going to need Grams's undivided attention for this. She grabbed a box of tissues from the counter and patted her soggy eyes as she waited. Her grandmother added her signature peppermint flavoring and continued stirring. Grams was always so calm—so patient. Clara wished she could be more like her.

On the other hand, was it absolutely necessary to make cocoa from *scratch* at a time like this? She was sure there was an instant cocoa fix for times such as these. Couldn't Grams hurry up the process, just this once? Clara laid her head down on her folded arms on the countertop. She closed her eyes and continued to wait. Her head ached.

Finally, she heard the splash of cocoa being poured into mugs. She raised her head to see Grams top off each one with a generous squirt of whipped cream and a dash of sprinkles.

"Now, let's go into the living room, and you can tell me what's going on."

Clara let out a breath of relief and stood. She walked to the sofa, followed closely by Grams and the beagles. The snow was falling outside, and they both stopped to gaze out the window to savor the scene. Even Clara could appreciate the momentary stillness.

They sat together on the sofa in front of a warm fire. The dogs sat at their feet. With steaming mugs of perfect cocoa, Clara felt calmer already, her entire body relaxing. She wasn't quite sure how her grandmother always managed to do that.

Grams placed a heavy patchwork quilt over their laps. They both took their first careful sip.

"What's wrong, sweetie?" her grandmother asked, holding her cup close to her chest.

"It's Brent." She sniffed.

"Did you have a fight?"

Clara shook her head. "He's being deployed."

"Oh?"

"For a year! And we don't even get to spend Christmas together."

"Oh, honey, I'm so sorry." Her grandmother took a long,

resigned breath. She set her mug down and reached for Clara's hands. She peered into Clara's eyes with that look of assurance that only she could give.

Clara gave her a faint smile and rested her head on Grams's shoulder, simply enjoying being next to her. Her Grams stroked her hair with a comforting rhythm.

Finally, her grandmother spoke. "You know, Clara, if you and Brent are meant to be, there will be other Christmases in your future."

Clara squeezed her fists in frustration. "But *this* Christmas was the one I needed to figure out if he's the one—like with you and Grandpa."

Her grandmother raised an eyebrow.

"This was going to be it, Grams. I just had that feeling. I *really* like this guy. More than I even knew." She gazed off into the distance, thinking about his dimpled smile and dreamy eyes. "He's exactly what I've been waiting for my entire life."

Grams nodded. "Well, maybe you just need to wait a little longer for him."

Clara sighed. "Honestly, I'm not sure I'm willing to wait until next Christmas for him. I don't think I'm cut out for this kind of relationship. It sounds so hard." She stared down at her lap, facing the difficult truth: As much as she wanted a future with Brent, this was *not* what she had signed on for. She moved her gaze to the floor. The dogs seemed to look up at her with sympathy. "I just can't see a future for us with all of this to deal with."

Grams stopped stroking her hair and took her by the chin. She had a serious expression on her face. "Clara, I know you like things done quickly, but sometimes life doesn't work that way. Sometimes, you have to play with the hand you're dealt."

Her grandmother's words felt like a sudden slap. Clara sat up straighter. She swallowed, unsure how to respond.

It was true. Life didn't always happen the way we wanted it to; she was old enough to know that. But in her defense, this seemed like an especially unfair situation. A little more sympathy would have been nice.

And yet, this was one of the things she loved most about her grandmother. She wouldn't just tell her what she wanted to hear. Grams's no-nonsense honesty was as valuable to Clara as her comforting hugs were. Sometimes in life we need someone to grab us by the shoulders and smack us in the face—metaphorically speaking. That someone for her had always been her Grams.

Still, it didn't make it any easier to accept, especially right now. Clara squeezed her eyes shut. She hadn't been looking for a lesson on the hard realities of life. Not tonight. No, right now she wanted shared outrage over the situation. She needed Grams to get furious on her behalf and come up with a plan to get her out of this mess. She needed a show of solidarity to fight this problem.

Clara took a sip of her cocoa too quickly. The heat burned in her throat, and her eyes watered. She took a moment to recover, waiting for her grandmother to say something else. She didn't.

Clara let out a long exhale. "I guess you're right. But isn't timing everything? And the timing for me and Brent .. . well, things couldn't possibly be stacked against us any more than they are. The circumstances are definitely not on our side."

Her grandmother remained quiet. She sipped her cocoa slowly, then set it back down. She looked out the window as the snowfall got heavier around the house. Finally, she turned toward Clara, a thoughtful look on her face. She pursed her lips and nodded. "Or, maybe they are."

Clara rubbed her temple with her free hand. She had no idea what her grandmother meant.

"Clara, I was a military wife for many years."

"Yeah, I know." Her tone was more curt than she had intended it to be. She knew her grandpa had been in the Army before she was even born. He'd even had military honors at his funeral when he died a few years ago. What she didn't understand was why her grandmother was turning the focus to herself right now.

Her grandmother reached out and held her by the elbows. Her expression was soft. "Distance can be hard on a relationship. But it can also create special connections too. In fact, sometimes it can bring a relationship even closer."

Clara rolled her eyes. Why was her grandmother not seeing her side on this? She didn't want a "Look at the bright side" speech—not now.

She pinched her mouth tight as she fought back a new batch of tears. "But Brent and I . . . our relationship never even got the chance to really get going, to see what would happen. He could have been the one, and now I'll never know."

Grams leaned in and whispered in her ear, "Don't deprive yourself of what could be a blessing in disguise. Remember, time is a gift."

Clara let out a breath of frustration. She closed her eyes to think. She wanted to continue arguing her side with Grams, to make her understand why this was unfair, no matter how you looked at it. But how could she do that when she didn't even understand what her grandmother was talking about?

She leaned her head back against the sofa and held the

warm mug against her stomach. It was no use. It didn't look like her grandmother was going to fix this after all. She wasn't going to find a way to get Brent out of the deployment. She wasn't even willing to give it the appropriate coddling it deserved. No, it looked like Clara was on her own.

Grams was quiet as she laid her head back on the sofa and pulled the quilt up over her shoulders. Clara decided to simply enjoy the warmth of the fire. Soft piano music played from the record player. The beagles had gone to sleep, and Clara recognized the familiar breathing pattern of her grandmother, who slowly began to drift off as well. She loved this about Grams—her ability to fall asleep anywhere, at any time. They could be mid-conversation one minute, and she'd be out like a light the next. Clara supposed that was one of the benefits of growing old—being so comfortable with your surroundings that you could nod off anytime you liked. Must be nice.

Clara lifted her head and passed an eye over the living room. All the familiar Christmas decorations were there. The garland over the hearth, the giant bow on the stair landing. The adorable Santa knick-knacks were scattered about. The room was dim, except for the bright lights on the tree and the glow of the fire.

Clara felt sick in the pit of her stomach. Her thoughts went right back to Brent. She wished he was with her right now, watching the snowfall from the window and enjoying the fire next to her. Instead, he was busy getting packed for his deployment—the deployment that would separate them. Probably for good.

Her eye landed suddenly on a worn brown box in the corner of the room, next to the tree: her family's decorations. Decades of old ornaments and handmade trinkets all sat patiently in the weathering box, waiting to be displayed again for another season.

She set down her mug, and stayed quiet as she rose from the sofa so she wouldn't wake Grams. She tiptoed over to the corner and knelt beside the box.

Peering inside, she was greeted by the sight of childhood relics, along with fluffy strands of garlands and a glittered-filled star. She dug farther into the box and was caught off guard by the blinding gleam of a golden ornament. She pulled it out, and it glistened against the bright lights from the tree. It was beautiful. Clara didn't remember ever seeing it before. It had a small clasp on one side and a shiny braided chain attached. It was perfectly round and the size of a compact mirror. It had to be an antique.

She turned it over in her hands and opened it with care. It was a pocket watch. A timepiece sat on one side. On the other was a black-and-white photo of a young couple. She recognized the familiar faces—her grandparents. She pulled it out. Her grandpa, in his Army uniform, appeared handsome and happy. Her Grams, in a party dress, with a huge open-mouthed grin. Clara flipped the picture over. Someone had written on the back.

Christmas 1967.

Clara thought for a moment about the stories her grandmother had told her. This would have been their first Christmas together. This was the Christmas they had fallen in love, never thinking twice about it. They had simply known. She looked closer and saw a tiny inscription on the ornament that had been covered by the picture.

Time is precious when love is new,

A Christmas wish will soon come true.

She narrowed her eyes. A Christmas wish? She looked at the picture of her grandparents, young and carefree. Clara thought about what that first Christmas must have been like for them—meeting when he had just returned from a deployment during the Vietnam War.

Was a magical Christmas wish what had brought them together? Is that why everything had been so perfectly simple for them?

A Christmas wish will soon come true. Was it possible? Clara thought about the magical Christmas she had been expecting to have with Brent, and then about the long and complicated year that was in store for them if they stayed together. All she really wanted was to skip right over it entirely.

She felt ridiculous for wanting something so impossible, so badly. Still, Clara knew she needed to try this—for herself, for Brent, and for their relationship. She had nothing to lose, anyway. If a magical wish worked for her grandparents, then maybe it could work for her and Brent.

Clara closed the pocket watch with determined focus. She wrapped her palm around it and squeezed it tightly. She pressed her lips together and took a slow breath in through her nose. In that instant, Clara made the decision to believe in Christmas magic with her entire heart. Without thinking any further, before she could chicken out, she closed her eyes and made a wish for the one thing she wanted more than anything in the world at that moment. Brent was worth it.

She squeezed her eyes tighter and held the ornament in one hand, her fingers curled around it. *I wish I could skip right past the next 365 days.*

The ornament became hot in her hand, which Clara found equally thrilling and terrifying. Even so, she couldn't bring herself to loosen her grip on it. A strange euphoria enveloped her. Her body felt an intense tingle all over, both warm and sedating, as if she'd swallowed a shot of brandy.

She cautiously opened one eye to find the tree lights pulsing with a brilliance she had never seen before. She opened both eyes. The splendor of the ordeal was over before she knew it.

The next second, the ornament went cold. The tree lights were still again. Clara furrowed her brow, wondering if she had imagined the whole thing. She stared at the ornament in her hand. It now appeared insignificant.

Clara felt ridiculous, suddenly realizing how outlandish the idea of a magical ornament was. She looked over at Grams, still asleep. She let out a sigh of relief that her grandmother hadn't witnessed any of it.

She dropped the ornament back in the box, hopped up, and wiped her hands on her thighs. She backed away from the box carefully with her hands up in defense. Of what, Clara wasn't sure—perhaps her own sanity. She took one last sideways look at the box, then turned around and headed back to the sofa—to Grams, her cocoa, her blanket, and her snow-filled window. For tonight, anyway, it was all she needed.

Clara thought about what she wouldn't give to actually have a magical ornament to fix all her problems. She shook her head and laughed inwardly at the absurdity of the idea.

It was a nice fantasy. But Clara knew the truth. The next morning, she would be forced to face reality.

CHAPTER EIGHT
CLARA

Clara woke up with a start. Had she missed it completely?

She looked over at the alarm clock beside her and lay her head back down with relief. No, she still had a couple of hours before she needed to be on base. The faint light of Sunday morning was beginning to come in through her window.

She had barely slept. After leaving Gram's house she had come home, changed straight into her pajamas, and fallen into bed. She had only wanted the long day—and its many complications—to be over.

Sleep cruelly eluded her, though, as thoughts of Brent and his deployment kept her up most of the night. She had tossed and turned for hours, replaying the things he'd said in her mind. Clara was still trying to grasp the fact that he wanted them to try to make the relationship work, even with the distance of a long deployment.

The crazy thing was that she wanted that too. She just had her doubts about whether it was even possible. The simple truth was that she didn't like the idea of it at all.

They really hadn't been dating long enough to endure something like this.

Still, she had to show up for him today. When he'd asked her to come to the base to see him off, she'd been flattered. She hadn't realized she was so important to him already. How could she possibly say no to that? No, Clara could never let him leave without being there to show him that she cared about him—for whatever it was worth. And to Brent, it seemed it was worth a lot.

Lying on her back, she placed her hands over her chest. Her heart grew warm at the idea of them staying together. The romantic side of her was ready to run to him with a long embrace, ready to fully dive into a long-distance relationship. But her practical side was second-guessing the entire situation. Maybe showing up wasn't such a good idea. Perhaps it was a sure way to inflict more pain upon herself. How was she supposed to watch him fly away from her for a whole year? Was she supposed to simply go home afterward —lonely and broken-hearted—just in time for Christmas?

Even though she hadn't spent one with Brent yet, a Christmas without him sounded miserable. A *year* without him sounded unbearable. Maybe it would all be easier if she didn't go. Maybe watching him leave would be another cruel twist of the knife.

Clara blew out a breath. She lifted her head from the pillow again and crawled out of bed. What was done was done already. She had agreed to go, so she would keep her word. Besides, it was all too overwhelming when she let herself think about it too much. She needed to get herself out of the quicksand of her thoughts for a moment. Grams was right. Clara needed to stop thinking about what she *wanted* and instead accept the fact that she was in this position, whether she liked it or not. She needed to get ready and get herself to the base. She would think about the rest later.

She showered and dried her hair, then applied her makeup quickly. She wanted to give herself plenty of time to find Brent before his plane left. Clara had no idea how any of this worked or what she was expected to do. She did know, however, that she could not be late. Military precision wasn't merely an expression.

Clara realized she had no idea what to wear to the base. She pulled out her phone and searched:

what to wear for a military

She stopped. What was this situation called, anyway? A farewell? A deployment departure? An unjustified ripping apart of two perfectly happy people? She gave up and threw her phone on the bed. This would be the last time her boyfriend would see her for a year, possibly forever. She wanted to make an impression, one he couldn't easily forget. On the other hand, what did it matter at this point? This time next year, he probably wouldn't even remember who she was.

Clara sifted through the closet half-heartedly, finally landing on a gray wrap dress with a pair of tan leather heels. It seemed an appropriate enough outfit to match the lack-luster mood of the occasion. Her hands trembled as she threw her wavy hair up into a neat ponytail, then added some earrings and a necklace. She hoped her light makeup was enough to hide the dark circles that had already formed under her eyes. She pulled on her favorite ivory dress coat with gold buttons down the front to add a little touch of elegance to an otherwise muted outfit. She gave a nod of approval to her reflection in the full-length mirror.

Then she stopped, caught off guard by a change in her appearance she hadn't noticed until now. She tilted her head to inspect herself. She looked different in a way she couldn't exactly identify. Was it her hair? Her skin? She seemed more mature somehow. It was amazing what one poor night of sleep could do to someone's appearance.

She waved it off with the flick of a hand. She didn't have time to worry about that right now. She grabbed the written instructions Brent had given her, telling her how to get on base, and headed out the door.

Dozens of questions swirled around her head as she made the thirty-minute drive from Cranberry Pines to the Air Force base. She was still trying to come to grips with everything and understand exactly what was being asked of her. Was she really expected to say goodbye to him for a year and act as if that wasn't going to change—well—everything? How could Brent be so optimistic? And how, she wondered again, could the military just ruin people's holiday plans like this? That constant thought kept repeating itself: It was all so unfair.

A rumble of jet engines in the distance let Clara know she was getting closer to the base. The water tower donning the official seal of the US Air Force loomed on the horizon. She nervously swallowed as she turned off the highway toward the main entrance. *Well, here goes nothing.*

The Air Force base was busier than she had imagined. It was like its own little town—plopped down in the middle of nowhere—surrounded by iron gates and armed guards. Planes flew overhead, and dozens of flags waved in the wind. She bent her head to see out the window, looking at the sky. A fighter jet was taking off into the clouds with the impressive roar of combat air power. A helicopter appeared larger before her eyes as it quickly approached from the distance.

Clara was taken off guard by a sudden surge of patriotism. She supposed being on a military base would do that; it was just that up until now, she had never been on one. Since Brent lived off base, this was her first opportunity to see it all up close.

Or was it? A fuzzy memory popped into her head of a time when her father had taken her to an air show as a young child. Now that she thought about it, it must have been right here on this base. She didn't remember too much about it, but she could recall the look on her father's face as he looked to the sky in awe. Or perhaps it was gratitude. The loud engines had scared her at the time, but her father had held her hand. He said they were the most comforting sounds in the world.

She supposed she understood now what he'd meant. There was something impressive about the Air Force, and she couldn't help but feel a sense of security, knowing the country was in good hands.

Clara parked her car at the security office, just outside the gate, as Brent had instructed her to do.

"Ms. Jenkins?" A young man in a security uniform was standing behind a desk. "We'll need to see your photo ID and have you fill out a little information. Senior Airman Peck will escort you out to the flight line as soon as you're ready."

Clara smoothed down her coat. She fumbled through her bag for her wallet, casting a glance over at Airman Peck, standing by a door.

He was a short, stocky man with dark hair and a solid mustache. He wore a camouflage top that looked like something between a shirt and a jacket. The matching pants were baggy, but tight at the ankles above a pair of heavy black boots. Clara was instantly intimidated by him. He looked like the typical boot-camp commander in an Army movie who would shout orders in the faces of new recruits. Why was *he* going to escort her anywhere?

She handed over her ID with a trembling hand and began filling out a form.

Airman Peck tapped his boot and let out a sigh.

Clara chewed on her lip.

He cleared his throat. "The bus is ready when you are, ma'am."

She looked up from her paperwork. "The bus?"

"To take you out to the flight line."

She shook her head to indicate she didn't understand.

"To meet the aircraft." Airman Peck turned to the door and walked outside.

She had assumed Brent would be the one to meet her here. Where *was* he anyway? Clara quickly handed her paperwork over the desk and followed close behind.

"Excuse me," she said to the airman's back.

He didn't seem to hear her.

"Shouldn't we wait for Major McNally?"

"The jet should be landing in about ten minutes," he said, ignoring her question. "I'll have you out there in time to see them arrive if you hurry."

"See them arrive?" She rushed around to the front of Airman Peck, forcing eye contact. She held up both her hands. "Wait, you must have me confused with someone else. I'm here to see a flight depart. Major McNally is leaving on the . . ." She pulled the notes from Brent out of her bag " . . . the C-17. It should be departing soon."

Airman Peck tapped away at his tablet, still walking toward the bus. "No, ma'am. No departures today. But there is a C-17 arriving. And Major McNally—I assure you —is on it." He stopped and turned around to give Clara an arrogant smile.

She let out a sigh. This guy obviously didn't know what was going on. If he was going to be difficult, there was nothing she could do about it. She was not about to argue with him here at the security office. Clara could just imagine having to tell Brent she'd been kicked off the base for insubordination. She supposed she'd have to wait to get out to this flight line—whatever that was. She'd get things straightened out there. Once Brent arrived, surely everything would be cleared up.

She followed Airman Peck onto the small shuttle bus. It reminded her of going to the airport, where every trip started with an overcrowded bus from the parking lot to the terminal. This one was also packed with people, all in their seats, waiting to depart. All eyes shifted to her—the one holding things up.

Clara looked from row to row at all the other passengers. It was mostly women and children. There were a few men. Several other airmen in uniform were scattered throughout. She supposed these were the other friends and family who came to see their loved ones off. She let out a quick breath. She was in the right place, after all. She would just have to wait and see Brent once she got out to wherever they were going.

She walked down the bus aisle, feeling like the new kid on their first day of school. Everyone seemed to be in good spirits, oddly enough. How happy could they really be when their Christmas would be so lonely and sad? These women were all about to lose their husbands for a year. The whole situation was depressing.

Clara managed to find an empty seat in the back of the

bus. She wasn't in the mood for small talk, and she wasn't a military spouse. She had no idea what she would even talk about with these ladies. Just being around them made her uneasy—in a way she couldn't explain, even to herself.

As the bus began to move, she closed her eyes for a moment to think. No, she wasn't a military spouse, and thank goodness for that. She let out a long exhale. So how, exactly, did she get herself into this situation?

When the bus slowed, she looked up to see a gray jet making a slow taxi down the runway. Clara tried to spot Brent. He was nowhere to be found. She tugged on her necklace and fiddled with the tiny charm. What would happen if she didn't find him? What if she *was* in the wrong place? What if he left for his deployment thinking she never showed up at all? The thought of that alone broke her heart —for both of them.

She disembarked the bus with the others. Even more families were standing around, already waiting. They were holding signs, balloons, and American flags. Nobody else seemed to be confused. In fact, they all seemed rather excited about something.

She looked over at a young woman standing nearby. She was dressed in a fitted black coat with a pair of high-heeled boots. Her shiny brunette hair had obviously been professionally blown out, and she had a full face of makeup on. Clara glanced down at her own sensible shoes and tightened up her ponytail. She suddenly felt underdressed.

"Excuse me," she said to the woman. "I think I'm in the wrong place. Where can I find Major Brent McNally?"

The woman's face lit up, and a perky southern accent came pouring out. "Oh, you must be Clara!" She was holding a little girl on her hip, and two others stood beside her. All three girls had bouncing blonde curls. They wore matching red peacoats and huge white bows in their hair.

The woman shifted her toddler to the other hip as she held out her hand. "I'm Janie, and I've heard so much about you," she drawled.

Clara looked at her, trying to place the unfamiliar name.

"Don't worry." Janie laughed. "You're in the right place."

"I don't understand. You've heard about me?"

"Of course I have. My husband is Will."

"Who?"

"Will! He said Brent talked about you the entire deployment. I bet you can't wait to see him after all this time." Janie bounced her daughter happily. "I know we're excited to see Daddy. Right, LuLu?"

Clara shook her head. "After all this time?"

Janie gave her a tight smile.

Clara cleared her throat, trying again for some information. "I'm supposed to meet Brent *McNally*. Here."

"Of course."

"To see him off before he leaves for his deployment."

"Mm-hm." Janie wiped some crumbs from her daughter's mouth.

"Isn't that what you're doing here?" Clara pressed.

Janie immediately dropped the smile and turned to Clara, looking at her through narrowed eyes. She shook her head at her. "Honey, we did that last year."

"What do you mean?" Clara's eyes widened.

Janie laughed. "Look, I know you're excited, but he'll be coming off that plane real soon. You need to calm down, girl."

"What do you mean, coming off the plane? You mean,

he's already back?" She gave a fake chuckle at the ridiculous idea.

Janie let out a ladylike snort. "Already? Well, I'm glad to hear the time flew by for *you*." She leaned over the older girls and made a quick fix to each of their bows with her free hand. "Lizzie and Gracie, I want you two to go hug your daddy as soon as he gets off, okay?"

The girls nodded with perfect sweetness. The adorable all-American family looked as if they were cut straight from a catalog page of expensive dolls.

Clara couldn't be sure what was happening. Was this some prank Janie was playing on her? Perhaps this was a kind of weird hazing ritual for new Air Force girlfriends. She continued to stare at her.

Janie looked back at her underneath a judgmental brow. Something in her expression told Clara she wasn't joking.

"You mean, he's coming back—today?" Clara asked, her tone serious.

Janie's face softened. "Look, I understand you're nervous, and you're new to all this. But just try to relax a little. You're getting yourself all spun up." She pointed a perfectly manicured nail at something in front of them.

Clara looked over to see the taxiing plane coming closer. She couldn't blink. She took in a shaky breath and held it, trying to figure out what was going on.

"Everything will be okay once you see him get off that plane," Janie whispered.

Clara wasn't sure if she was talking to her or to herself. All she knew about Janie at this point was that she wasn't making any sense.

Clara grabbed her phone from her purse to make sure she had the time right. Yes, it was 10:15 a.m. on December 5—as it should be.

Suddenly, the memory of the night before at her grand-mother's house barreled into her mind. The wish she had made on that ornament! Clara stood motionless, her body completely paralyzed with fear. She stared at the people around her, having no idea where to set her gaze.

"No . . ." She said it out loud to nobody in particular. It couldn't be—could it? She couldn't possibly have skipped a whole year. That would be impossible. Right?

She quickly opened the calendar app on her phone and saw December staring back at her. December of next year.

Clara put a hand to her cheek. That didn't mean anything. She'd been looking at next year's calendar last night when she'd been thinking about Brent. She probably never closed it properly.

She needed to know. She could ask Janie point-blank, but she'd displayed enough of her cluelessness in front of this woman already. The last thing she needed was for her to think she was completely nuts.

Clara noticed Airman Peck standing off to the side. He was reading something on his tablet. As much as he intimi-dated her, she felt she could trust him. Someone like him wouldn't go blabbing about the crazy lady who didn't know what year it was, would he?

Her heart hammered in her chest as she approached him. "Excuse me, sir." She cleared her throat. "I know this is a strange question, but . . ." She bit her lip. "What year is it?"

He looked up from his reading, a deep frown under that thicket of mustache. He simply shook his head to indicate he didn't have time for her silliness. He pulled a piece of paper from a folder beneath his tablet and handed it to her, then walked off without answering the question.

Clara studied the paper. Her hands were shaking so

violently it took a moment for her to realize what exactly she was looking at.

52nd Air Squadron Homecoming Schedule

Below it was the date in small bold letters. It was today's date, except—NO! The year was wrong. Her jaw dropped. She felt dizzy and fluid as she entered some weird state of shock, as if her feet couldn't quite sense the ground. She was practically spinning in complete and utter disbelief.

It was next year's date.

"It actually worked," Clara whispered, her eyes unblinking. She took in a long breath and then let out a bark of laughter, before quickly covering her mouth with her hand.

She couldn't believe it. Her wish had come true.

She had skipped over the entire year.

CHAPTER NINE
BRENT

Brent looked out the window as the plane made a slow taxi. He was back.

He let the relief sink in after what had felt like the longest flight of his life. It hadn't helped that he'd been a passenger for the past twelve hours. He would have much preferred to have been piloting the plane to distract him from his nerves. He shook out his hands. Flying was the last thing on his mind now. He was focused on a different, much more terrifying, mission. His heart pounded. *What was taking them so long to bring this plane in for a stop?*

Brent got out of his seat, then realized he couldn't go anywhere. He sat back down. He couldn't wait to take in a breath of that clean New Hampshire air. Mostly, he couldn't wait to see Clara.

"So, you ready for this?" Will leaned over Brent from his seat to get a better view out the window.

"Sure am. No doubt in my mind." It was true. Brent had complete faith in what he was about to do. He had been planning it out for months now and had spent the last several hours going over it in his mind. Now, he needed to get it right.

"There are my girls!" Will pointed outside.

Brent looked onto the tarmac below. He recognized Will's family from the pictures he'd seen.

And there she was, beside them. He had to do a double take. Seeing Clara in the flesh after all this time made his head jerk back into the seat. Brent closed his eyes and felt his smile widen. It had been *so* long. A year of video calls just wasn't the same.

He peered out again to watch her. Her mouth was drawn in a tight frown. Clara clutched her purse tightly against her body. It made sense she'd be uncomfortable. She still wasn't used to this whole military scene. Even so, he wasn't sure what to make of her expression. The other waiting spouses seemed full of excitement.

For a moment, he reconsidered his plan entirely. Maybe this wasn't the right time. Would Clara be too nervous in this environment?

The plane finally came to a complete stop, and the engines shut down. He swallowed.

"You're up, McNally," Will said, raising his eyebrows.

Brent gave a faint smile. He couldn't possibly tell Will how scared he was, despite Will now being one of his closest friends in the world.

Prior to the deployment, Brent hadn't known the guy at all—Will being new to the squadron. Rooming with him for a year changed that. Will, blond and athletic, was an outdoorsy boy from South Carolina. He was married with three young daughters, laid-back, hilarious, and loved SEC football. Will had commissioned into the Air Force for "something interesting to do" after college, but had never planned a military career and had no idea how long he expected to stay in. His philosophy on life was so different from Brent's "plan everything" mentality.

That was what Brent loved most about being in the military. Meeting folks from all over, with different personalities, backgrounds, interests, and experiences—and working together for a common goal.

He stood up. His heart raced. He held the ring box tightly in his hand, waiting for the aircraft door to open.

No, Brent wasn't turning back now. He had passed V1 already—the term a pilot uses when it's too late to abort a takeoff. He was going for it now. He had to.

CHAPTER TEN

CLARA

Clara tried to compose herself as the massive airplane came to a stop right in front of her. Her head ached with confusion as she attempted to make sense of the situation.

Brent was about to come off that plane. The deployment was over. Had it even happened? Although she kept trying to explain everything to her brain, she was still having trouble believing it.

She could feel the energy in the crowd swell around her as the staircase was wheeled up to the aircraft door. The families beside her waited with enthusiasm, their eyes turned upward to the plane. Clara forced herself to do the same, realizing she was the only one in the crowd without a giant smile covering her face. She decided to temporarily shrug off her confusion; it was just too hard to fully understand. She'd sort it all out later. For now, she had a show to put on. Clara knew she should act somewhat normal, whatever normal would be in this situation. It would probably look strange to Janie if she greeted Brent with a casual "Hey, what's up?"—as if she had just seen him yesterday.

She *had* just seen him yesterday, but as far as Janie was

concerned, Clara hadn't seen her boyfriend in a year. She supposed she needed to act accordingly. She put on the widest eyes and happiest face she could manage.

And she *should* be excited—genuinely thrilled. He was back. It was exactly what she had wished for.

Clara noticed her perspective shift as she truly began to understand the incredible stroke of good luck she'd been handed. They hadn't missed Christmas together. They hadn't missed anything. How could they have when there was nothing to miss? She and Brent would now be able to pick up right back where they had left off yesterday, as if the whole deployment had never happened. Because it hadn't happened. They'd skipped over the entire thing.

What was she so worried about anyway? She'd hit the jackpot with that wish coming true. The most important thing was that this whole deployment problem was now behind them. They would get to spend Christmas together. *This* Christmas. So maybe it was now technically *next* Christmas, but who cared? It was happening right now, and their relationship could go on as originally planned.

Clara looked up at the sky and thanked her lucky stars—or, in this case, lucky ornament. She'd skipped over all that hard stuff and got straight to her goal—Christmas with her boyfriend. Wow, that really *was* easy. She said a silent prayer of gratitude for Christmas magic and watched with sparkling eyes as the aircraft door finally opened.

Brent was the first to come out onto the staircase. There he was, more handsome than she'd ever seen him. She was surprised he wasn't in his usual green flight suit. Instead, he wore a dressier military uniform, one she'd never seen before. An Air Force blue uniform jacket with matching trousers fit perfectly over his tall, attractive frame. The jacket had silver buttons down the front and a tie underneath. A gold oak leaf adorned each of his broad shoulders, and over his left breast sat a pair of silver wings over rows of military ribbons. He looked so official, so formal, yet so drop-dead gorgeous at the same time.

He pulled on his uniform cap, and his gaze made its way straight to her. He looked at her from underneath the brim and treated her to that familiar dimpled smile. Clara melted. She lowered her head, returning his gaze from beneath her eyelashes. She felt as though she were in a dream. Maybe she was. Brent looked even more fit than she remembered him looking yesterday. His hair was different too, cut a little shorter around the sides. His face had a deep sun-kissed tan. She supposed it all made sense since it had technically been a year since yesterday. At the sight of him, she felt the breath rush out of her. At that moment, one thing was clear—Clara definitely had a thing for a man in uniform.

He descended the stairs, holding a single red rose. Was this how they usually came home from a deployment? As the other airmen began to file out behind him, it seemed that Brent was dressed more formally than everyone else. Most of the others wore loose-fitting, sand-colored uniforms. Also, why was everyone watching *him*? Maybe he was someone more important in the squadron than she'd realized. Was Brent some kind of commander or something? Clara scratched her head. She gave up trying to understand the intricacies of the military. Trying to figure out anything about this absurd situation was complicated enough.

He made his way over to her.

Clara tried her best to act as if she hadn't seen him the night before—for the sake of those around them.

"Welcome home!" She gave him a wink and wrapped her arms around him.

He pulled her in and buried his face into her neck. He held her tight.

She inhaled the familiar scent of his favorite soap. She lowered her head and whispered in his ear, "I can't believe we skipped over it all."

Brent ignored the comment and pulled back. "Clara, I've missed you so much." His face looked serious, but also warm and affectionate. He handed her the rose, then reached into his pocket. "I couldn't wait to get home so I could ask you this . . ." He dropped to one knee and held out a small velvet box.

As he opened it, her heart stopped. There stood a shiny diamond.

Clara's mouth popped open. She stared at the ring, her eyes wide in disbelief. She stood motionless, feeling as if she had no concept of reality—and perhaps she didn't.

Her stomach became queasy, and her legs gave way to an intense wobble. She quickly put both hands over her heart to calm the racing. What in the world was going on? He wasn't actually—proposing—was he?

Down on his knee, holding out the ring, Brent looked up at her with total sincerity. "Clara, will you marry me?"

She stumbled backward. Her skin tingled like the sharp burn of an electric shock. No! This was way too soon. They'd only known each other for a couple of months. What could he possibly be thinking? Maybe this was some sort of act to throw people off to the crazy fact that they had skipped a year. Was she supposed to be in on it?

Clara couldn't be sure if she was imagining this or if she had actually manifested it into reality. Was she simply a character in a story who didn't realize her life wasn't real?

She remembered how she and Lily would discuss different scenarios like this when they were younger and had played with their Barbies. What if they were no different than their dolls, living a storyline in a world they didn't know was imaginary? She shook the thought from her head. This was no time for philosophy. The tremble in her legs and the pounding in her chest told her that this was as physically real as life could get.

Brent looked at her, still asking the question with his eyes.

She folded her arms across her stomach, hoping she wouldn't be sick. She felt as if she was living in another dimension. She supposed she *was* living in another dimension. The top of her head was weightless. Her nervous eyes darted aimlessly at all the families around them. They all stared back at her with excited faces. A wave of panic coursed through her veins as she looked at Brent. He was still looking up at her, waiting for an answer.

Clara nodded, too stunned to do anything else.

He looked at her, urging her to say something else.

"Yes," she finally added in barely a whisper. The word came out sounding more like a question than she had intended it to.

She forced a smile upon her fear-stricken face as Brent lifted her up in another embrace.

Everyone around them cheered. Why shouldn't they? They had no idea this couple had no business being engaged—that they had just met, really. Nobody knew, except the two of them, that they hadn't, in fact, spent an entire year in a long-distance relationship.

A question suddenly pummeled her so hard she almost collapsed. Brent *did* know that. Didn't he?

He seemed to notice her stiffen and immediately set her down so they were eye to eye. He grabbed her chin gently. "Are you okay?" he whispered.

Clara stared back into his concerned face. The reality of this entire situation—her magical Christmas wish—hit her like a freight train. As she looked deep into his eyes, she instantly knew the truth; he had known her a lot longer than she had known him.

Her eyes grew big. As if in a trance, she shifted the rose to her right hand as she held out her left so he could slip the ring on her finger. She held it up in front of her and frowned. She wished her hands would stop shaking.

Brent's face grew more concerned. She heard whispers around them—people wondering if she was feeling okay. She could only look back at them with wide eyes that had lost all ability to blink. She grasped the back of her head, trying to regain control of her body.

Clara suddenly realized that her simple wish was, in fact, a complicated mess. How could she not have thought this all the way through? Probably because she never actually expected it to come true. She had only been thinking of herself when she'd made that wish. Clearly, that had been a huge oversight on her part.

Still paralyzed with shock, she finally understood the massive complexity of the entire situation. She had traveled a year into the future. But Brent hadn't. Only Clara had skipped that year. He, however, had lived through it all.

CHAPTER ELEVEN
BRENT

Exhausted from the long flight and the emotions of the day, Brent arrived back at his house and changed out of his uniform. He flopped onto his couch and let out a long breath of gratitude.

Engaged to be married and home for Christmas. He pressed his palms over his eyes and thought about how lucky he was. But it wasn't actually luck, was it? He knew better than that. It was all thanks to a lot of hard work on both of their parts that he and Clara had gotten to this point.

Now, he could finally focus on celebrating the holidays with her. Their first *real* Christmas together. Although last year's Christmas was significant in its own right. It was certainly one of the reasons they were engaged today.

Brent looked around his house and took a moment to enjoy the peace and quiet. He hadn't had much of that over the past year, always sharing his space with someone else. He got up and ambled his way to the kitchen. He laughed when he opened the refrigerator to find it stocked with food and beer. Dave. He was always thoughtful like that. He grabbed a beer and cracked it open. When he sat down on his couch again, it felt better than anything in the world. He only wished Clara was there beside him.

What did it mean that she hadn't wanted to come over after they'd left the base? He'd asked her to join him for a Christmas movie, but she'd decided to go back to her house instead. She said she had an early morning at work the next day. She had to prepare for some big meeting coming up this week, insisting she'd be much better company tomorrow. He hadn't wanted to press. Still, something about that had him worried.

Had he done the right thing by proposing so suddenly like that? When he'd stepped off that plane, the only thing he wanted to do was run to her. So why did he get the feeling Clara had acted sort of distant? No, distant was an understatement. She'd seemed a million miles away.

Perhaps she was simply thrown off by the whole thing. Maybe she was distracted by everyone around them. Or maybe . . . The thought Brent feared most loomed in the back of his mind. Maybe a year apart had taken its toll on their relationship.

There was no question he wanted to marry Clara. He knew her better than anyone in the world. Over the past year they'd grown closer in a way he wasn't sure would have been possible otherwise. It was certainly a level of intimacy he'd never experienced in any relationship before. He knew, with certainty, that they were ready for the commitment of marriage. But did she feel the same way? That was the big question filling his mind.

Yesterday, out in the desert, Brent wouldn't have doubted for a second that his feelings were reciprocated. Today, though, finally being together in person . . . well, it was not what he'd expected.

His phone rang, pulling him away from his thoughts. He looked at the screen, hoping it would be Clara having changed her mind, and wanting to come over. Instead, it was Will.

Brent answered with a smile. "Miss me already?"

"Nah, I've had my fill of you for a while. I was just calling to let you know I have your deployment trunk. You lovebirds left so quickly; you forgot about the load of stuff you hauled around with you for a year."

"Oh, yeah, sorry about that. Thanks for grabbing it. I guess my mind was somewhere else."

"Understandable."

"Hey, Will, did you notice anything strange about the way Clara acted when I proposed?"

"Well, she seemed surprised. But that's probably normal, I think."

"I guess. It just has me worried. I hope she and I are on the same page."

"Dude, don't worry about it. It's the adjustment period," Will said.

Brent took a long pull from his beer. He swallowed. "What do you mean?"

"Trust me. I've been through this with my wife a couple of times now. It can be overwhelming to throw yourself back into your relationship after spending so long apart. Sometimes they need a little space before they warm back up to you."

Brent laughed. "That sounds more like advice geared for a puppy than a girlfriend."

"Believe me, she just needs to get used to you again. Didn't you read the redeployment packet the squadron gave us?"

"Not yet."

"Everything will be fine once you've been back for a while. Relax, man."

"You're probably right. Thanks. I'll swing by and grab my stuff later." He ended the call and immediately felt better. Is that really all it was? An adjustment period? It made sense, after all. He couldn't expect everything in their relationship to go back to normal immediately. Of course a transition period should be expected. They'd been apart for an entire year.

He let his head fall backward and blew out a stream of air through his mouth.

His phone was still in his hand, so he picked up his head and dialed his parents' number. They would want to know he had made it home safely. Normally, they would have come to the base to greet him, but today he'd only wanted Clara there to focus on his proposal. He had promised his parents he would come out to see them soon. At the very least, he owed them a phone call.

"Hi, Mom. Merry Christmas."

"Brent, you're home!" his mother shouted.

He smiled. "I'm home."

"I'm so relieved to hear your voice. I can finally relax now and enjoy the holidays."

"And there's something else too."

"Oh?"

"I'm engaged."

His mom gasped. "Oh, Brent. Your father and I were hoping to get that sort of news. We think Clara is wonderful. We had a feeling . . . you know, after everything that happened."

He nodded, taking another sip of beer.

"We just didn't expect it so soon. When did you propose?"

"As soon as I got home."

"Wow, you didn't waste any time, did you?"

"Nope. After a year apart, I'm ready to get the rest of our lives moving. I figured enough planning; now it's time for action."

His mom laughed. "Well, I see you haven't changed much over the past year. Oh, sweetie, I'm so happy for the two of you."

"Thanks, Mom."

"And, Brent, I want you to know how proud of you we are, of everything you did during this deployment. This year was a lot for all of us." She sniffed. "You are truly a hero." She paused, then let out a long sigh. "I'm just so glad you're home safe."

Brent blushed. He could always count on his mom to gush over him and make a big deal of any accomplishment, big or small. He suddenly regretted not inviting her to be on base to greet him today. He knew she would have been thrilled to welcome him home with all the warmth in the world.

"Well, I'm glad to hear someone thinks I'm great, even if it is my own mother." He couldn't stop his mind from jumping to the stiff homecoming reception he'd received from Clara by contrast.

"Oh, I know I'm not the only one. So how did Clara react? Was she surprised?"

He wasn't sure how to answer the question. "She was . . ." He considered his next word. *Uneasy. Shaken.* Instead, he said, "Yeah, I think she was pretty shocked."

"Well, that's wonderful, honey. I assume the two of you will be at our Christmas party?"

"We wouldn't miss it. I'll see you then."

Brent hung up the phone and lay his head back on the

sofa again. He closed his eyes and thought about what he had told his mom. It was true that Clara had seemed shocked. But he couldn't quite shake the feeling that it was more than that.

He thought back to this time last year when he'd found out about the deployment. She'd been so upset about it. He remembered she'd been unsure they'd be able to make the relationship work. Brent thought about the day he had left, how he'd been so scared that she wouldn't show up at all, unwilling to get involved in a long-distance relationship.

But they *had* made it work. Shouldn't any doubts she'd had then be gone by now? Especially after the long year they'd just gone through together. Especially now that he was home. Shouldn't their relationship be stronger than ever at this point?

Brent's eyes popped opened, and he took in the welcome sight of his house. It was clean and unlived in. It needed a touch of Christmas. He decided to brush aside his insecurities for now and instead focus on enjoying the holidays with Clara. They would get through this adjustment period in no time. He sprung up from the sofa and walked over to the kitchen drawer where he kept all his important papers. Right on top was the one he was looking for—his Christmas checklist. Sure, he had written it a year ago, but it was finally time to get started on it. He glanced at the first item on the list and smiled.

Get a Christmas tree at the Cranberry Pines Tree Farm.

Perfect. This was exactly what they needed to get things back on track. It was time to pick up right where they had left off last year. The only difference was that, instead of a new girlfriend, Clara was his fiancée. Instead of someone he was getting to know, she was the person he knew better than anyone in the world. Instead of a new relationship, they were in a lifelong commitment together.

Thoughts of Christmas filled his mind as he moved about the kitchen with energy. He needed to do some shopping, to spruce this place up. Brent was going to make sure the next few weeks were memorable. He thought back to Christmas morning last year when Clara had opened the gift that he'd made for her. Her reaction had justified all the work involved. It had been time well spent to see the sincere gleam in her eyes. Now, he just needed to do that again with the perfect Christmas itinerary.

Maybe her tepid reaction to the proposal today was simply a reminder that he needed to put a lot more work into their Christmas *this* year. He needed to come to terms with the fact that things wouldn't automatically become easy just because they were now together. In fact, it could get more difficult.

He wouldn't let that happen. Brent pulled a pencil from the drawer and immediately got to work, updating his checklist. He needed to make sure he covered everything so that no mistakes were made. Yes, he was going to make sure this would be a perfect Christmas for the two of them.

Brent just hoped he wasn't a year too late.

CHAPTER TWELVE
CLARA

The early Monday streets were deserted. Clara stepped outside her townhouse into the frigid morning air.

Cranberry Pines was not a place that changed much from year to year, especially at Christmas—to her relief. After the chaos of yesterday's events, she craved consistency. At least she could count on her town for that, even a year in the future. Yes, a walk down Main Street was exactly what she needed to clear her head.

The early-morning hours had always been her favorite time for wandering around. The streets had just been plowed, and the sidewalks were freshly shoveled after the most recent batch of snow. The sun was beginning to rise over the powdery ground. The smoky aroma of a wood-burning fire drifted from a nearby house. Clara took a deep breath and savored the feeling of comfort.

She had always appreciated the beauty of her town in the winter, especially after a fresh snowfall. It made everything revert to a state of simplicity. It erased the ugliness of everyday life and covered it with a fresh blanket. Clean and simple. That was exactly what she needed.

Clara shuffled along the quiet street in her fur-lined snow boots and heavy down coat. Her favorite coffee tumbler was filled with steaming-hot gingerbread tea. She took her first sip and felt the warmth travel throughout her entire body. The soothing smell of gingerbread made her eyelids soften. The heat of the mug against her chilled lips felt just right underneath her favorite scarf. She took in her surroundings and admired the delightfulness of her little town. She appreciated all the familiar decorations, looking exactly as she had seen them yesterday—just as she had seen them for years.

The stores were still closed at this early hour, but the storefronts were as inviting as ever. A bright electric candle sat in each shop window. The standard-issue town garland surrounded each door frame. With their polished version of quaint village life, the Cranberry Pines downtown association made sure each business on Main Street was not only uniform in their holiday decorations but also utterly charming. The cranberry-filled wreath on every lamppost was the signature touch that made sure the town lived up to its name.

Clara walked past the historic town hall, the anchor of the downtown area. It looked like a small castle lit up from within. In front stood a giant Christmas tree with white lights and thick strands of cranberry garlands. The snow-covered mountains looming in the background only added to the picturesque sight. She looked around and let out a contented sigh. The vapor from her warm breath rose like smoke before her. Clara had always thought her town looked like a jigsaw-puzzle image of an idyllic Christmas village. Yes, even a year in the future, everything looked exactly as it should—just right.

Unfortunately, she couldn't say the same for anything

else in her life. The quiet of the usually bustling downtown gave her a chance to gather her thoughts. This morning, they were all over the place. She still couldn't believe Brent had proposed. How could he possibly think they were ready for this? Well, maybe it was because she'd wished him into thinking they'd been together for a year. She clenched her fists, annoyed with herself for her short-sighted stupidity.

As much as she had wanted to go home with him yesterday, Clara knew she needed to get a handle on everything before she could talk to him about it. Every time she glanced down at the diamond on her hand, another round of nausea would sweep over her at the reminder of what she'd done. She had no idea what to say to him about any of it.

She still couldn't believe this was really happening—that her wish had come true. When she woke up that morning, she had expected everything to go back to normal. That it all would have been a crazy dream. But when an early-morning text came in from Brent—wanting to see how his fiancée was doing—Clara knew she hadn't imagined it at all. Unless she was still in some sort of dream.

No, everything seemed far too real. A check of her phone let her know that it was December 6. It was the day after Brent had been scheduled to leave—instead, the day he had returned. Other than the incorrect year still staring back at her from her calendar app, everything seemed just as it should.

Clara walked past the Darlington Hotel, grateful she wouldn't be going to work today. She'd sent a quick text to the front desk as soon as she'd woken up, letting them know she was sick. It wasn't a lie, exactly. She *was* sick over this whole thing, and the last thing she needed after the weekend she'd had was to think about work. She had no idea what the situation would even be like at the hotel one year in the future. *Was* the hotel in the future, or did this absurd situation apply only to her relationship? She wasn't sure. All she knew was that, in the real world, she only had a few days before her big meeting with Mr. Spencer. She needed to get things sorted out and under control before then.

She had bigger things to worry about than the hotel, though. Clara cringed at the reminder that Brent would expect her to spend any time she wasn't at work with him. As excited about that as she'd been mere days ago, she now had no idea how to celebrate Christmas with him. Fake engagements may be cute and romantic in the movies, but pretending to be engaged to someone who *thought* it was real did not sound like her idea of holiday fun. It sounded mean.

What she really needed was to get them both out of this mess. As much as she liked Brent, marriage was a huge step and a commitment they certainly weren't ready for. It was her fault they were in this situation. She needed to get them out of it.

Clara looked off in the distance toward the mountains. The tops were covered by a white, hazy fog. As she scanned the horizon, her eye caught an unfamiliar shape a few blocks over. It appeared to be a new building—one she had never seen before. She squinted, trying to identify it in the faint dawn light. The building appeared to be tall and modern, unlike anything else in town. She walked toward it. Her boots trudged through a heavy slush along the wet sidewalks.

As she got closer to the mysterious building, she suddenly realized what she was looking at: the new hotel on Fifth Street. Of course. It had been a year since her last walk through town. At that time—two days ago to her—it had been a large construction zone. Now, here it stood—shiny, new, and fully built. It didn't look quite right with the rest of the architecture in the downtown area. Maybe she just needed some time to get used to something new in town. Perhaps she just needed some time to get used to everything.

She continued with her walk and tried to untangle things in her mind. So, Brent hadn't skipped the year as she had. He had gone through it all. And he was ready to get *married?*

Clara shook her head, closing her eyes in frustration. She still couldn't comprehend how Brent got from where they were in their relationship the other day to being ready for marriage—in an instant. Even if he *had* known her for a year now, they hadn't actually been together. How well could he really know her when they'd spent the past twelve months thousands of miles apart?

Clara crossed the street. The Cranberry Pines Elementary School sat on the other side. She sped up her walk, eager to get to one of her favorite places in town.

She sat on a swing and cast an eye over the deserted school playground. The morning sun illuminated the snow-capped scenery. Clara couldn't help but smile as she glanced over at the school. The handmade paper snowflakes hanging from the windows inside flooded her with a wave of nostalgia. They were the same ones she had made when she was a kid going to school there.

She stared down at her feet, planted firmly on the ground beneath the swing. She suddenly felt overwhelmed by how fast her life seemed to be moving. She rubbed at her forehead. Clara still couldn't believe she had agreed to marry someone she'd only known for two months.

She remembered the simple decision she had made at Buddy's the other night—that Christmas with Brent was all she needed to know if he was the one. She had just told Lily that three days ago, with all the confidence in the world. That plan, that simple plan, seemed so stupid to her now. Had she really thought that she could make such a huge decision by spending one holiday with him?

She felt more distant from Brent than ever. She needed to talk to him about this. She needed to explain what had happened. She needed to set things right and tell him that she wasn't ready to be engaged.

Clara pulled her phone from her pocket to call him, then immediately reconsidered. She stared at the phone instead. How could she possibly explain any of this to him? What was she supposed to say—that she had made a wish on a magical ornament and then traveled a year into the future? She was still having a hard time believing it herself. No, she couldn't tell him that. He would think she was crazy. *Was* she crazy?

Clara dialed her grandmother's number instead. As absurd as this was all going to sound, she needed to tell someone, and Grams was probably the only one who could help her make any sense of it. Instead of a ringtone, she got a recorded voicemail greeting.

Hi, you have reached Phyllis Jenkins. I am currently on vacation in Paris and won't have cell coverage in the meantime. Please leave me a message, and I'll return your call when I get back in a few weeks.

Clara scratched her chin. She remembered what Grams

had said the other night about going to Paris next Christmas. Was that *this* Christmas? She went to Paris without her? Leave it to her grandmother not to spring for an international phone plan just when she needed her most. She rubbed the back of her neck. At least her parents had cell coverage, and they would be with Grams. She dialed the number for her mom, and it went straight to voicemail too. The same happened when she tried her dad. She let out a heavy sigh.

She stared at her phone, not knowing where to go next for information. This wasn't exactly a situation she could google. Clara clicked on her social media app and instantly noticed that she was logged out. She blew a stray hair off her forehead as she typed in her password. Access denied. She tried again and received the same error message. She clicked on the button to indicate she had forgotten her password. A security question popped onto the screen.

What is your most valuable possession?

Clara tapped a gloved finger against her lips. That was strange. She couldn't, for the life of her, think what her most valuable possession would be. She wondered why she had chosen that security question in the first place. It was so vague.

She entered in *family*. She supposed her family wasn't exactly a possession. Even so, she couldn't see putting a tangible item above that.

Access was denied.

She quickly tried again with *phone*.

Also wrong.

She glanced back at the school. It made her think of the toys she'd had as a child. It was the last time she could remember having possessions she truly valued. Clara decided to send a quick text to her mom, knowing it was more likely to get a response than a missed call.

> Hey, Mom, quick question . . . do you remember what my favorite toy was as a child?

She knew better than to expect an immediate answer. She loved her parents, but with them spending so much time traveling internationally lately, it was becoming increasingly hard to communicate with them. They were usually asleep when she was awake, and vice versa. She couldn't help but get frustrated with the communication delays, even though she knew it wasn't their fault.

Clara closed the social media app and decided to give Lily a call instead. She answered after a few rings.

"Hey, Clar."

Clara could tell from Lily's gravelly voice that she had woken her up. "Lil, I'm sorry to call so early, but I need to ask you something."

"Sure."

"Where have I been for the past year?"

"Uh . . . what?"

"When was the last time you saw me?"

Lily cleared the morning voice from her throat, probably realizing this wasn't going to be a quick call. "Well, I saw you the other day at Buddy's."

"Yes. At Buddy's . . . right after you got engaged."

"Um, no. I got engaged last year. I'm talking about *this* year, as in, a few days ago."

A long silence followed.

"Clara, it was just the other day. We talked all about Brent coming home, remember? Speaking of that, how did it go? Was it super romantic, like those military homecomings you see on the news?"

She squeezed her eyes shut at the reminder. "Well . . ."

Lily was silent, obviously waiting for her to continue.

Clara bit her lower lip. "He proposed." She braced herself for the reaction she knew was coming.

"What!? Clara, that's incredible." Her best friend was clearly fully awake now, her voice brimming with enthusiasm. "Congratulations!"

Clara cleared her throat. "Thanks."

Lily paused. "I mean, that's great, isn't it?"

She didn't say anything in return.

"Uh oh," Lily said.

Clara knew Lily was able to interpret that silence in an instant. She tried to recover. "No, sorry, I was drinking my tea," she lied. "It's great. So great." She continued to chew on her lower lip.

"Okay, what's up? Why aren't you more excited? It isn't like *you* to be playing it so cool with a huge announcement like this."

"I know, it's just that—" She wasn't sure how to finish the sentence.

"Clara?"

"I mean, I like Brent and all, but—"

"Like him? You're crazy about him."

"I am? I mean, I am. Of course I am."

Lily let out a sigh. "My dear friend, you've talked about nothing but Brent for the past year. All I've heard lately is how much you love him and can't wait for him to get back. He comes home after all this time away, proposes to you, and you're *not* ecstatic? And you talk about me holding back my emotions."

"I said I loved him?" she asked, then immediately

regretted it. "No. Of course I'm excited. I guess I'm still getting used to the idea."

"Are you sure?"

"Yeah."

"Clara, is there something else going on?" Lily asked, her ever-present patience coming through in her voice. Clara could imagine her using that voice on her students.

"It's complicated," she said. As nurturing as Lily could be, Clara was not one of her third graders. She was a fully grown adult in a very adult situation.

"Clar, what's the matter? You're not sounding like yourself."

With her eyes still closed, Clara blurted out the truth before she could chicken out. "Lil, I think I time-traveled."

Lily was silent.

"Are you there?" Clara asked.

"Yeah. Um, what are you talking about, exactly? Are you getting philosophical on me again?"

Clara balled up a fist in frustration. "No. I actually time-traveled. Listen, I know this sounds nuts, but I made a wish the other day—well, technically, last year—to skip over a year. You know, so I could skip over that whole deployment thing. And it worked. I'm in the future now."

Lily snickered. "Okay, Clar. Well, that sounds fun."

Clara pinched her lips together. "I'm serious, Lily."

"Hm. Well, you're obviously up in your head about this engagement."

Clara swallowed, the frustration building.

Lily exhaled, probably realizing her best friend was off her rocker. "Listen, I realize whatever is going on is stressful for you. Why don't you come over later and we can talk more about it. You probably just need some time to get used to Brent being back. But I'm going to need to wake up and have some coffee before I can properly help you through this one."

Clara blew out a slow puff of air and shook her head. It was useless. None of this made any sense at all. Of course Lily wouldn't believe her. How could she?

Clara gave an unconvincing chuckle. "Never mind. I think I'm tired too. I'm still a little overwhelmed from yesterday and haven't processed everything. I probably woke up too early. I just need to go back to bed and reset. Forget I said anything."

"But Clar—"

"I'll call you later." Clara hung up before Lily could say anything else.

It did sound crazy. *She* sounded crazy. If she couldn't explain this to her best friend, there was no way she'd be able to explain any of this to Brent.

She looked down at her phone to see she had missed a call from her mom while she'd been talking to Lily. She clicked on the voicemail message.

Hi, sweetie. I hope Brent got home safely. We hate that you can't be with us for the holidays this year, but we completely understand. We hope you two have a great Christmas together, and I can't wait to hear about everything. We're in London now, but we're about to take the train to Paris. I'll call soon. Oh, and your favorite toy was that Magic 8 Ball, remember? Love you!

Clara hung up, annoyed with her family for all being together without her. She knew it wasn't rational. Why shouldn't they be enjoying a European holiday together? Even so, she shook her head in frustration. Clearly, not much had changed with her parents over the past year—still traveling the globe and having a great time. She could feel the miles between her and her mother now more than ever. She wanted to tell her everything that was going on. To ask her about everything she'd missed over the past year.

Instead, as usual, she'd have to wait. Once her parents got to Paris and met up with Grams, she was sure she'd get this sorted out. She just needed to explain everything to her grandmother. Grams would help her figure out this whole mess.

Clara wrote back a simple text message in reply.

> Have fun!

She tried again to log into her social media account, entering *Magic 8 Ball* this time. She scoffed. Wasn't it just like her to want a magic ball to fix her problems? Some things never change, she supposed. Still, no access was allowed. She threw the phone back into her pocket. It may as well have said what that ball used to tell her back then: reply hazy, try again.

Clara let out a tired breath. She remembered that she and Brent had plans to go to the tree farm together after she got off work, which she was no longer going to. The thought of facing him, of pretending to be his fiancée, sent a new wave of hysteria through her already stressed body. She could feel her palms beginning to sweat. She set her tumbler on the ground. She took off her gloves and began to fan herself with them despite the cold. This entire situation was out of control. She wanted to stop the rapidly spinning world and hop off for a moment to gather her thoughts. To come up with a plan. She just wished she had a little more time for everything. To figure out this situation with Brent. To get a hold of Grams. She needed more time before this major meeting with Mr. Spencer.

She needed someone to step in, slow her life down, and work out everything for her. And right now she needed someone to calm her down. But the someone who was always able to do that was somewhere over the Atlantic at the moment.

She thought about calling Matthew. If there was another person who could fix a problem for her, it was him. She realized how ridiculous it would be to bring this up with *him,* though. If Lily had thought she was crazy, Clara couldn't imagine what Matthew's response would be. No, she had nobody to help her out of this mess. She was on her own.

She took a few minutes to breathe slowly and focus on the beauty of her surroundings—instead of her anxiety-inducing circumstances. It was a method Grams had taught her a few years ago after an especially tough breakup with Matthew. It was all about letting go of what you couldn't control and instead finding the positive in each situation. There was opportunity in everything, no matter how hard it seemed at the time, her grandmother had told her. Sometimes, it just took a change in perspective to find it.

Clara could feel it beginning to work. The scenery around her truly was breathtaking, and she forced her mind to focus on that. The combination of morning sun and freshly fallen snow made everything look like a frosted cake. She could hear the light padding of snow falling from the tree branches above her. The feathery, cold touch of the flakes fell gently on her face.

Taking a few deep breaths of the clean winter air made

her thoughts slowly turn to the holidays. She thought about the plans Brent had made for this Christmas—well, for last Christmas. They would bake cookies, decorate a tree, and go to parties. They would sit by the fire with cocoa, listen to music, and exchange gifts. Clara smiled, thinking about it all, and began to feel a twinge of excitement for Christmas again—just as she had before all of this deployment nonsense.

She grasped the chains of the swing that hung on each side of her, pushed off the ground, lifted her feet, and leaned backward. She swung forward and threw back her head, her legs stretched out in front. A relaxed feeling came over her as she suddenly thought about the simplicity of being a young child—pure joy, simply magical.

Magic. That was it!

They still had Christmas. She now knew that Christmas magic was undoubtedly a real—and powerful—thing. If it could make her time travel, it could certainly make her fall in love. Just like it did for her grandparents. If all went well, she would be ready to be engaged *for real* after the holidays were over. As simple as that. Brent would never even need to know about the wish. As far as she was concerned, they would pick up right back where they left things last year, have their romantic Christmas, and move forward with the rest of their lives. It would be like the deployment never even happened. After all, isn't that exactly what she had wished for?

Clara put her feet back on the ground and nodded with resolve. She gazed off into the distance, taking a long look at the mountains, and noticed they seemed to curl up in a coil, just as the poet Robert Frost had noted in his famous poem about her home state, "New Hampshire". She remembered learning the poem, written by New England's most famous poet, right here in this school for her fifth-grade graduation. Each student had been responsible for memorizing a few lines, which they performed at the graduation ceremony. Clara could still remember hers. She couldn't possibly sum up her thoughts any better than that. Yes, she had made a decision, and now, she could finally rest. Christmas magic would make her fall in love with Brent.

Renewed with Christmas spirit and hopeful optimism, Clara felt revitalized. She stood and brushed the snow off her jeans. She took one last look around the playground and drank her last sip of gingerbread tea. She had an extra bounce in her step as she started the walk home, this time offering a friendly wave to everyone she passed.

When she'd woke up that morning, she couldn't bear the thought of facing Brent. Now, she couldn't wait for him to pick her up, to go pick out a tree together. It was all she'd wanted to do from the start—spend the holidays with him. She stopped and pulled out her phone to send him a quick text message.

> Hey, called in sick to work today. Want to go to the tree farm early?

He wrote back immediately.

> Definitely! Pick you up in an hour?

> Can't wait!

Her heart seemed to glow with the holiday spirit and relief over finding a simple solution. Everything was going to be okay—thanks to Christmas magic.

CHAPTER THIRTEEN

BRENT

The Cranberry Pines Christmas Tree Farm was more charming than Brent could have imagined. He stepped out of his truck and clasped his hands behind his back. Fresh evergreens dotted the white blanket, glistening under the morning sun. He breathed in the scent of fresh balsam fir and felt his muscles loosen. The snow was completely untouched throughout the scenic acres of winter's impressive display.

He'd been thrilled to get Clara's text, and he couldn't imagine a better time to be there than a perfect winter morning. It looked like they had the place to themselves, along with the first pick of the day from the wide selection of trees. The only sounds were the soft whistle of a light wind and a tractor off in the distance.

Brent beamed, enjoying the results of all that waiting finally coming to fruition. It was the first item on his checklist to celebrate their Christmas together. He had dreamed about this moment for twelve months. The air was crisp. The sky was clear. The fresh snow shimmered. It would be the perfect date. Aside from the fact that it had been delayed a year, everything was going according to his plan. Better than his plan.

Brent held his breath, more nervous than he'd realized. He jogged over to Clara's side of the truck to open her door for her. She seemed to remember that he liked doing that instead of hopping out like she had when they'd first started dating. He knew some would say it was an outdated practice. Still, he loved that she seemed to appreciate the chivalry behind the gesture.

He had no idea what to expect from her mood today. Had she adjusted yet? He'd spent the entire drive to her house stewing over how this date would go. He crossed his fingers that she'd be more comfortable around him today. Now that she'd had the night to herself to process the proposal, Brent was hopeful they could get back to normal— whatever normal was for them.

It almost felt as if he was on a first date again—back when he never knew what to expect from a woman. He supposed it *was* sort of like a first date again. He couldn't shake the uncomfortable feeling that it seemed like they were starting all over.

He thought back to their actual first date in the lounge of the Darlington Hotel. He'd struggled a bit with the small talk initially, as he often did when he was nervous. Still, there was a gentleness behind Clara's eyes that had made him grow comfortable with her very quickly. That date turned into one of the easiest conversations of his life.

Remembering this now caused his shoulders to lighten. Brent knew he needed to get over this insecurity about her awkward reaction to the proposal. Besides, Will was right. It would be unreasonable to expect a seamless transition, wouldn't it? He just needed to be patient while she got used to being around him again.

With his favorite handsaw tucked under one arm, Brent offered his other hand to Clara as she stepped out of the truck. She placed her hand into his, and he instantly regretted the bulky gloves he'd worn. After not getting to touch her for a year, he wasn't going to waste an opportunity to have the feel of her skin on his. He pulled his hand back to slip off his gloves. He stuck them in his coat pocket, then held out his hand again. She looked up at him. Her soft palm molded perfectly into his. He gave it a squeeze before intertwining their fingers together. A slow smile spread across her face as her familiar blue eyes held his gaze. Brent felt his heart skip a beat. He brushed her cheek with his thumb. Maybe he had been worrying too much. This *was* still Clara, the girl he had become so close to, not some random first date.

They walked into the farm together, holding hands. The entrance was flanked by two fully decorated trees and connected by an archway of lighted greenery. Clara pulled out her phone to take a selfie of the two of them. He smiled for the camera, his arm around her. With her puffy white coat and matching knit hat with a pom-pom on top, Clara looked like a perfect snowflake, pretty and unique. She suddenly leaned in closer and surprised him with a kiss on the cheek for a picture-perfect moment. He laughed. Yes, everything was looking better this morning. None of the brutal awkwardness from the day before seemed to linger between them. She already seemed more comfortable and more enthusiastic today. Simply an adjustment, he reminded himself again.

Brent took some time to appreciate the moment. He was struck with a sudden sense of tranquility, and it seemed to him that she felt it too. He watched her as she took in the snowy solitude with a peaceful smile on her face. It felt as if they were the only two people on Earth, alone in a vast wilderness of beauty—a paradise. If only their relationship could have remained in such an unspoiled state without the complications of a deployment imposed on it so early on.

Clara's eye landed on his, and she smiled, realizing he'd been watching her. He gently took her chin into his hand and gazed upon her face. He leaned in and gave her a soft kiss on the lips. His entire body shivered. He pulled back to gauge her reaction. She smiled up at him.

Brent pulled her in again, and she stepped up onto her toes. Her mouth landed on his, and their bodies pressed against each other. The kiss deepened. A soft wind blew; her hair smelled of cinnamon. He closed his eyes and slowly breathed it in. A year of longing was worth all of it for this one moment.

She pulled back, her hands still cupped around his head. "I'm so excited for Christmas," she said. "I can already feel the magic in the air."

He let his head fall backward, his eyes looking to the sky as he tried to catch his breath. "I'll say." He put his arm around her and pulled her close as he led her farther into the farm.

As he strolled with Clara through the scenic rows of trees, he forgot any feelings of distance between them. Everything felt right again. It was like last year, back when any time they'd been together felt blissful.

On second thought, it was better than that. Being with Clara today felt as if he had finally come home again after a long journey. Which made sense since that's exactly what he'd done. Strolling through the tree farm with her was all the assurance Brent needed that everything in their relationship was back under control—an assurance he had been desperate to have.

Clara stopped in front of a fluffy Douglas fir. "This is the one."

"You sure?" He loved how quickly she could make a decision. It was a refreshing change from his—at times—paralysis by overanalysis. "You don't want to take your time? Look around a little more?"

"Nope, this is the one."

"Well, that was easy."

She looked at him. "What do *you* think of it?"

He looked at the tree, walking around it to get a view from all angles. Brent could imagine it with the perfect addition perched right on top. That reminded him, the tree topper was probably still at his parents' house. He'd need to get that back.

He pretended to be sizing it up, but he already knew the truth—if she loved it, he loved it. He looked right into her eyes and said exactly what he was thinking, although it wasn't about the tree. "This is the one."

"I knew it." Clara clapped her hands together. "See, we're perfectly in sync. Just like an engaged couple should be."

Brent couldn't help but wince at her words. Were they in sync? He worried for a moment that she was trying to convince herself—or him, for that matter—that they were. And there was something about the way she had said "should be" that made him feel a slight sting of judgment. He brushed off the comment and squatted down to the trunk of the tree, his saw in hand.

He decided to lighten the mood a little. "Don't worry. Once I get this tree cut down, I'll shake it out." Brent laughed. "And I'll make sure to give it a full inspection before we bring it inside." He looked up at her to see her reaction.

She was quiet, holding onto the tree to keep it upright while he cut. Maybe she hadn't heard him.

Brent tried again. "I'll make sure we get anything out of here that you don't want—if you know what I mean." He looked up at her with a wink.

Clara stood over him with a blank stare. "Like what?"

His eyes widened at her, still waiting for her to catch on. The confusion was written all over her face. She didn't know what he was talking about. He let out a nervous laugh as he continued to saw.

"Timber."

He was out of breath by the time he'd sawed his way through the thick trunk. The tree was slow to tip over and they watched together as it fell with a thump to the snowy ground. Brent looked over at Clara with a proud grin. He decided to go for another attempt now they were standing on the same level.

"Crickets?" Brent nudged her arm.

"Crickets in a Christmas tree?" She laughed. "Is that a thing we should be worried about?"

His mouth opened in surprise. He wasn't sure if she was playing around. He gave an anxious chuckle and shook his head. "Come on, let's get this tree in the truck, and then we'll go get some cider."

She nodded, looking at the ground. Brent still couldn't tell if she was kidding or not. He wasn't exactly sure *what* was going on with her.

He grabbed the trunk of the tree and dragged it through the snow, heading toward the truck. Clara, beside him, was quiet. Brent knew he should probably let it go, but he couldn't seem to do it.

"So, I guess you really were traumatized by those bugs

last year if you've already blocked it from your memory." He smiled at her, hoping to keep the mood airy.

"Oh! Last year. Of course." Her eyes got wide. "It must have slipped my mind for a moment. Of course, I remember the bugs." An awkward laugh escaped her throat. "Crickets, right?"

Brent could feel his face fall. It slipped her mind? They had talked about that Christmas-tree incident for *weeks* last year. He'd thought it was hilarious when she'd first told him what had happened.

IT WAS the week before Christmas. Clara had been at home sitting by the fireplace, watching a movie, when she heard the loud chirp of crickets. Assuming she'd left a window open, she walked over to close it, only to have one jump out of her tree and right onto her head. She had screamed so loudly that her next-door neighbor had called to check on her. Once she'd calmed down, she went to inspect the tree with a flashlight and found a whole nest of baby crickets setting up home right there in the branches of her tree.

Brent hadn't been able to stop laughing when she'd told him the story. He could just imagine her surprise, and terror, to find this Christmas bonus. He'd especially loved the part when she opened the door to her backyard and tossed the tree outside, fully decorated, stand and all. She hadn't thought about anything other than getting those bugs out of her house.

His favorite part of the story, though, had been when her neighbor offered to take the tree to the dump for her. Clara had declined, stating that the babies needed a nice home to spend Christmas in. She had left that tree there in her tiny backyard for the rest of the season. She said they would stay there until they could grow up and venture out on their own. He loved this about her. As panicked as she was over those bugs, she still had a caring heart that showed itself at every turn.

Brent remembered how she would update him daily as she checked in on her cricket family. At first, she'd felt bad taking up so much of their precious phone-call time to burden him with her trivial problems, like insects in a tree. But he had soon convinced her that hearing about life—and Christmas—at home was the best way to keep his spirits up. Besides, he loved that story.

HE FROWNED, his worry about Clara—and their relationship—back at the forefront of his thoughts. Why did it seem as if she didn't want to talk about it? In fact, it didn't even seem like she remembered the incident at all. How could a memory that was so important to him be so easily forgotten by her?

She seemed to notice his concern as they approached his truck. "Brent," she started, "I feel like I should tell you something."

"Okay." He stopped, still holding the tree by its trunk. He looked at her and waited for her to speak.

"Well, this past year . . ."

"Yes?"

"Well, it wasn't quite the same for me as . . ."

He nodded, urging her to continue. He noticed an eerie feeling in the pit of his stomach.

"It's hard to explain, but—"

Elvis Presley interrupted her as "Blue Christmas" sounded from her phone. She looked at him, confused. He could also detect a hint of relief in her face. Whatever she had been trying to say to him, it seemed she welcomed the interruption. Clara obviously didn't realize the song was coming from her pocket, though. She looked behind her, frustration on her face, trying to identify the source of the music.

Brent laughed. "I think that's you."

"Huh?"

He pointed to her pocket. "That's your ringtone."

She fished around her coat for her phone. "What? No. My ringtone is 'Jingle Bells'."

"You changed it." He opened the bed of his truck. "Remember?"

She looked at him with a blank expression.

"You changed your ringtone from 'Jingle Bells' to 'Blue Christmas' as soon as I left last year, remember?" Brent noticed his nervous laugh return as he waited for a hint of recognition.

"Oh, yeah," she said. "I must have forgotten about that." She pulled her phone from her pocket, still playing music, and looked down at the screen. "I'm sorry, Brent, but I have to take this. It's the hotel."

"Of course." He lowered his head and slowly backed away, giving her some privacy. Unbelievable. Had she really forgotten that "Blue Christmas," *their* song, was her ring-tone—that it had been for a year now? She had never changed it back, even during summertime, saying it meant too much to her. From the looks of it now, she'd never heard that song coming from her pocket before. How was that possible after everything that song had meant to them?

What was going on with her memory today? Perhaps it

was stress. Brent shook his head. He hoisted the tree into the back of the truck. Stress could certainly cause forgetfulness, right?

He felt terrible that their relationship was causing her any stress at all. He hated that this transition had to be so hard on her. Clara had seemed to be doing so well during the deployment. She always seemed so strong. So positive. So open about everything. When they'd had their hard days, they had always talked things through. She was never closed off to him, the way she seemed to be now.

Perhaps he had simply been blind to the truth. Maybe things were so much more difficult for her than he'd ever known. Brent lay his forehead on his arm, resting on the edge of the truck bed. Everything seemed so right between them at times. But then there were others when it felt as if they were completely distant from each other. He lifted his head and firmed his jaw. Maybe some of his memories from the past year weren't as meaningful to her as they had been to him. Or perhaps it was worse than that. Maybe their *relationship* meant more to him than it did to her.

No. Brent shook his head and closed his eyes. He knew deep down that wasn't true. Besides, it wasn't like him to give up, to accept defeat. No, he would figure this out. He would make a plan and work through the problem. He banged the edge of his truck with an open palm and raised his chin. Yes, that's what he would do.

Perhaps this was the reminder he needed that relationships take work, not only during the tough times, but on a daily basis. Perhaps all he needed was to work harder to make new memories for them *this* Christmas.

CHAPTER FOURTEEN
CLARA

"Clara, we need you to come in right now." The frantic voice of the hotel's longtime front-desk agent, Lucy, was on the other end.

"Why, what's going on?"

"Look, I know you called in because your boyfriend just got home. I get it. But things are a mess. You need to get here immediately."

"What things? What's a mess?"

"Mr. Spencer. His meeting room wasn't ready when he arrived this morning, and his clients are all waiting out in the hallway. He's mad, Clara. He's threatening to take his business somewhere else."

Clara gasped. "Mr. Spencer? My meeting isn't for another few days. He's not supposed to be there until Thursday."

"Well tell that to him. Because he's here now, and he's asking for you."

The reality of her situation hit her again: It was a year in the future. She clapped a hand over her mouth. "Mr. Spencer! You mean, we got that account?"

"Yeah—and we're going to lose it soon if you don't get here and smooth things over with him."

Clara squeezed her eyes shut, knowing what she needed to say next, but also knowing how much she didn't want to say it. "I'll be right there." She put her phone back in her pocket and looked over at Brent.

He stood next to the truck, their perfect Christmas tree in the back. His arm rested against the edge of the truck bed, giving her a glimpse of his perfect physique. He wore a red-and-black flannel shirt, and his face showed the beginning of beard growth—one of the perks of post-deployment leave, he'd told her. He looked just like that gorgeous lumberjack guy from the paper-towel ads. Clara let out a puff of disappointment. The perfect tree, with her perfect boyfriend, on what should have been a perfect day. Instead, it was all such a mess.

She walked over to him, offering him a look of apology before he could even see it coming. "I'm so sorry, Brent, I have to go to work. Something has come up with a big client."

His face fell. "That's okay." He rubbed the back of his neck.

She could see the disappointment all over him, and an immediate guilt enveloped her. But Brent, of all people, should understand that sometimes your job can cancel your plans. As far as inconveniences go, this was nothing compared to the one he'd pulled on her.

Seeming to read her thoughts, he winked at her. "I understand. Duty calls, right?"

She offered a thankful smile. She appreciated him for being so nice about it. Still, she felt awful.

"I'll drop you off there now."

Clara nodded and got into the truck as he held the door

for her. He walked around to the back, shut the truck bed, and climbed into the driver's seat. She glanced over at him with one last look of apology as he started up the engine. She felt terrible that she hadn't known anything about the crickets or the new ringtone. What must he think of her? Either that she had the world's worst memory or that she was a total fake of a fiancée.

She supposed the latter was true.

How would she possibly explain any of this to him? She was about to tell him *something* right before the call came in, although she hadn't known exactly what. Perhaps it was for the best that she'd been interrupted. As welcoming a distraction as that phone call had been in the moment, though, Clara felt nothing but disappointment over having to end their date early. Brent didn't deserve this after all the work he had put in to planning this outing. She should've kept the date scheduled for that evening as planned. Leave it to her to allow her impatience to get in the way. She rolled her eyes at herself. Typical.

The truth was, she was having a great time with him today. If only he'd stop bringing up memories from the past year. Clara cringed at the thought of those awkward moments. Still, she knew she needed to have a conversation with him at some point. He certainly deserved her honesty, if nothing else.

She watched Brent as he drove them away from the tree farm. His expression was difficult to read. He looked over at her, met her eye, and held it for a moment. She smiled at him. Later, she would think about how she should explain all of this. Right now, she needed to get to the Darlington.

CLARA RUSHED into the hotel and recognized Mr. Spencer right away. In his sharp suit, with his white hair, and thick glasses, he looked the same as he had in the video conference she'd had with him last week. Or, last year, rather. He paced back and forth in the center of the lobby. It looked the same as it had the other day. At least she'd had the good sense to use that decorator again this year.

She took off her puffy coat and ran a hand through her hair that had been stuffed underneath a hat. She winced. She was dressed for a Christmas tree farm, not a client meeting. This was not the first impression she had wanted to make, but from Lucy's tone, Clara had known she couldn't risk a stop at home to change first.

She approached him with caution. She had never actually met the man in person.

Mr. Spencer met her eye and gave a frustrated shake of his head. "What in the world happened, Ms. Jenkins? I arrived this morning, and the conference room was empty. No chairs, no tables, and no food." He looked at his watch. "I have clients here from all over the area for a one-day meeting. Their time is valuable. *My* time is valuable."

"Of course it is." Clara's voice gave way to a slight shake. Her professionalism had already taken a hit with her attire. Now her status as a competent sales manager was at risk as well. "Please don't worry, Mr. Spencer. I will get things fixed immediately." She gave him an unconvincing smile and then motioned to the front desk. "I need to find out what's going on." Wasn't that the truth?

Mr. Spencer tapped on his watch.

She rushed over to Lucy at the front desk, who was busy with a check-in. Clara pulled her aside. "What exactly is going on?" she asked under her breath.

Lucy's ash-blonde hair was pulled into a neat bun. The

polished navy-blue blazer and tailored trousers she always wore were a stark contrast to the casualness of Clara's clothes.

Lucy gave a quick look of apology to the guest she had been helping. "Excuse me for a moment, please." She turned back to Clara and widened her eyes to ask what the sudden interruption was for.

Lucy had been a front-desk agent at the Darlington for years. Though she was twenty years older than her, Clara considered her a close friend in addition to a coworker.

She looked at Lucy with a desperate plea in her eyes. "I know Mr. Spencer's account is my responsibility, but I truly am not feeling well right now."

Lucy gave her a pointed look to indicate she wasn't buying the "I'm sick" excuse one bit.

"Lucy, I need . . ." She wasn't sure how to finish the sentence. "I need some help with this," Clara said with complete honesty.

Lucy nodded, her frown giving way to a bit of sympathy.

"Can Matthew take care of this for now?" Clara asked. She wondered how much longer she had left on this awful arrangement of shadowing him in his job. Surely, one year in the future, she should be nearing the end of that whole thing by now.

Lucy drew her eyebrows together. "Matthew? But why—"

"Ma'am." A voice cut off Lucy.

Clara looked up to see the man who had been trying to check in.

"Is there some sort of problem here?" he asked.

Clara smiled at him. "No, sir, I just—"

"Excuse me," a new voice boomed through the lobby, stopping her mid-sentence.

Clara looked up to see another man, middle-aged and heavily built. He hurried over with urgency, unwilling to look out for anyone who might be in his way. And he was holding a plunger.

Clara's eyes widened. A tingle began to creep up from the bottoms of her toes. Whatever this guy had to say, it wasn't going to be good. He didn't have shoes on, only a Celtics sweatshirt, a pair of jeans, and wet socks.

"I seem to be having some plumbing issues in my room." His voice lowered to a whisper as he realized his entrance had attracted the notice of the other people bustling around the lobby. "Sorry, I didn't mean to be so frantic." He looked to the floor and stroked his beard. He cleared his throat. "But I've tried everything."

Clara shuddered. Plumbing was definitely not in her wheelhouse. She tossed a sympathetic smile at the man. "Of course. We'll get you all fixed up in a minute, sir." She held up a finger. She shared a peripheral look of panic with Lucy. "Where's Matthew?" she asked her under her breath.

Lucy didn't answer, turning her attention back to her check-in. Clara let out a breath. She didn't have time for these guests. She needed to figure out how to fix this situation with Mr. Spencer.

"Call Matthew in his office. Tell him I need him—now," she said to Lucy.

Lucy shrugged and picked up the phone.

Clara breezed past the plunger-wielding man, through the lobby. "If you wouldn't mind waiting . . ." she said to him as she hurried past.

"It's kind of an emergency," she heard him say to the back of her head.

She closed her eyes in frustration as she sped up her steps. She ached with shame at the sound of her rubber boots squeaking against the marble floors, but moved quickly through the corridor that led to the conference rooms at the back of the hotel until she was practically running. Her forehead was covered in a thin layer of sweat. She wiped the sleeve of her sweater against it.

The Darlington's four conference rooms opened to an oval-shaped vestibule. A poinsettia arrangement filled the glass table in the center of the space. A dozen people dressed in business attire stood around it, many looking at their watches. The sound of holiday music felt out of place in the current atmosphere, heavy under the strain of inconvenience. She could only imagine what Mr. Spencer's clients thought about the Darlington's service. Where were the banquet staff? She tried to open the conference rooms. Only one was unlocked, and it was completely empty.

Clara's office sat a few yards away. There, she would be able to look up Mr. Spencer's event order and figure out what he needed. It would have all the information to throw his meeting together in no time. This wasn't the first time she'd had a meeting pop up at the last minute. The only difference now was that this whole situation was entirely her fault. That and the knowledge that this account had the potential to make or break her career.

She hurried to her office and opened the door, going straight for the computer. She entered her password to unlock it and found herself denied access. Not this too. She threw her hands in the air.

Clara only knew one thing at that moment: She needed Matthew. As much as she hated to admit it, she couldn't solve these problems on her own. She sprinted back to the front of the hotel and hopped behind the desk alongside

Lucy, who appeared to be having trouble with the check-in. A line had formed.

"He's still not here?" Clara asked her.

"Who?"

"Matthew."

Lucy shook her head.

"Do you even work here?" The man checking in asked.

Clara lowered her gaze to her rubber wellies and jeans and felt her face heat up.

"Well, I first noticed the water on the floor . . ."

She cringed. The man in the Celtics sweatshirt was now telling the newest guest in line, an older woman, all about his plumbing issues.

Clara stood up on her toes to get as high as she could, which wasn't very high in her boots. She looked past the guests in all directions in a desperate attempt to locate Matthew. Maintenance was *not* her area of expertise. She needed to be dealing with her client instead of these hotel guests.

Really, she shouldn't be here at all. It was her day to be sick, and if there was one thing she certainly was, it was unwell. Where *was* Matthew anyway? His office was right behind the front-desk area. What could possibly be taking him so long to get out here?

The man with the plunger continued to drone on, unaware of everyone's increasing discomfort around him. "And then when *that* didn't work—"

"May I see the general manager, please?" the voice of the older woman interrupted him. It was clear she'd had enough of this man's story and wasn't willing to wait any longer. She was tiny and elderly, with short white hair. She had one of the hotel's chunky throw blankets wrapped around her shoulders.

Before Clara could speak, Lucy chimed in. "Yes, ma'am, she's right here."

Clara whipped her head around, narrowing her eyes at Lucy, who was motioning with an open hand to Clara.

Clara froze, her eyes flying open wide. A song ended at the exact same time the purr of the heater kicked off. The Darlington lobby was completely silent. Clara's face didn't move except for the frantic darting of her eyes. It felt as if every person in the lobby had stopped what they were doing to look at her. Her heart hammered in her chest. She swallowed. She said nothing, paralyzed by the spine-chilling tension of the moment. She looked from face to face, not sure where to focus. Everyone was looking back at her, waiting for her to say something. Her eye finally landed on the brassy plaque hanging right over the front desk.

The Darlington Hotel

Clara Jenkins—General Manager

Clara blinked and rubbed her eyes in disbelief. She squinted to make sure she was reading that correctly. *She was now the general manager of the Darlington? Already?*

Of course she was. Her jaw dropped in sudden understanding. She had skipped it. She had made it through that year—a year she had certainly never wanted to do anyway. She had gotten to the other side of it after all. A year of trying to impress Matthew. A year of learning the boring operations side of the hotel. A year of awkward conversations about their relationship. All of it done in an instant. No more complicated history. No more emotional roller coaster. The new hotel must have been ready ahead of schedule and thank goodness for that.

Her open mouth quickly transformed itself into a wide grin. She felt like the Cheshire cat, having won a prize thanks to her own cunningness. Or perhaps she felt more like Alice, lost in some magical wonderland. Clara still wasn't entirely sure she wasn't going to wake up at any moment and realize it was all a dream. She pressed a finger against her smiling lips. She couldn't believe her luck. That wonderful, magical, very convenient wish. This was certainly an unintended benefit. She had only wanted to skip the deployment. She hadn't even thought about skipping that awful year of work. What a stroke of good timing that she was also able to hop right over all that and get straight to her promotion.

Clara gave a confident nod as she gazed upon the Darlington lobby. This was now *her* hotel. She did it. She got straight to her goal without all the mess. Well, that was easy.

Elated over her new circumstances, she quickly shifted her mindset and put on her best professional smile for the older woman. She cleared her throat and raised her chin. "Yes, I am the general manager. How may I help you?"

"Oh, well, my thermostat seems to be broken. I'm not getting any heat in my room," the woman said.

Clara's posture straightened with the weight of her prestigious new title. "Well, that's no problem. We'll send maintenance up to take a look. We'll have it fixed in no time." Clara gave her a closed-mouth smile and cocked her head to the side. She was already beginning to feel confident in her new role. She was in charge now. *She* was the general manager. She squealed internally, just thinking about it.

Lucy's voice suddenly interrupted. "Maintenance isn't available. They're fixing an issue on the roof right now." Lucy was on the walkie-talkie, waiting for someone to answer at the other end.

"What?" Clara asked, her eyes drifting down to the computer in front of her.

"Maintenance isn't available," Lucy repeated.

Clara pressed her lips together. She refused to allow any insecurity to show on her face. She waved off the maintenance problem with a confident flick of the wrist. "Okay. Well, we'll just give her another room then."

"We're sold out," Lucy said.

Clara clenched her fists from behind the desk, throwing an annoyed glance in Lucy's direction. Well, this was what being the manager was all about—solving problems. How hard could it be? She had watched Matthew solve these types of problems for years. Hadn't she?

She stared at the computer. She didn't know what anything on the screen meant. It had been a long time since she'd worked the front desk, and the reservation system had been completely updated since then. The program she used in the sales office was entirely different from the complex web of numbers and letters she was looking at now.

An angry voice sounded from out of nowhere. "Ms. Jenkins, what about my meeting room?"

Clara looked up, her eyes widening in horror. Mr. Spencer. She rushed away from the desk to approach her most important client. These issues would have to wait— Mr. Spencer could not. His business was vital to the Darlington, and she could not lose that account. Not on her watch.

He waited for her to say something. The only problem was she didn't have any idea what to say to him. It was as if she had lost any ability to form sentences, or thoughts for that matter. She stood still, completely frozen. To say she was in over her head was an understatement. It was as if she were buried under several feet of snow.

She glanced over at the other guests in line. The first guest, who had still not been checked in, was growing more impatient by the minute. The Celtics man was still holding that plunger—now resting upon his right shoulder—and eyeing her. Clara looked at the older woman and knew she needed to do something for her. But what?

Clara's bottom lip quivered. She pursed her lips together and took a deep breath, trying her hardest to hide the fear that was building inside her. "I'm so sorry, every-one," she managed to say. She looked at the floor, her eyes landing on her ratty old rubber boots. Her cheeks burned. She had no idea what to do.

A familiar wave of panic began to course through her body. She tried to take a deep breath, but felt it get caught in her throat. "I will . . . I . . . I don't know how to . . ." She looked around, desperate to focus on anything besides all the faces staring back at her. She wanted to run out of the lobby and never come back. Perhaps she would have if it weren't for the familiar face that suddenly entered the hotel.

"Clara, hey." It was Matthew, panting and out of breath.

She breathed a heavy sigh of relief. She had never been so happy to see anybody in her whole life. Matthew's normally perfect hair was a sweaty mess as he removed his hat and hung up his coat on the rack. "Lucy called me. What do you need?"

"Where were you?" she asked, a rush of air escaping her lungs.

"At my hotel." He appeared winded, but alert with concern.

Clara gave her brain a moment to get caught up with everything. "Ah, yes. The new hotel on Fifth," she said, explaining things to herself. "Of course." She nodded in understanding, then looked at Matthew to see what he would do next.

"You came all the way here to help me?" She thought about how fast he would have had to run to get there so quickly. The new hotel was at least five blocks away. At that moment, her heart softened toward him. He always did seem to show up to help her when she needed it most. And right now, she definitely needed it.

He flashed her that signature smile of his. The one that had always made her heart quicken, the one that had usually made it impossible to avoid a coquettish blush.

Clara didn't blush this time. In fact, she found herself slightly annoyed by his lofty demeanor. She forced herself to bury the feeling. Like it or not, she needed him to help her out of this mess. She looked at him, pleading with her eyes. "Matthew, I really need your help right now."

He looked down at her. She couldn't tell if it was pity, or judgment, or something else she detected in his eyes. It was almost as if hearing those words stirred something up in him, a power he seemed to enjoy. He pursed his lips together. "Clara, you can do this, or at least you *should* be able to do this. You should know how to handle this stuff by now. We've gone through all of this over the past year."

"I know. But—" She stopped, unable to finish the sentence. She had no idea how to handle any of the hotel's operational issues. All she knew was sales. But she certainly couldn't explain *that* situation at the moment.

Matthew quickly nudged Clara out of the way and

hopped behind the check-in counter. He typed with focused vigor.

Clara leaned toward Lucy. Lucy nodded to indicate she was listening, though her attention was on what Matthew was doing.

"Is there a new sales manager?" Clara whispered.

Lucy pulled her to the side, out of earshot of Matthew. "You tell me. Last I heard, you were still interviewing."

"I was?"

Lucy let out a sigh. "Look, I know the new hotel being ready ahead of schedule threw us all for a loop, but you've been working too hard doing both jobs. You need to hire somebody to take over sales already."

Clara didn't respond. She watched as Matthew walked around the desk and over to Mr. Spencer. He shook his hand. "Nice to see you again, sir. It seems your meeting room issue was simply a clerical error. It looks like you'll be in meeting room B today instead. Everything is set up and ready to go. The banquet staff has it all prepared the way you wanted it; they just unlocked the wrong room by acci-dent. We apologize, but I'll come down and personally check in on you there in a few minutes to make sure it all looks good."

Mr. Spencer nodded at Matthew and clapped him on the back. He looked over at Clara, his brow furrowed, and shook his head before walking away.

She stood behind the desk, mortified and feeling like a complete idiot. She felt more than incompetent. She felt useless. Maybe she *was* useless.

Matthew returned to the desk and addressed the guests in line. He quickly checked in the first man with no trouble and gave him a complimentary bottle of the hotel's finest wine for his patience. The man seemed pleased enough, although he made sure to throw an annoyed glance at Clara before he left.

To the Celtics man, he said, "Sir, I think we can get an emergency plumber in here in no time. How about a drink at the bar, on us, while you wait?"

The man relaxed his posture, and he nodded in agreement. The plunger was still slung over his shoulder as he headed toward the bar.

Matthew looked at the older woman. "Ma'am, for you, a complimentary hot meal in our restaurant while we wait for maintenance to get to your room. It shouldn't take more than an hour for that thermostat to get fixed."

"Oh, thank you so much," she said to him with a warm smile.

He turned to Lucy. "Make sure maintenance gets straight to the thermostat when they finish on the roof and get a hold of that on-call plumber that the Darlington has a contract with."

Lucy nodded and got on the phone. The mood in the lobby seemed to lighten instantly, and the holiday music went back to playing with ease in the background. Everyone seemed more relaxed—except Clara, who stewed in a pot of self-loathing.

She pulled at the collar of her sweater. *She* was supposed to be the general manager? After that embarrassing display of her management skills, it was clear the Darlington had made a huge mistake in promoting her. Did she really think she was capable of doing this on her own? It looked like Matthew had been right. She obviously *had* needed that year of training to learn the operations side of running a hotel. How was she going to be the general manager without that?

Matthew pulled her aside as if to drive home the point.

"Look, Clara, I gave my recommendation to corporate that you could manage this hotel."

Clara flinched, internally begging him not to say anything else. She did *not* want to talk about this. She couldn't take any more humiliation today. She only nodded and bit down hard on her lower lip to still the quivering.

He went on. "It's only natural that you're still dependent on me, and you probably will always be in some ways. It's okay. I understand."

Clara swallowed the lump in her throat. "Thank you, Matthew. I don't know what I would have done without you."

Her head ached with embarrassment. As much as she hated this feeling, she knew she only had herself to blame. She shouldn't be mad at Matthew. He'd helped her out of this mess. No, she was furious at herself for not having the skills she needed to handle things on her own. She had done this to herself, missed out on a year of experience—experience she badly needed.

She covered her face with her hands and tried to wrap her head around the complexities of her messy wish. She moved her hands to her temples and began to rub them in pure exhaustion.

Matthew gave her a pat on the shoulder. "Well, I'm going back to my hotel now. I've put out enough of your fires; now it's time to take care of things on your own. Good luck."

"Thanks, Matthew," she replied, trying her best to sound appreciative while internally seething over his patronizing attitude.

Clara watched his back through narrowed eyes. He made his way through the lobby toward the door with that trademark swagger, as if he owned the place. Her head pounded with anger, and her hands trembled with frustration.

"Oh, and Clara," he added as he turned back to her. "How's that boyfriend of yours?"

Her brow furrowed. "Brent? He's fine, why?"

"Well, he's been gone a long time now. I was wondering how you're doing with all that. Seems like it may not be an ideal situation."

She pressed her lips together. "It's fine. He's back now."

Matthew raised his eyebrows, taking his time putting on his coat. "That's great. It's important people can be there for you, right? Glad I could help today." He gave her a quick wink and walked out the door.

Clara fumed. How dare he cast judgment on Brent for not being around. He'd been off doing something far more important; he was serving their country. How could Matthew make it sound like such a selfish thing?

Rage filled the top of her head as she wondered how Matthew could make her feel so incompetent with just one look. It was no wonder the two of them had never worked out. He was always the one in the driver's seat. Why had she given him so much control over their relationship? Over her happiness? She should have put Matthew in his place long ago. She couldn't, for the life of her, remember why she'd been so enamored with him for so long. He was so arrogant, so condescending—so convinced that Clara needed him.

She shook her head in slow reflection, terrified by the idea that despite all those flaws, perhaps he was also right.

CHAPTER FIFTEEN

BRENT

The annual squadron Christmas party was always held on a Saturday night in the middle of December. Brent was thrilled to be home for it this year.

He stood tall, ready to show the officer's club to Clara, especially on a night like this. He knew the Christmas party would be the perfect way to show squadron life through a different lens. All she had experienced of the Air Force up to this point had been the sacrifices involved; the hardships of a long separation. Tonight, Brent was ready to introduce her to the other side. The fun side.

He turned to her with a beaming smile and placed a hand on her back as they walked up the stairs to the entrance of the club. She wore a red satin gown with a high jeweled collar. Her hair was pulled up in a loose twist, soft blonde curls framing her face.

Brent normally hated wearing his military mess dress, accented with the formalness of the bow tie. The pants were stiff, the jacket short, and the cummerbund ridiculous. But tonight, he felt good in it. Over his left breast sat a collection of his military accomplishments, including the most recent ribbon earned for his latest deployment.

As they entered, Brent looked up at the soaring cathedral ceiling. He'd never really noticed the architecture of the club before. Stately chandeliers descended from wooden beams; dozens of plaques hung in perfect formation with squadron logos and awards from years past; tables were sprinkled throughout the room, each one covered with a white tablecloth and an arrangement of roses. A Christmas tree towered in the corner, and a four-piece string band played an array of holiday favorites.

"Wow," Clara said. "I had no idea the officer's club would be so elegant."

He nodded, agreeing completely. "Well, you can thank most of the spouses for that. They did all the hard work for this party." He watched her, his chest swelling as she admired the surroundings. He offered her his arm.

Clara smiled as she took it. "An officer *and* a gentleman."

Brent led her to the bar. It was true; he did seem to have an extra confidence about him tonight. Maybe it was the mess dress or the impressive state of the officer's club. Really, he knew it was from having her there on his arm.

The bartender handed them each a glass of champagne. Brent gazed around and was struck with an appreciation to be there. Everything his eye landed on seemed to glow with perfection. The band started to play "There's No Place Like Home for the Holidays." He closed his eyes and pressed the champagne to his smiling lips. He couldn't possibly agree with the sentiment more.

The squadron cleaned up nicely, he had to admit, and there was something special about the pomp of a formal military event. Brent could tell that Clara was impressed with it all, and that made him feel happier than he realized it would. He wanted her to like this part of his life. Once they were married, it would become her life too.

"Well, this must be Clara," said that deep southern drawl Brent had grown so accustomed to over the past year.

He turned around. "Will! Merry Christmas." He tapped his champagne glass against Will's beer bottle in greeting and touched Clara on the elbow. "Clara, this is my buddy—and for the past year my roommate—Will."

Clara shook Will's hand. "It's so nice to meet you, Will."

"You as well. I've heard plenty about you already. Trust me." He gave Brent a playful nudge. "And I'd like you to meet my wife." Will waved over his wife, who had been talking to someone nearby.

Brent noticed Clara's face form a tight frown as Will's wife approached. Her black dress sparkled, and her lipstick was the brightest shade of red Brent had ever seen. She bounded over with an enthusiastic grin and introduced herself to Brent with a handshake and a drawl even more honeyed than her husband's.

Her head tilted with sympathy as she took Clara's hand into hers, placing her other one on top. "It's so nice to see you again, Clara," she said in a hushed tone.

"You too," Clara said, in barely a whisper.

Brent noticed Clara's eyes drop to the floor. He hadn't realized she'd met Will's wife before, but figured it must have been the day he got home.

"Are you feeling better?" Janie asked her. "You didn't seem to have your bearings the other day on base."

Brent's ears perked up at the mention of her behavior. He met Clara's gaze for a second before she shifted it away. Everyone was quiet.

"Clara, are you okay?" he finally asked.

Her glance quickly turned back to Janie. "Oh, I'm sorry. Yes, of course. I'm fine," she said. "I think I was just a little nervous about everything. And then it was so shocking. You know, the proposal and all. I guess for a moment I got myself all turned around mentally."

"Oh, well, that's completely understandable," Janie said. "I've been there too, when everything feels a bit catty-wampus. That's what we call it in Charleston anyway. It happens to us all."

Brent shared a look with Will, who nodded at him. "See?" he mouthed. "Adjustment."

Brent relaxed, knowing Will was right. At least it hadn't been his imagination. Clara *had* acted odd, and other people had noticed it too. At least he knew why now. She'd said it herself—she had just been nervous. It made complete sense when he thought about it. She hadn't been expecting a proposal on top of the pressure of a long-awaited reunion. Maybe he should have dropped some hints beforehand instead of springing it on her so suddenly. Looking at it now, that probably would have been a better plan. None of that really mattered now, though. Their relationship was quickly getting back to where it needed to be.

Janie's mouth popped open as she looked past them. She waved at someone on the other side of the room, then turned back to them. "Now, please excuse me, but I'm in charge of running the games tonight. It looks like they want me to get things started." She gave Will a quick kiss on the cheek and hurried off toward the dance floor.

"Well, I believe congratulations are in order for you two," Will said once it was the three of them.

Brent caught Clara's eye, and she gave a timid smile back.

Will set his beer on a cocktail table and folded his arms across his chest. "I couldn't be happier for you both. You two clearly have what it takes to make it in this chaotic military life. And, Clara, I want you to know how much it meant to Brent."

"What's that?" she asked.

"Everything you did for him during the deployment."

Her eyes popped open, then they shifted to the floor.

"You know, the letters, the gifts, the care packages—they certainly kept his spirits up."

A silence followed. The band stopped for a moment before starting up again with a jazzy rendition of "All I Want for Christmas Is You."

Clara appeared to be lost in thought, her focus elsewhere.

Will waited for a response, but she said nothing. He chuckled and picked up his beer again. "I've never seen anyone spend so much time on video calls. You two must have set a new record."

Brent noticed her stiffen. He offered up a nervous laugh, but she remained quiet.

"Not all girlfriends are willing to commit that kind of time to a boyfriend that's out of sight," Will continued, oblivious to any awkwardness.

"Uh-huh," she said.

"Brent knowing that you cared as much as you did, well, it made all the difference in the world for him."

Brent watched Clara from the corner of his eye. He couldn't help but notice the discomfort all over her face. She shifted her weight and moved a stray piece of hair out of the way.

Clara cleared her throat. "That's nice to hear," she said. She let out a breath of annoyance that couldn't be hidden.

"In fact—"

Brent interrupted before Will could go on any longer. "Enough about the deployment. It *is* a party, after all. Right?" He laughed.

"Okay. Sure," Will said.

Brent gave him a look of appreciation. He knew he needed to end this conversation; he just wasn't exactly sure why. He patted Will on the shoulder and took Clara by the hand. "Well, we're gonna go grab some food. Will, we'll see you out on the dance floor later?"

"You know it."

The two men shook hands. Clara looked up to give Will a slight smile before they walked away.

"Come on, those hors d'oeuvres look delicious," Brent said.

Clara let out an obvious sigh of relief.

He had no idea what was going on in her mind, but he was certain of one thing—she did *not* want to talk about the deployment. But why? Did thinking about the past year make her sad? Maybe there was an underlying resentment for what she'd endured.

Brent had nothing but fond memories from the past year as far as their relationship was concerned. Yes, it was hard at times. There were definitely some tough days. But, overall, he enjoyed thinking back on it to appreciate how much they had gone through—together. Obviously, Clara didn't feel the same way. Maybe she wanted to just forget it had happened. If that was the case, then maybe they weren't on the same page at all. What did that mean for future deployments? If this one had been so bad she couldn't even talk about it, would she be willing to go through one again?

Brent felt a quiver in his stomach. No, things were not

as they should be. He had his work cut out for him still. He needed to remind her of the positive things that came out of that year. He needed her to see how well they knew each other—to understand their connection was stronger than ever. He needed to prove to her that their relationship then and now was worth everything they had been through.

CHAPTER SIXTEEN
CLARA

Clara tried to relax and enjoy the party, but her thoughts kept going back to that conversation with Will.

She and Brent stood by the Christmas tree with a group of airmen and their dates. She sipped her champagne as someone told a story from a previous squadron event. Everyone around her found it hilarious, especially Brent. Clara laughed when the others did, a look of interest pasted over her vacant eyes.

Had she really done all Will said? When she'd first been faced with the idea of a long-distance relationship, she knew it wouldn't be easy. But to spend *hours* on a phone call? To take the time to actually write letters? Putting together care packages? None of this sounded like her at all. The truth was, that slow-burn type of romance had never really appealed to her. What she had wanted with Brent was a sudden, sweep-you-off-your-feet kind of love.

She supposed it was a good thing she had skipped over all that stuff. It was exactly the type of relationship she feared when Brent had suggested they stay together—a hard one.

Even so, the thought of it now—of putting in all that effort—made her feel something she couldn't exactly identify. Was it pride? Perhaps it was simply a feeling of accomplishment, of perseverance. Clara laughed at herself, quickly realizing the ridiculousness of her thoughts. She hadn't actually done any of it. She'd skipped right over it all and was just getting the credit now.

No, Clara knew exactly what she was feeling. Guilt. And it served her right. Shame burned deep in her stomach as she thought again about the compliments Will had paid her. She didn't deserve any of them. Everyone, including Brent, thought she was the perfect girlfriend. Really, she was a complete fraud.

Clara watched Brent as he stood beside his friends, all doubled over in laughter. He looked up and met her glance. His brown eyes shined in the soft reflection of the tree lights. She could see the creases along his mouth, his cheekbones raised. A shiver of attraction ran through her body. Something *was* happening between the two of them. Whether or not it was magic, she couldn't tell yet. The sparks were there, though, floating around, if not flying. Her feelings for him only seemed to grow stronger over the past week as she got to know him better. She appreciated his generous heart and his bright outlook on life. Brent was also really fun to be around. It certainly didn't hurt that he had the dreamiest dimples too. Clara smiled back at him and felt a lightness in her limbs. What exactly *had* she missed out on in that yearlong relationship?

"Ladies and gents, it's time for our annual newlywed, not-so-newlywed game," Janie's voice boomed over a microphone, interrupting her thoughts. "We need three couples to volunteer for our first game. Who wants to come on up here and show everyone how much you know about each other?"

Brent's hand shot in the air.

Clara's eyes widened. What was he doing? "We're not newlyweds," she muttered to him under her breath.

He took her by the hand. "Close enough." A mischievous smirk spread across his face. "Come on, we got this. Nobody knows each other like we do, right?"

She didn't know how to answer that. She grabbed a new glass of champagne from a passing tray and followed him. He led her over to the dance floor where three pairs of chairs were set up, each with their backs to each other. She sat down in one and crossed her legs. Brent sat in the chair directly behind her. Two other couples, both clearly excited to be playing, took the seats that had been set out next to theirs.

Clara's high-heeled foot bounced with nerves as she sipped on her drink.

"Okay, couples," Janie said. "Y'all know how this works, right? I'll ask you a question about your partner or your relationship, and you have to write the answer down on your board." She handed out whiteboards and markers to each of the players. "Your partner will write down their answer as well. We will then reveal your answers to see which ones are a match and—ultimately—to see who knows each other best. Whoever gets the most points is the winner. Simple. Men, you're up first. Then we will switch to the women." She wagged a finger. "And no peeking."

Clara stood and set her drink down on a nearby table so she'd have her hands free to write. She cracked her fingers, then sat back down in the chair. She observed the room. Everyone seemed to be in good spirits as they talked, laughed, and cheered on the three couples in the game. She tried to shake off her nerves and loosen up too. It was just a game.

Janie quieted down the crowd to begin. "Okay, first question, y'all—we'll start with an easy one. Men, what is your wife's"—she motioned to Clara—"or fiancée's, favorite Christmas movie?"

"Easy," Brent said. She could sense from behind her that he was quickly putting a marker to the whiteboard in his lap.

Clara scribbled down the name of her favorite Christmas movie. She noticed her hand tremble as she wrote, and she reminded herself to relax. Would he know this? She couldn't remember if they had ever talked about it before. She shrugged.

"Question two, gentlemen," Janie continued. "When your partner was a child, what did she want to be when she grew up?"

Again, Brent went straight to writing. He seemed to have a lot of confidence on this one too.

Clara swallowed. She wrote her answer, crossing her fingers that they had talked about it at some point over the past year. She seriously doubted it, though. This was a topic that didn't come up much in casual conversation. She knew they hadn't talked about it during their real, short relationship. Her only hope was that it had come up at some point during the deployment.

"Question three," Janie said. "What is your partner's dream vacation destination?"

"In the bag," Brent said from behind her. "Three for three." His marker squeaked against the whiteboard.

Dream vacation destination? Clara tapped her marker

against her chin. She wasn't even sure she knew the answer to this herself. Had the two of them talked about going on vacation yet? No, the only plans they'd ever talked about were for Christmas. She racked her brain, trying to come up with a place she would dream of traveling to—one that she would have mentioned to him.

She thought again about Grams and how she'd wanted to go to Paris. Did Clara stay behind to spend the holidays with Brent? She must have, and it made sense that she would. Still, she hated the idea of spending her first Christmas ever without her family.

She needed to write an answer down on the board. Everyone else had finished, and they were all waiting for her. Clara wrinkled her nose. She supposed she had always wanted to go to Italy. She jotted it down.

Clara closed her eyes and said a quick prayer that she and Brent wouldn't embarrass themselves with what they didn't know about each other. She made a last-minute bargain with herself that she would tell him everything if only she could make it through this game without revealing the entire hoax. She just needed to convince everyone there that they were a real couple, in love, who had spent the past year getting to know each other the old-fashioned way.

"Now. It's time to reveal your answers," Janie said.

The first team flipped over their whiteboards. They were a young couple—actual newlyweds. Clara wasn't sure if the wife had been enjoying the open bar, or was particularly amused by the game, but she giggled at everything. The husband got two out of the three questions correct, but every answer he revealed caused his wife to dissolve into a fit of laughter that filled the room. When he missed the question about what she'd wanted to be when she grew up—

wrongly guessing a dolphin trainer—she practically fell out of her chair. They both were pleased with their showing. They stood and high-fived each other, the wife clutching her husband to keep herself upright.

"Not bad for the first year of marriage, y'all," Janie said. She moved to the second couple—quite a bit older than the first. "Now, let's see how a not-so-newlywed couple fared. Let's see what kind of knowledge twenty years of marriage gets you."

The veteran husband and wife turned over their whiteboards at the same time. A loud whoop roared through the crowd. It was a perfect match.

"All three correct!" Janie said.

The husband stood up and circled his fist in the air in celebration. The crowd erupted with whistles and cheers.

Clara's heart pounded. She tried to calm herself with a deep breath. That couple had been married for two decades. Of course they would know everything about each other. Besides, the newlywed couple missed one themselves, and they were actually married. As far as everyone was concerned she and Brent had only been together a year. Maybe she could fake it enough to fool the crowd—and to fool him.

"A good run so far," Janie said. "Now, Brent. Let's see what you know about Clara."

"Everything," he said as he flipped his board and showed it to the crowd.

Clara did the same with hers. Another round of cheers erupted from the audience. They turned around to face each other so they could compare the boards for themselves. Her mouth dropped. There—written in his neat handwriting—were Brent's perfectly correct answers.

1. White Christmas
2. Professional ice skater
3. Italy (Tuscany, to be exact)

Clara shook her head in awe. She glanced down again at her answers to make sure she hadn't imagined them.

1. White Christmas
2. Ice skater
3. Italy

How? It seemed impossible. She hadn't even known herself—until that very instant—that Tuscany was *exactly* where she would pick to go in Italy. It seemed like Brent know her better than she knew herself. She remembered what Will had said about their phone calls. They must have discussed these things at some point over their long chats. The ice skater thing, though, really? They'd talked about *that?*

Clara swung her legs around so she could give Brent a high five and a peck on the lips. He stood up to showboat for the crowd as the other guy had done. Everyone went wild. She shook her head and rolled her eyes with a smile. Pilots.

She felt her entire body relax with the knowledge that they hadn't embarrassed themselves. In fact, they were on par with a couple married for twenty years. She was struck with a sudden boost of confidence—not only about the game, but about them as a couple. Besides, playing a game with Brent was fun. Really fun.

Clara wiped the answers from her board to start the next round with a clean slate.

Janie continued the game. "Okay, ladies, now it's your turn to show what you know about your men."

Clara nodded. Her mind quickly reeled as she tried her best to conjure up as many random facts as she could based on the conversations they'd had over the past couple of months.

"Okay, first question," Janie said. "What is your partner's favorite Christmas dessert?"

Clara's mind drew a blank. It was just another annoying reminder that they hadn't spent a Christmas together yet. She chewed on her fingernail. They'd talked about Christmas plans plenty, but did he ever mention a dessert? She set her marker on her lap and rubbed a nervous palm up and down her thigh. They had talked about making cookies. Maybe that was it. But what kind of cookies? She needed to write something down. Everyone else had finished writing, and they were all waiting for her again.

"Is everyone about ready to move on?" Janie asked, looking straight at her.

Out of time, Clara wrote down *her* favorite Christmas dessert—those peanut butter balls she and Grams always made. She remembered how they'd form the creamy dough into perfect drops before covering them in a thick layer of melted milk chocolate. Clara would shake the red and green sprinkles over the top before putting them in the refrigerator to set. Maybe a favorite Christmas dessert was something they had in common. She shrugged. It was worth a shot.

"Number two," Janie continued. "What is the name of your partner's favorite pet—ever?"

A pet? Brent didn't have a pet. But had he *ever* had a pet? Probably. What about when he was a child? She had to come up with something. *Come on, Clara, think.* Her mind raced with hundreds of potential pet names.

Clara squeezed the marker tight in her balled-up fist. Why couldn't they ask an easy one, like his middle name? She knew that—Robert. Or what about his major in college? Easy—engineering. But a pet's name? It was so specific. So personal. Sadly, it was exactly the sort of thing you should know about the man you were going to marry.

She racked her brain to come up with a name she could imagine Brent giving to a pet. It would be practical, masculine, something like . . .

Hank! She faintly remembered him mentioning a Hank once. Well, it was something. She wrote it down.

"Finally," Janie said, "what would your partner say was the best gift he ever gave you?"

Clara pressed her left hand to her heart, her shoulders rolling back. Now, this was one she could answer. He had only ever given her one gift, and it sat right there, sparkling on her finger. At the very least, she would get this one right. She nodded with confidence as she quickly wrote down *engagement ring*. Maybe that was her most valuable possession. She made a mental note to try logging into her social media account with that as the answer. On second thought, she wouldn't have had the ring yet when she created that password, right? She let out a frustrated sigh.

Her eyes scanned the room. Everyone seemed to be having a good time. It was just a game, something she needed to keep reminding herself. How they scored on this didn't mean anything. Still, she was a little worried about those first two answers.

"Okay, y'all, let's see how the ladies did," Janie said. "Couple number one, please reveal your answers."

The wife of the young couple turned over her board to

reveal her answers. A loud gasp went through the crowd, followed by a stunned silence. Then, an explosion of laughter from everybody in the audience. The good-humored bride had somehow managed to infuse some adult content into the otherwise G-rated game. Her husband turned to read her board, and his face went crimson. His mouth dropped open, and he threw his hands over his face. Then, he picked up his own board and turned it around. He had answered one of the questions more innocently than his wife had. Still, as somebody shouted from the crowd, the two answers were similar enough when you *really* thought about it. Both wife and husband were in hysterics now, along with everybody in the audience. The entire room was filled with laughter and whooping.

Janie snickered. "All three answers, correct . . . sort of. Nicely done, couple number one." She moved on to the older couple as the laughter continued around them. "Couple number two, show us what you've got."

Clara would have been laughing herself if she hadn't been so worried about her own performance. Couple number two flipped their boards, showing another perfect match. The cheers from the crowd swelled around them as the cocky husband performed some more of his moves.

She bit her lower lip as Janie approached them. "Couple number three, Clara and Brent, please show us your answers."

Clara squeezed her eyes shut and held her breath. Here went nothing. She flipped her board to reveal her answers.

1. Peanut butter balls
2. Hank
3. Engagement ring

She waited. Her heart pounded.

Behind her, Brent turned over his board. Silence followed. Clara thought she could hear a cricket chirp. *Crickets.* She didn't need that reminder. The cheerless quiet around them told her everything she needed to know—she had failed, badly.

Janie put a sympathetic hand on her shoulder. Whispers sounded from the audience.

She and Brent turned toward each other again to compare their answers. He looked at her board with a grimace, then showed her his.

1. Gingersnaps
2. Ruffles
3. Blue star

She got every single one of them wrong? Clara stared down at his board, trying to understand the meaning behind any of the things he had written. None of those answers made any sense. Neither one of them spoke. The entire room remained silent; all eyes focused straight on them.

Janie finally let out a nervous laugh. "Well, it looks like these two need to get caught up after a long year apart, don't you think?"

Several people chuckled to be polite.

Clara remained glued to her chair; her eyes fixed on her lap.

"Our winner is couple number two!" Janie brought the winning couple an obnoxious-looking trophy that they seemed thrilled to receive. The music started up again, and people got up from their seats and resumed mingling. The conversations continued to flow, and the fun atmosphere of the party was back in full swing—for everyone except Clara. She just wished the floor would swallow her up completely.

Brent scooted his chair around so they were looking at each other face to face. Clara's chin dipped to her chest.

"I'm sorry," she whispered.

He leaned forward, his elbows resting on his knees. He ran his fingers through his hair. "Well, I'm sure peanut butter balls are delicious." He rubbed his forehead. "If only I weren't allergic to peanut butter."

Her eyes widened, and she clapped her hand over her mouth. Her fiancé was allergic to peanut butter—and she didn't know. She felt sick to her stomach. She could not have possibly messed this up any worse than she did. Clara dropped her face into her hands and squeezed her eyes tight to suppress the tears of humiliation. She raised her head, still refusing to meet his eye, and cautiously reached over for his hand. "I'm so sorry," she said. "I guess I forgot some things. Maybe I was just nervous."

Brent gave her hand a tender squeeze. "That's okay. I understand." He put his hand to his heart as if he had been wounded and gave her a pained look. "But Ruffles? You forgot about my dog?"

He had a playful smile on his face, but she could tell he was genuinely hurt. And why shouldn't he be? She just showed him, along with everyone else at the party, that she knew nothing about him. The man she was planning to marry.

"I thought I remembered something about a Hank."

He pursed his lips. "Hank is my dad's name."

Clara gritted her teeth, the increasing buildup of embarrassment physically hurting her entire body. She didn't dare bring up the blue star, whatever that was. Maybe he had named a star after her. Maybe he bought her some star-shaped jewelry. She didn't know. Either way, how could an engagement ring not be his best gift? Well, she knew one thing for sure—she was *not* going to ask.

A hot panic crept over her chest as she realized the reality of what all this meant. She was going to marry someone she didn't know anything about—even something as simple as his favorite Christmas dessert. But how could she? They'd only known each other for eight weeks.

Clara ran her gaze around the room, trying to focus on her surroundings to calm down, the way Grams had taught her. She glanced over at the tree, and it appeared to spin, the lights creating a haze of tension. She looked toward the band, and it seemed to scream at her. She looked at Brent and could see nothing but the look of disappointment all over his face. She couldn't calm down this time. No, she needed to get out of there. She popped up from her chair, desperate to leave.

Brent looked up at her with obvious concern on his face.

She forced herself to sit back down. She stared at him, her eyebrows pulled together. Clara knew she should stay and come clean about her wish. This would be the moment to do it, to be honest with him about what was going on. But she couldn't. She was mortified enough. She couldn't take this feeling for one more second. Her breathing became shallow, and she felt her skin flush. She couldn't seem to get enough oxygen into her lungs. Her eyes darted around the room, looking for somewhere to escape.

"Clara?" Brent's expression grew more worried by the second.

She covered her face with her hands and dropped her chin to her chest. No, she couldn't tell him the truth. It would be too hard. Her eyes squeezed shut, and she pinched her forehead. Then, she raised her chin and stood from her chair, leaving the dance floor in a hurry.

As Clara bolted away, only one thought went through her mind: She wished she were braver. Why was she always too scared to do the hard things? After all, it was why she was in this mess in the first place.

CHAPTER SEVENTEEN
BRENT

Brent fidgeted with his bowtie. He sat in the lobby of the club, waiting for Clara to return from the restroom. He scrubbed his hands over his face, kicking himself for volunteering for that game. He'd thought it would remind her of how close they'd grown over the past year. Instead, it seemed to set them back even further.

He glanced at his watch, wondering how long he should wait before going to look for her. He needed to understand what had upset her so suddenly. It couldn't simply be that she got those answers wrong. Why *did* she get all those answers wrong? They had talked about all of it. Every single one of those topics had come up over the past year at one point or another. So why did she seem to have no recollection of it? That nagging feeling loomed in the back of his mind, the one that told him things were not as they should be between them. As much as he wanted to chalk it all up to an adjustment period, he knew there was real reason for concern.

His jaw unclenched when he saw Clara return. He looked up at her with a timid raise of the eyebrows.

She greeted him back with a look of apology. "Sorry. I just needed a minute to myself."

"Clara, are you okay?"

She nodded.

"I'm worried about you."

"Don't be."

"Clara—"

"I've been letting myself get overwhelmed. I can't seem to think straight lately." She waved her hands over her face as if to reset. "I'm fine now, really."

Brent studied her expression. He gazed into her eyes, those familiar pools of shimmering blue, and remembered the woman he'd met a year ago. She looked the same tonight as she had then. Her cheeks still glowed. Her smile could still give his stomach a kick of excitement. The difference now was that he was also completely in love with her. He only hated that he'd caused her so much hardship with this deployment. He wished this process could be easier for her.

He stood up from his chair, unsure how to proceed. "Would you like to dance then?" he tried, preparing himself for rejection.

Clara smiled back at him and nodded.

He took her by the hand and led her to the dance floor. Brent held his breath as they moved through the crowd. He felt as if every move he made with her tonight was like walking over eggshells. One wrong step or topic of conversation, and she'd be upset again—or worse, heading for the door.

He hated how fragile their relationship seemed to be, especially after watching how strong and resilient it had become over the past year. He wondered what had happened to all that fortitude they'd gained through the deployment. Where was all that determination to make things work between them? Was it ever really there, or had he imagined it entirely?

Brent stopped before they approached the dance floor. His eyes widened in surprise. The band was playing "Blue Christmas." He let out a hearty laugh.

"What?" she asked.

"Listen." He watched her, waiting for her to recognize the tune.

"What is it?"

"They're playing our song."

Clara strained to hear. "Oh, yeah. My ringtone." She gave him a casual shrug, waiting for him to lead her in a dance.

Brent felt his shoulders fall. He was disappointed it didn't get a stronger reaction from her, but he brushed it off as the two began a slow sway on the dance floor. What were the odds of this song playing at that exact moment? Perhaps this was fate stepping in to give them a nudge, a nudge they desperately needed. Maybe it was a serendipitous reminder of what they'd been through together. Maybe it was simply a coincidence. Either way, Brent knew he couldn't have planned this moment any better if he'd tried.

He sang along to the lyrics in his head. The ones about snowflakes falling and memories calling. He smiled. Blue memories, indeed. The truth was those memories now made him anything but blue. They made him happy. Brent only feared that Clara didn't feel the same. There was something about rehashing the past year that distressed her. At times, it seemed as if it was torture for her to think about. If that was the case, what did that mean for their future? They would face more separations throughout their marriage. Now, he found himself wondering if she'd be willing to sign on for a lifetime of that.

Brent held Clara close as they danced. He could smell that faint hint of cinnamon in her hair again, a scent that was now becoming familiar and comforting. This song was no coincidence—how could it be? In fact, Clara had probably requested it from the band while she'd been off by herself. The idea of that alone gave his heart a shockwave of warmth. While listening to *their* song playing, while holding Clara in his arms, Brent knew he hadn't misinterpreted their relationship at all. It *was* strong. How could it not be, after all it had endured? It didn't matter how they did in some silly trivia game. Nothing mattered at all right now except the two of them being together. He felt a return of confidence that everything was going to work out. It had to. He had put too much work into this relationship to see it fail.

He gazed down at her and studied her eyes. The soft candlelight reflected off her face. He leaned in closer and whispered in her ear, "I don't want you to worry about that game. Let's move forward."

Clara looked up at him and nodded. "I agree."

He pulled her in closer and rested his cheek against the top of her head. The song mesmerized him. He shed the extra breath he'd been holding, and his steady heartbeat pulsed in time with the music. His focus slowly moved to the corners of her mouth. They were turned up in a relaxed smile. She looked at him from underneath her lashes as he lowered his face closer to hers.

Clara looked into his eyes and raised her chin.

Brent felt as if he was under a spell, unable to resist the pull. He took her face between his hands and pressed his mouth against hers.

She leaned into his body, her lips melting into his.

He closed his eyes as a wave of euphoria pulsed through

him. If a kiss could talk, this one was worth a thousand words. It calmed him in ways he hadn't realized he needed. It brought refreshment to a heart that had been through so much over the past year. It bubbled up a spring of excitement that had been sitting just below the surface since he'd been home.

He felt weightless. His entire body tingled as the feeling of Clara's sweet breath hung against his mouth. He didn't think about the mistakes he'd made. He didn't worry about what would happen next. The present moment was all that mattered. Brent knew everything he needed to: They were finally together again, they had their whole future ahead of them, and they were undoubtedly in love.

He was slow to pull away. His mouth fell open slightly in disbelief as if it was the first kiss they'd ever had. He stroked her arm and felt tiny goosebumps run along its length. Her face was flushed with color.

They held each other's gaze. They really *were* in love. He knew she felt it too. The moment between them was a renewed hope for everything he trusted to be true.

"Time for another game!" Janie's perky voice suddenly drawled through the microphone, stopping the music.

Brent pulled back in a startle, the effervescence of the moment over.

"We need some volunteers," Janie said.

He raised a teasing eyebrow at Clara.

She looked back at him with warning.

They smiled at each other. The intimacy of the moment lingered between them. Perfectly in sync, they said what they were thinking at the exact same time. "We'll pass."

CHAPTER EIGHTEEN

CLARA

Clara couldn't pull her thoughts away from that kiss. Was that some kind of Christmas magic, or what? Maybe it *was* magic. Or maybe she simply got caught up in the romance of the moment.

Whatever Clara felt, it was unlike any kiss she'd ever had before, even with him. Sure, they'd kissed plenty of times before. In fact, the entire two months of dating were full of those spine-tingling kisses. Still, there was something unique about the one they'd just shared. Something that made her wonder if some enchanted element could really be at play here.

Clara and Brent sat at a table with several other couples as coffee and dessert were served. For the first time that evening, she felt relaxed. All thanks to that long-awaited moment of connection. She hadn't realized how much she'd needed it—some sign that she wasn't chasing a romantic pipe dream. She'd been craving that spark, a little nugget of hope that the splendor of the holidays *could* bring them together, for real. Above all, she'd needed confirmation that

Brent really did have the potential to be the one. Well, she got it.

It was a good thing too, since they were already engaged. She laughed inwardly at the absurd irony of the whole situation.

Clara sat back in her chair and sipped her coffee. Brent chatted with his squadron commander seated on his other side. It sounded as if there was some big Christmas Eve mission coming up—something important. She gleaned from the conversation that Brent wouldn't be assigned to it since he was on post-deployment leave. It was a tidbit she was relieved to hear. The last thing they needed right now was to miss Christmas together after all this. Even so, his eyes remained glued to his commander as he detailed the plans for the mission.

Brent's attention focused elsewhere; Clara took the opportunity to think about the evening. When he'd kissed her on the dance floor, any of the reservations she'd had about their relationship seemed to fly out the window. Maybe that magical ornament really could bring her and Brent together. Well, it had brought her this far. And at this point, she was willing to believe in anything. It looked as if this Christmas magic thing could take care of this whole problem on its own. If that was the case, she didn't need to tell Brent anything about the wish. Right?

She still wasn't sure, but the one thing Clara *was* sure of was that she was having a great time with Brent. He was fun, charming, and thoughtful—everything she had known him to be over the past couple of months. There seemed to be *more* about him tonight too, something new she hadn't discovered previously. Whatever it was—it made her smile.

Clara took in the officer's club, quietly observing the other men and women who were part of this squadron.

People chatted away about all sorts of things—flying airplanes, having babies, moving bases. She picked at her cake, content to be on the outside listening in.

Normally, Clara hated not having someone to talk to at a party. That feeling of insecurity, the concern that others may interpret it as aloofness. Tonight, though, she found it oddly comforting. She appreciated this time to be alone with her thoughts and soak up things around her without outside voices to distract her. Besides, she was feeling relaxed from the champagne and that kiss with Brent. He looked over at her to make sure she wasn't bored. She gave him a smile to let him know she was happy to be right where she was.

A small group of women at a table behind her were making ambitious plans for an upcoming girls' trip while their husbands discussed last season's fantasy football league. Clara glanced over to see a small group of men in civilian clothes hanging out by the bar. She gathered these were the husbands of some of the female pilots in the squadron. She heard accents in the room that sounded like they came from everywhere, from Birmingham to Boston. Every race, gender, and background seemed to be represented here. She could have listened in all night like a fly on the wall. She wanted to hear more about these people and their stories. Clara was beginning to enjoy this peek into squadron life, as much as the feeling surprised her.

Even so, there was still no part of her that wanted to be a military spouse herself—a hard truth she would need to deal with eventually. It seemed to be such a lonely existence. Constantly moving around the country. Leaving your friends and family behind. Leaving any career behind—all for a man who would leave you alone in a strange place for months on end. No thank you. It was one thing to date someone like that, but it was a totally different thing to consider marrying them.

The worst part was that she hadn't been given the chance to properly consider marriage with Brent. This had all been sprung on her so suddenly, with no time to really think about things. When they first started dating, she assumed she'd have plenty of time to think about a possible future with him before jumping into any big commitment.

Again, she felt that desperate need for her life to slow down. It was spinning out of control faster than she could keep up. She needed more information or perhaps more experience. Really, she just needed more time.

Clara thought again about her relationship with Matthew. Though that relationship may have been complicated in its own way, at least he'd always been around for her. Although, maybe that had been the biggest problem with Matthew. He was *always* around—to help her out, to solve her problems, to influence her decisions. She never could seem to detach from him, even now.

This past week at the hotel had been the hardest of her entire career. Without Matthew around to help, she still wasn't sure how any of this was going to work, how she'd get a handle on her responsibilities as general manager. Work life aside, Clara knew she'd needed him a little too much in other ways too. Maybe some independence in a relationship wouldn't be such a bad thing for her. But to marry someone in the military? That was another extreme entirely.

She wondered what it would be like to be married to Brent. To be part of this life. She had to admit, she could understand the appeal—for some people. She thought about what it would feel like to be a part of something so important. Being a part of the history of this squadron and its vital mission over the years must feel like an incredible honor.

She looked over at Brent, who caught her eye with a warm smile. She was proud of him and impressed with the things he accomplished—both at home and overseas. She considered how it must feel for the spouses of these airmen to be part of that service to their country. To contribute to the overall mission in their own way.

Maybe she was beginning to understand what people meant when they said, "Being a part of something bigger than yourself." She'd never been connected to anything significant like that before. She'd never really thought about life in that way at all. Her choices always seemed to steer themselves toward what most naturally fit into place for her. Whether it was going to college, working at the Darlington, or dating Matthew, she had always done what simply felt like the most sensible—or perhaps the easiest—thing to do. She had never made any tough decisions, gone out on a limb, or contributed to something more meaningful than her own small-scale existence.

Clara looked back at Brent, still focused on the conversation with his commander. He nodded along to everything he said. Whatever that Christmas Eve mission involved, Brent was enthralled.

Even after knowing him for only two months, it was obvious to her that Brent was sharp and skilled at the controls of a plane. But there was a stronger force that moved him. She could tell that he had a heart that was calling him to do what he did, that his military service wasn't only a way for him to fly airplanes. He truly believed in the mission.

Still, as much as Brent was committed to this life, she knew her reservations couldn't be ignored forever. If only magic could take care of that problem too.

CHAPTER NINETEEN
CLARA

Clara left the Darlington, stepping into the cold afternoon air. She bent over and rested her hands on her knees, letting out a long exhale. Her breath rose in a cloud of frost before her.

It had been an intense couple of weeks at the hotel. Although relieved to be finished with her workday, she was now emotionally and physically drained. Finally, it was the week before Christmas.

The first weeks of December were always the busiest of the year at the hotel, and this year had been no exception. As interim sales manager, Clara was still responsible for the end-of-year sales report, not to mention the booking, planning, and perfect execution of dozens of parties throughout the month.

This year, she'd had the additional challenge of acting as the general manager too. And to her, it did feel like acting. Clara was racked with exhaustion, not to mention a severe case of impostor syndrome, over the whole thing. Sure, she was slowly beginning to find her footing, but she still had a long way to go. She'd had to fight the urge—or habit—to call Matthew on more than one occasion. Whether it was to solve a problem or simply answer a question, she was tempted to go for the quickest fix—him.

Clara knew, though, that she needed to figure it out without him, so she'd decided to use the staff as the valuable resources they were. She'd been following them around to learn the ins and outs of each department. Over the past couple of weeks, she'd soaked up as much information as she could about maintenance, reservations, housekeeping, even the restaurant. Now, she was just relieved to have gotten through it in one piece.

With Christmas only a week away, the party rush was now behind her. Things slowed down a lot at the Darlington over the week leading up to Christmas, as the hotel's hordes of business travelers were replaced with a much lighter holiday tourist crowd. Clara was thrilled to finally be getting some badly needed time off—time she'd get to spend with Brent. As busy as she'd been at the hotel all week, she hadn't seen him since the squadron party last weekend.

Clara glided down Main Street, the weight of her work week disappearing with each step away from the hotel. She headed straight for the Sugarberry Bakery. The bell jingled as she opened the door to be greeted by the sweet aroma of sugar and butter. She peered at the cakes behind the glass. They looked too good to eat—like a display case full of art. Clara went to the counter to pick up her order, packaged in a pink box tied with their signature gold ribbon. It was worth the small fortune she'd paid for it. The Sugarberry Bakery was famous for its decadent cakes, especially around Christmas. It would be the perfect gift to take to Brent's parents' house for their Christmas party that evening. Clara swallowed. Their first time meeting.

Cake in hand, she made a last-minute decision to visit Lily before heading home to get ready. She pulled out her phone to double check the address she'd stored for Kyle, knowing Lily had planned to move to his place after the wedding. Clara hadn't seen her at all since this whole time-travel thing, and she needed Lily's calm right about now. She was more nervous about meeting Brent's family tonight than she realized. Were they going to see right through her? Would they take one look at her and know she didn't have any idea who their son really was? She was beginning to feel more like a con artist at every turn.

SHE KNOCKED on Kyle's door and was instantly greeted by her best friend waving her inside. Clara set the cake on the kitchen counter and untied the ribbon to give Lily a quick peek. They had both been in awe of the boutique bakery's cakes ever since they were kids.

She thought about the time when they were in third grade and had gone to Sugarberry to pick out a cake for Clara's birthday party. Her mom had given them money and told them to pick out whatever looked best to them. Clara, in true fashion, had wanted something basic and beautiful. Lily, of course, had tried to talk her into a confetti cake. It was full of colors, all of them bright, exploding with sprinkles in all directions. Instead, Clara chose a classic white cake with pink roses on it. The whipped cream flowers looked as if they had bloomed from a real garden. She loved that cake and could still remember how happy it made her that day.

She thought back to that time in their childhood, back when life was so simple. It didn't seem all that long ago, but now here they were. Lily's students were now that age. She was married, and Clara was about to be as well. It all seemed to go by in the blink of an eye, and perhaps it did. Clara thought about what she wouldn't give to slow time down, even just a little.

"Oh, that looks amazing," Lily said, peering inside the box, her eyes wide. The two of them both inhaled at the same time, the scents of buttercream and gingerbread pouring out from the cardboard box. Lily leaned in and stuck a finger toward it. Clara swatted it away.

"This is sure to make a good first impression," Lily said. She looked up at Clara. "But from the way you'd talked about his parents before, I assumed you'd already met them."

Clara frowned and closed the box. She sat at the table while Lily poured her a cup of hot tea. She pretended to be more familiar with Kyle's house than she was. She'd been there before but hadn't paid much attention at the time. Surely she must have been to Lily's new place at least a dozen times over the past year, and she needed to act accordingly. The last thing she wanted was to revisit the awkward conversation they'd had the other day.

Lily hadn't believed her for a second, and Clara supposed that was for the best. It was becoming more obvious each day that this was a phenomenon she needed to keep to herself, at least until she understood it better. No, Clara wasn't going to try to explain this to Lily. She was already stressed enough about meeting Brent's family. What she needed right now was the familiar company of her best friend. She just hoped that Lily had forgotten their weird conversation.

Clara took out her phone to quickly check for any missed calls. Her thoughts turned to the one person who could make sense of this—her grandmother, who she still couldn't get a hold of. She needed her more than ever right now, and things were beginning to feel more desperate the longer she went without talking to her.

Clara fired off another text message to her mom.

> Call me when you can.

Every time her parents had called lately, she'd either been asleep or working, and any calls Clara had returned went straight to their voicemail. If it weren't for the regular texts she received from them, she'd be worried. But with the time difference, she knew better than to count on consistent communication. Even so, this was longer than she was used to going without talking to them, especially Grams.

Her mind returned to Lily's comment about Brent's parents. Clara bit her lower lip and thought about what she knew about them. "They live a couple of hours away, so there hasn't been an opportunity to meet them," she said, unsure if that was true. She *hadn't* met them before, had she? Clara squinted as she racked her brain for any clues, knowing the chances were almost nil. Still, she needed to be careful. She never knew what to expect with a conversation these days and didn't want any more mortifying moments like at the squadron party. Between that painful encounter with Will and her embarrassing show during the newlywed game, she'd had enough humiliation to last her the season.

She made another attempt to get onto her social media account, using the word *car* this time. The day after the party, she'd tried both *engagement ring* and *blue star*.

Neither had worked. She just knew the clues she needed to piece things together were there online. If only she could get in. Access was denied again, though.

Clara passed an eye over the kitchen, taking in the sights of her best friend's grown-up house. It was a small bungalow on a great street near downtown. Lily, of course, had decorated it all in her typical style. Clara chuckled to herself, appreciating how very "Lily" it all was. Some things never changed—even a year in the future.

She sipped her tea, enjoying the moment of calm in what had otherwise been a chaotic week. Even if the house wasn't familiar, it was still nice to be in Lily's comforting presence. While life seemed to be changing so quickly around her, she needed the stability of their rock-solid friendship to ground her in reality.

Clara was quickly learning that her life was just a series of changes she was forced to adapt to, whether she liked it or not. Perhaps a moment of patient reflection was all she needed to reset and not feel that things were moving at a thousand miles per hour. She took a slow breath, smelling the fresh flowers Lily had set out. She closed her eyes and enjoyed the warmth of the mug against her hands. Lily's cat purred in a soothing rhythm from underneath the table. When did Lily get a cat? Clara shook her head and smiled, appreciating the surprises as they came. She reached down to rub him on the back. In return, he rubbed his head against her leg as if they'd known each other forever. Yes, she needed this time to relax and get out of her head for a moment.

Lily sat in the chair across from her. "So, are you nervous for the party tonight?" she asked, taking Clara away from her peaceful escape too soon.

Clara nodded with her lips pressed together. "It's not only his parents I'll be meeting. His entire family and all their friends will be there too."

"No pressure," Lily said. She raised her mug to her lips.

Clara chewed a fingernail.

"Seriously though, Clar, I know they're all going to love you."

Clara only shrugged, hoping Lily was right.

"So how was the squadron party last weekend?" Lily asked, changing the subject.

"A little awkward at times." Clara stopped herself from saying more. She had no idea how she could possibly explain *that* situation to Lily. She couldn't imagine how it would sound that, through a party game, she realized she knew absolutely nothing about the man she was engaged to. It was probably best to leave that part out.

Lily raised her eyebrows.

Clara waved it off. "Overall, it was amazing." It was true. After that night, she was more convinced than ever that Brent could be the one. Sure, it seemed as if he knew everything about her already, and she still had *a lot* to learn about him. When they'd danced together, though, none of that seemed to matter. She smiled to herself as she remembered it now.

Lily looked at her, urging her to go on.

"We kissed." Clara let out a deep sigh while gazing into the distance as she thought again about the moment. "It was incredible. No, it was magical." She felt a shiver run down her back. She had no doubt in her mind that magic was what she had felt on the dance floor that night. It had been the first time since Brent's return that she had simply enjoyed being with him without the worry of saying something dumb. She'd been replaying it in her mind all week.

The way he held her, the feel of his cheek against hers. And that kiss. It was all she'd wanted when she made that wish: to be on the other side of the deployment and back in Brent's arms.

Lily laughed and got up from the table. "Well, I guess after a year apart, it would feel like first kisses all over again. Can I get you some sugar for that?"

"No thanks, I'm good." She took a long inhale of her tea, which was steaming with the scent of spiced oranges.

"Hey, Clar, about what you said the other day about time traveling . . ."

Clara flinched. Of course her best friend wouldn't forget her making a comment like that.

"What exactly were you talking about?"

Clara let out a nervous laugh. "Oh, that? You were right. I was being philosophical about life. Like, I guess it felt like the year flew by—or something like that. I was just overthinking everything, and I wasn't making sense."

Lily came closer. She bent down and studied Clara's face. "You sure you're okay?"

"Perfect." Clara broke eye contact. "I'm more interested in knowing how you are now that you're married."

Lily retreated. She seemed unconvinced, but was willing to drop the subject. "Now that I'm married? It's been six months already."

"Of course," Clara said. "I mean, well, just getting a status update."

"Okay. So far so good." She gave Clara a wink. "You'll find out what it's like soon enough, though."

Clara inwardly rolled her eyes at the reminder. She took a long sip of her tea. The heat burned her chest. It wasn't that she didn't want to be married—she did. It was just that Lily and Kyle's relationship was so solid before they had made that commitment to each other. She thought back to her outlook on relationships from the other day. She had wanted so badly to rush through all the time involved in a long relationship. To get straight to the good stuff—ending up together. It seemed so enticing at the time. Now, what she wouldn't give to have the option to slow things down even a little—to simply have the time to breathe a bit, to really figure out if Brent was right for her.

Clara narrowed her eyes as she watched her best friend move around the kitchen. Lily looked different. Her hair was curlier and shorter than it had been the other day—well, last year. She wore a flirty animal-print skirt with a bright-pink blouse; the gym-clothes phase clearly behind her already. Beside the new diamond on her left hand that Clara had seen the other day stood a shiny solid gold band. Lily was married. She had missed her best friend's wedding.

"Hey, Lil, can I look at the photos from your wedding?"

"Sure." She pointed. "The album's over there in the bookcase."

Clara set down her mug and moved to the living room. She found a black leather photo album embossed with Lily and Kyle's initials in silver. She sat on the sofa and flipped through the pages. There, smiling back at her, was Lily, looking gorgeous in her one-of-a-kind wedding dress. There were pictures of her walking down the aisle toward Kyle. She saw them waltzing for their first dance and feeding each other cake. It was all so beautiful.

There—next to Lily in almost every photo—was Clara. It was the proof she needed that the year she skipped had actually happened. It was now painfully clear to her that she had, in fact, been present. Like the age-old question about a tree falling in the woods, she wondered: If a whole year passes, but there's no memory of it—did it really even happen? According to the pictures in front of her, the answer was yes.

In the photos Clara wore a bright-purple dress she had never seen before, clearly a Lily-chosen bridesmaid dress. Her hair was up in her perfectly styled ponytail, her blonde waves falling down her back. She looked happy in the pictures—dancing, laughing, having a blast with the other guests. On the pages in front of her sat a summary of one perfect moment in time. All her closest friends together, celebrating an occasion that would never come again.

She bit her lower lip. A sadness washed over her as she stared down at the pages of everything she had missed. She wished more than anything that she had been there. Clara pinched the bridge of her nose to stop a tear that was beginning to form. She continued to flip.

Past the pictures of the wedding, she came upon a few additional shots that showed the events leading up to the big day. A bachelorette party at a local winery, the bridal shower at the Darlington, and the rehearsal dinner at Buddy's Tavern—complete with extravagant martinis and all.

Her attention narrowed in on one picture in particular. It was a photo of Lily in a makeshift veil standing beside Clara and her other bridesmaids. There, off to the side of the frame, was Grams. They were all standing in front of the Darlington, huge smiles on their faces. It appeared to be sometime in the spring, and they all wore floral sundresses. Grams had a peaceful smile on her face, her gaze directed at Clara. A longing stirred inside Clara's heart. She had missed that season with her grandmother, with everyone she loved.

She rubbed her hands over her face. A heaviness set deep into her chest. She had missed it—all of it. Well, she had been there, obviously. She even had the pictures to prove it. She simply didn't have any recollection of it. Wasn't that the same as not having been there at all?

How precious can a moment in life be if you don't have the memory of it to take with you?

CHAPTER TWENTY

CLARA

Christmas lights perfectly outlined the single-level brick house. The cul-de-sac was filled with cars, and every window of the modest home glowed with activity.

Clara stood beside Brent on his parents' front porch. Her hands trembled as she held the cake box against her stomach. Meeting a boyfriend's parents was nerve-racking enough. Meeting her fiancé's parents for the first time in this nonsensical situation instantly topped the list of things Clara wished she could skip right over.

Her thoughts jumped back to the first time she'd met Matthew's parents. They'd had a brunch planned at the hotel for their visit to town. Clara had arranged everything for an elegant meal, excited to meet the parents of the man she'd become so close to. But Matthew had canceled at the last minute for a meeting that "couldn't wait." He'd insisted the brunch go on without him, so she'd had the pleasure of spending a wildly uncomfortable afternoon with his parents —alone. That incident had always bothered her and was just one of the many flags she seemed to overlook when it came to Matthew. Maybe he hadn't been as dependable over the years as she'd thought.

Clara knew this was an entirely different situation. She could tell Brent genuinely wanted her to get to know his family. Besides, she supposed it was a necessary step. If this Christmas magic thing was going to work out, they'd be her in-laws before long.

Brent turned to her with a playful grin. "I should warn you, there are a lot of McNallys in there, including some honorary ones. And they are all excited to meet you."

"Can't wait," she said through gritted teeth.

Under normal circumstances, she would be excited to be there. But these were not normal circumstances. She was still getting used to the fact that life had gone on without her for an entire year. Every conversation seemed to serve as a cruel reminder of that. She was tired of constantly feeling as if she was in the dark about everything.

Brent stood beside her, his hand on her back for support. They both wore the gaudiest Christmas clothes they could find. He'd told her that the typical attire for his parents' annual party was Christmas tacky. They'd had fun shopping online for their outfits together. Clara had picked out a colorful dress with a battery-operated wreath. He chose a sweater with a pom-pom-nosed reindeer on it.

Clara shook off her nerves with a shudder and decided to focus on the positives. This was an exciting moment in their relationship—a huge step forward for them.

"Clara! Brent!" Mrs McNally, Christine, answered the door with a warm smile. She had shoulder-length, sandy blonde hair and a pair of dimples that looked exactly like Brent's. She wore a Christmas vest with so much festive bling going on that Clara wasn't sure where to look. "It's so nice to have you here." She held the door open for them to enter.

Brent's dad, Hank, stood just inside the hallway. He was a tall man with a full head of gray hair and a vest to match his wife's.

They stepped inside. Clara's mouth popped open, and her eyes brightened. The house smelled incredible, as if someone had been cooking all day. She handed the cake to Brent's mom, somewhat distracted by the music and laughter coming from the next room.

"It's so nice to meet you both," she blurted out before she could even think. She clapped her hand over her mouth, willing the words back in.

She still hadn't been sure, especially after Lily's comment. Asking Brent hadn't been an option. Even with the two-hour car ride out to their house, she couldn't seem to come up with a way to ask, "So have I met your parents before?" without sounding like a total lunatic. Between the distance and the fact that he'd been gone, Clara figured the odds they had met were pretty low. Judging by the looks on their faces now, she had figured wrong. Her face began to flush as she realized one thing: This wasn't their first meeting.

Clara felt her shoulders slump. There was that feeling again. It was a combination of frustration, confusion, and shame—an emotion that was becoming way too familiar to her now. She had just arrived, and already she was steeped in humiliation.

She lowered her eyes to the floor, feeling ridiculous as she watched the blinking lights from her dress pulse through her coat. She wished she was wearing an outfit more her style. None of this was her, and she was tempted to shout it out loud for everyone to hear. The dress only made her feel more like a phony than she already did.

"Well, let me take your coats," Christine said, glossing over her comment. "It's so nice to see you for some holiday fun, Clara, as opposed to the circumstances last time."

Clara took off her coat and tugged at her dress. "Yes, I agree," she said. "So, so much better." She heard the crack in her voice.

Hank gave her a kind smile and stuck his hands in his pockets.

Clara cleared her throat. "So much better that I feel like this is the first time we're meeting." She cringed as soon as she heard the words leave her mouth. She avoided Brent's eyes. What *were* the circumstances last time they met?

Entering the house, Clara was blinded by the tinsel, lights, and loudness of the annual McNally Christmas party. Dozens of friends, relatives, and neighbors had all descended upon the household in their tackiest gear. Everyone seemed to be in a festive mood. Music played, and the drinks flowed.

The large open kitchen appeared to be the hub of the party, and Brent immediately led her over. It was brightly lit and packed with people. Clara squinted through the crowd to peek at everything up close. The countertops were heavy under the weight of some of the most delicious-looking food she had ever laid eyes on. There was a giant veggie tray shaped like a Christmas tree. Dozens of cheese balls sat alongside an array of crackers and nuts. Sweet-smelling loaves of fruitcake were already sliced. There was a baked ham with pineapples on top and side dishes of green bean casserole and candied sweet potatoes. It was so different from the upscale menu of prime rib and beef wellington she'd been serving at the Darlington all month. It was perfect. On the kitchen table sat a punch bowl of eggnog covered in a fat layer of frothy foam.

They each ladled a glass and headed to the living room. A wood-burning fireplace warmed the space, and a Christmas tree glowed brightly from the corner. Clara put a hand to her chest, admiring the idyllic scene. It reminded her of the Christmases growing up in her house, back when her parents would throw a party for all their friends and neighbors every Christmas Eve. She felt a thickness build in her throat as she thought about the Christmases of her childhood. She closed her eyes and took a moment to miss her family. Her eyes prickled.

She drew in a deep breath, letting the air fill her lungs before gradually letting it out. She let the feeling give way to an appreciation for being exactly where she was—with Brent and his family. Clara liked the feeling that his family reminded her of her own, and she was happy to be starting new traditions—and memories—with him.

She hadn't felt it much over the past few days, but here was that feeling again, both welcome and familiar—the simple joy of Christmas.

A handsome, silver-haired man played a piano in the center of the living room. Guests sipped on cocktails and sang along. Clara wondered if she'd met any of these people over the past year. She had no idea how to keep it all straight or how she could possibly know what to say without seeming like an idiot again.

Clara looked over at Brent and watched his dimples deepen. She made a decision to shrug off her worry and instead simply enjoy the evening. She'd follow his lead. She snuggled in close to him as he welcomed her into the living room.

Christine came around with a platter of cookies, and

Clara helped herself to one. She grabbed a gingersnap for Brent, remembering this tidbit from the game at the squadron's party. She loved that she now knew his favorite Christmas dessert. See? Christmas was bringing them closer together already.

They approached the piano, where the charming man played a tune while simultaneously engaged in a boisterous conversation.

"Clara, this is my uncle Pete." Brent clapped Pete on the back, then he greeted the others gathered around with hugs and handshakes. He introduced Clara to the group.

"Nice to meet you, Clara. Do you have any requests?" Pete asked.

She thought for a second. "Well, I've become particularly fond of Elvis these days." She winked at Brent.

She chalked up the huge smile he threw back at her as a further win. It was another thing she had in common with him—the song "Blue Christmas." She still didn't understand why, but that song seemed to be important to him in some way. Maybe she was finally beginning to catch on to some of the shared memories, even if it was from something as dumb as a ringtone. Although Clara had to admit, after the dance they'd shared at the party, she definitely liked that song now too.

"The King I can do," Pete said. He banged out the opening notes of "Here Comes Santa Claus."

Everyone sang along to Pete's attempt at an Elvis impersonation. Clara was having a good time with Brent already. She always did. She took a moment to appreciate the picture-perfect scene. She glanced over at the kitchen where his parents were busy filling drinks and hosting friends. Her gaze slowly rotated around the living room. She watched the other guests. They hugged in greeting.

They laughed. Everyone was happy. It was a beautiful illustration of the importance of being together with loved ones for the holidays. Time together with friends and family. Sharing in the joy of the season.

It all served as a necessary reminder that she and Brent really *had* needed to spend Christmas together. She thought about what they would be doing right now if she hadn't made that wish. He would be off in the desert and all alone at Christmas. He would be missing out on all of this—and she would be too.

They would have been deprived of experiencing one of the best moments that life can offer. Despite all the messiness, at that moment, Clara knew one thing with certainty: She had made the right decision in making that wish.

As she perused the room, her eyes stopped on the Christmas tree. Her gaze landed on the star that stood atop. Her mouth opened and something stirred inside her. It was familiar. A tingle coursed through her spine. Her eyes remained glued to the star. There wasn't anything extraordinary about it. It didn't sparkle like the one at the hotel. It didn't light up. There was little grandeur about it at all. It appeared to be made of simple wood and painted a basic shade of blue. Still, there was an allure about it that she was drawn to.

Brent noticed her staring and nodded toward it. "Our tree is still missing something, isn't it?"

"Huh?"

"Don't worry. I told my parents we'd be taking that with us tonight. They just wanted to show it off for the party."

She looked at him, not understanding.

"It was nice of you to loan it to them last year." He laughed. "Since the crickets had other plans for your tree."

"Yeah, they sure did," she said with a fake laugh. *Those crickets again.* She rolled her eyes.

"But this year, and for every Christmas from now on, that star goes on our tree."

Clara was silent. Her brow furrowed. She tried to piece together clues so she could make sense of what he was saying.

"I made that for *you*, after all."

"You made that?"

Brent turned to face her and sucked in a breath.

She shook her head, still not understanding. She stared at the star again. It was impossible to take her eyes off it. Clara saw a faint vision play out in her mind. It didn't feel like a memory exactly, not from real life—more like a memory of a dream.

Brent's jaw became firm. "Yes, Clara. It was the gift I made for you last Christmas."

The sharpness of his tone broke the spell she was under.

An abrupt laugh escaped her throat that she'd never heard come out of her before. "We didn't even know each other last Christmas."

Clara covered her mouth with her hand, forced her lips together, and squeezed her eyes shut. She knew better than to say something stupid like that. It felt as if the words had jumped out of her mouth before she could even stop them. It was as if she had been so lost in thought over that dumb star that she lost all ability to think.

Maybe she'd been so relaxed she got caught up in the nostalgic feelings of Christmas and forgot about their current situation entirely. Or maybe the stress of this overwhelming lie was becoming impossible to handle. Maybe she was beginning to crack. Either way, she was overcome with a desperate desire to end this whole charade. She couldn't keep up with this act much longer.

Part of her wished Brent would just tell her everything she'd missed instead of quizzing her all the time. Every conversation with him was a test of her memory—a test she continued to fail. The only way it would stop, though, was if she told him the truth. But if she did that, he'd probably run for the hills, or at least a psychiatrist.

Brent lowered his head and ran his hands through his hair. His frustration was becoming impossible to hide.

Clara felt her chest tighten. She didn't blame him for reaching the end of his rope with her inexplicable and all too frequent lapses in memory. No, it wasn't his fault. He had been incredibly patient with her up to this point. Nothing about this ridiculous situation made any sense. There was no way to explain it to him—why she hadn't remembered meeting his parents, or those dumb crickets, or that aggravating ringtone, or his peanut butter allergy, or his adorably named dog—and now, this Christmas gift?

Clara shook her head as if erasing an Etch A Sketch to start over. "I'm sorry, Brent. I'm not sure why I said that." She felt a pain in the back of her throat. She closed her eyes and took a deep breath as she tried to think of what to say next.

She remembered his answer about a blue star from the game at the squadron party the other night. The best gift he'd ever given her—apparently—was this tree topper. She folded her arms across her stomach and looked down at her feet. She still didn't know why this simple gift was such a big deal. All she knew was that, by the look on his face, it was.

She blew out a stream of air. "Of course I remember the gift. I'm so sorry," she said.

Brent stared at her. The usual warmth in his expression was missing.

Clara turned away, unable to look him in the eyes. She glanced out the window to the backyard. It was dark, except for the orange glow from a wood-burning firepit. She needed to pull herself together. She needed to sort out everything he'd told her. Right now, she needed some air.

"That fire out there looks nice; I think I'll go sit for a minute."

Brent said nothing as she hurried to the back door.

She stepped out into the backyard. The fire blazed with heat. She sat down and sank deep into a chair, her head falling backward. She was relieved nobody else was out there. She needed a minute alone to wrap her mind around everything. She couldn't keep doing this. They couldn't possibly pick up where they left off last year, especially now that they were on entirely different timelines.

What would happen to their relationship if this Christmas magic thing didn't make her fall in love? They were in two totally different places, and she had no idea how to get them back to a shared reality.

Clara knew she *could* fall in love with Brent. If this was a normal relationship, it would probably happen anyway, all on its own time. But she didn't have that option anymore. No, she needed Gram's magic ornament to finish what it started and see this thing through to the end.

"Transitions are hard," said a voice from behind her.

Clara turned around to see Christine, a plaid blanket wrapped around her. She handed Clara a new cup of eggnog.

"Thank you," Clara said, taking the cup. "Is it obvious?"

"Let's say I know a thing or two about it. I dealt with plenty of tough transitions in the twenty years that my husband was in the Air Force." She sat down in the chair beside Clara. "Sometimes we build up their return in our minds. We have this expectation that it will be all romance and roses once they're back, that it'll all be easy again. But the reality is that, initially, you're just out of sync sometimes." She took a sip of her eggnog and looked up at the sky. "And it takes some time to get back on the same wavelength."

You have no idea. "Thanks," Clara said. "I think you're right."

"You know, Clara," she continued, "when you drove out here to see us when Brent had been injured—"

Clara sat up straight in her chair. He had been injured?

"It meant a lot to us that you came to be with us. It was hard in those first few hours when we had no idea if he was even alive."

Clara leaned forward, her eyes widening.

"When we finally got the call that he was okay—with only a few bumps and bruises—there was nobody we would have wanted there with us more than you."

Clara only nodded, but her mind was racing. Brent had been injured. He had been in actual harm's way for a whole year. Clara took a moment to think about all he must have endured during his deployment. Meanwhile, there she'd been, back home safe and sound, complaining to him about something as trivial as crickets in her Christmas tree.

And now, here she was, finding herself frustrated with *him*. And for what—having memories? For the first time since she'd heard the word *deployment*, Clara began to think about what she should have thought about much earlier—what it would mean for Brent. She had been so focused on herself and how this experience would affect *her*. She had never stopped to think about what it must have been like for him. What *had* he gone through over the past year?

How could she have been so self-centered? She wished she could have been more supportive of him and all his deployment involved. She wished she had been there to help him through it.

"Room for one more?" Brent's voice sounded behind them. He took another seat by the fire.

Christine stood up. "I should probably go inside and make sure everyone's good on drinks." She touched Clara gently on the shoulder before turning toward the house, leaving the blanket behind for her.

It was just the two of them by the fire. Clara reached over and took his hand.

"Brent," she said, placing the blanket across both of their laps. "I'm sorry."

He shrugged.

"I'm sorry for the way I've been acting lately. I know I've been out of sorts since you've been back."

He nodded, gazing at the fire.

"I don't want to talk about me though. I want to know what you went through over there while you were deployed. I mean, like really know."

Brent was quiet, his eyes focused on his lap. He seemed deep in thought.

Clara waited patiently in silence. The crackle of the fire was the only sound.

She was surprised at the heaviness of his back as she watched him ponder something. Brent had always seemed so self-assured, so optimistic. He'd never seemed particularly stressed to her. Probably because he planned everything out so perfectly. His checklists seemed to provide him with stability and confidence. Now, he looked as if he had the weight of the world on his shoulders. He appeared to be wrestling with whatever was on his mind, feelings he couldn't control. To see something push against him so strongly like this caught her off guard.

She wondered if the deployment version of herself had known about all he'd been carrying around with him. She wondered if she had helped him through any of it. At that moment, she wished she'd been the one to do it.

Brent raised his head. "There will be plenty of time to talk about that kind of stuff—again." He smiled. "I think I'd rather enjoy being here at this party with you tonight."

She nodded, understanding the part that went unspoken. She was relieved to see his smile return, the one she'd come to expect over the past couple of months. It was always full of hope. Although, she couldn't help but wonder now if there was another side to him—one that she found herself wanting, more than anything, to get to know.

He looked her straight in the eye, his expression turning serious. "I do have one question for you, though."

Her stomach knotted. It was only reasonable that he was going to finally demand some kind of explanation for her memory loss. He certainly deserved one. She closed her eyes, bracing herself for the question she could no longer avoid.

He looked at her from underneath his eyebrows. His intensity gave way to a flirtatious smile. "Would you like to make some cookies with me tomorrow?"

Clara let out an exhale of relief. She nodded with enthusiasm. "I would love to," she said.

Now just wasn't the right time. And timing, she was quickly learning, was everything.

CHAPTER TWENTY-ONE

BRENT

The next day, Brent crouched on the floor of his garage in front of his toolbox. He turned a wrench over in his palm. He'd missed working with his hands. He needed to make something again. To construct something. To create a plan and see it through. He'd considered getting started on a new woodworking project. Maybe another gift for Clara. But he was finding it hard to get inspired since finding his last project had been so easily dismissed. He tapped his fingers against the wrench, trying to wrap his mind around everything.

Brent shifted his focus to his truck, propped up on jack stands. He lay on his back and slid underneath it. Changing the oil in his truck wasn't anything to get excited about. Even so, he was thrilled to be doing it. It was a process he could control. He knew each step he needed to take and how it would turn out in the end if he did it right. If only everything in life could be that simple.

He opened the drain plug and removed the filter, then watched as the oil began to drip into the pan. Brent slid back out from underneath and sat up, wiping his brow with the sleeve of his flannel shirt. He organized the contents of his toolbox while he waited, needing to find some purpose for his jittery hands. He frowned. His thoughts were impossible to steer toward anything other than last night's conversation.

Brent knew Clara had been out of sorts, but forgetting about the gift entirely? This wasn't leftover stress from the deployment. And it certainly wasn't as simple as an adjustment period anymore. No, there was something much more serious going on.

It was almost as if she'd intentionally blocked the gift from her memory. It certainly wasn't the only thing she'd chosen to forget from the past year. Perhaps she had shut the entire deployment from her mind. But the question he continued to struggle with was, why?

He thought about those counselors who would come into the squadron every now and then to talk to the airmen. The Air Force was taking the mental health of its pilots seriously these days, and efforts had only increased over the past few years. Brent knew memory loss could be a way of blocking out painful circumstances. He wondered if Clara needed to talk to a professional about all of this. She seemed to be having trouble opening up to him, but maybe someone with more experience with this type of problem could help her.

Brent thought back to that Christmas morning nearly a year ago now. He'd been so excited for her to see the gift he'd made, and nervous too. He'd worked on it for weeks before the deployment. Brent hoped she would love it. It wasn't just about the time it took, though. It was also heavy with a significance that he hadn't been entirely sure she was ready for.

When he'd first planned the gift, it had been a simple

wooden star—a homemade tree topper for her Christmas tree. He felt it was an appropriate enough gift for a relatively new relationship—something made by his hand, suitable for the holiday, and not too serious for a first Christmas together.

But once he'd received the call about the deployment, everything in his plans had changed. Suddenly, Brent had been faced with a new question. Did he see a future with Clara? As he held the star in his hands that night, not knowing what their fate would be, he looked at it in a new light. At that moment, he'd realized he no longer wanted it to be just a casual gift for a girlfriend. Brent had wanted her to have this star on top of her tree that Christmas and perhaps every Christmas afterward as well.

Right then, he'd decided to paint it blue. A blue star in the military represented having a family member serving on active duty. It was the best way he could think of to let her know how important she was to him. Although she wasn't his family yet, it was his way of telling Clara that he wanted a future with her.

Brent was well aware that when someone served in the military, it wasn't only the service members who sacrificed, but also their families. Between frequent moves, long deployments, and long separations, military families served their country right alongside their loved ones.

Brent knew this better than anyone. He'd grown up as an Air Force "brat," after all. He remembered how military kids had been compared to dandelions because of their ability to grow anywhere and thrive in difficult conditions. He'd never fully appreciated being compared to a weed, but now he could understand what a special thing that was. To be able to constantly move around and take root in a new environment—and grow.

Yes, military families really were special; he realized it now.

This blue star had signified to Brent that he wanted Clara to be his partner alongside him through it all. It hadn't been part of his plan, but something stronger than a checklist had compelled him to move forward with it anyway.

Brent scooted himself into position and slid back underneath the truck. He screwed in the new filter and replaced the drain plug before he shimmied his way back out. He thought back to Christmas morning last year.

BRENT HAD CALLED Clara early to wake her up. He'd wanted their first moment of Christmas to be spent together. He'd told her to go out onto the front porch to find the package Dave had left for her, then instructed her to go sit by the fire and turn on some Christmas music to set the mood. He'd wanted everything to be exactly right.

She started up a Christmas album from her phone. A soft version of "Away in a Manger" was the first tune to play. It was perfect until an incoming call interrupted the moment with Elvis's "Blue Christmas"—her new ringtone. Clara immediately tried to silence the call to stop the interruption and not ruin the mood, but she kept fumbling with her phone, and Elvis kept crooning. They couldn't stop laughing. It ended up setting a more perfect backdrop to the moment than either of them could have planned for.

Brent had enclosed a card in the package.

Clara, I hope this star guides us through this year apart and will bring us back together for another Christmas. May it adorn our future Christmas trees.

*   —Brent*

Clara's reaction to the gift had been genuine happiness —pure and simple—just as he'd hoped. She'd teared up and held the star close to her heart, seeming to know why it was important. She hadn't known quite what to say, but the look in her eyes, even over a video call, told him everything he'd needed to know. She was in it too, for the long haul. It had been the major turning point in their relationship. That was the moment when they both realized they were in for a commitment—and a future.

The song had been more fitting than they could have imagined. A perfect anthem for their first Christmas. They may have been missing each other and, of course, they wished they hadn't been apart—but deep down, they both knew there was something special about their blue Christmas. With the handmade blue star at the center of it all.

———

AT LEAST, that was what he'd thought at the time. After last night, Brent was rethinking everything. He lowered the jack stands, bringing the truck back down to the floor. Maybe he had been wrong about all of it. Maybe he had misjudged her reaction. Brent began to doubt everything he believed to be true. He didn't know what to think anymore. If Clara hadn't viewed the gift with the same significance he had, then could the same be said for their entire relationship?

Brent popped the hood and opened the fill cap. He

poured in a new bottle of oil while making a mental note to get in touch with one of the squadron counselors, just to be safe. In the meantime, Brent knew he needed to relax and try not to make too much out of it for Clara's sake. He reasoned there must be some logical explanation for her strange behavior. Perhaps they simply needed some more time together. When they put the topic of the deployment behind them, everything seemed to be perfect. Perhaps he needed to stop focusing on the past year and instead look forward to the new memories they were making.

He screwed the fill cap back on, then checked the dipstick. Flawless. He wiped his hands with a cloth. Brent put away his tools, eager to turn his attention toward more pleasant things.

With perfect timing, the blare of a car horn jerked his head up and away from his thoughts. Clara pulled into his driveway, a mischievous smile peeking out above the steering wheel.

His mood instantly lightened. At least she was still showing up, still eager to share in all of his well-planned Christmas activities. Besides, there was one thing he knew for sure; they were going to have fun together. They always did. He just needed to make sure the topic of the deployment didn't come up.

Brent watched Clara as they went inside together. He noticed her eyes brighten at the sight of his kitchen. It was small and homey—but now—it was also full of Christmas. He was thrilled to finally get to use it with her today, his first time since being back. He wasn't much of a cook, and with Clara at the hotel most evenings, he'd been picking up his dinners from the café down the road. His white granite counters and matching cabinets were clean and sparkling, having been completely untouched for the past year.

Brent had gone to the base exchange when he'd returned to stock up on some items he thought would add some flavor. He'd hung a large wreath over the window and two snowman dish towels draped from the oven. A long garland full of lights now lined the tops of all the kitchen cabinets.

He had all the ingredients they needed for several types of cookies, all lined up and ready to go. He'd spent nearly an hour getting the kitchen organized for baking that morning. Just like with anything else, good preparation was the key to success. Whether it was making cookies or making plans for the future, Brent needed to know he still had some control over his life. Even printing out a recipe or two gave him that warm and fuzzy feeling that hard work would yield results.

"Here, got you this." He tossed Clara a gingerbread-style apron with a row of colorful gumdrops down the middle.

She caught it in her free hand. The other picked up a red spatula with white snowflakes on it. "Love it," she said. "But where's yours?"

Brent pulled out a matching apron from the bag and tied it around his waist.

"You're full of surprises today, Major McNally."

Brent could tell Clara was happy to be there, and that made him feel more relief than he knew he needed. He never knew with her lately. So far, things today seemed to be rolling along nicely, ready for a smooth takeoff.

He started a Christmas playlist on his phone. "All I Want for Christmas Is You" began to play, and he instantly skipped to the next song. Brent loved Christmas music and all, but he must have heard that song at least a thousand times over the past couple of weeks. Even he had his limits.

Instead, someone else started singing about a Christmas tree farm. He smirked at the reminder of their outing the other day.

"So, what are we making today, chef?" Clara tied on her apron and grabbed a mixing bowl.

"A lot of cookies." He glanced down at his list on the counter. "Sugar cookies, chocolate chip cookies, snickerdoodles . . ." He looked up with a grin. "And, of course, gingersnaps."

She raised her eyebrows. "Is that all?" she joked. "What in the world are we going to do with all those cookies?"

"Don't worry. I've got a plan for that."

"Of course you do."

Brent reached over to grab his organized bundle of note-cards. "I've got the recipes for each, all printed out with the necessary ingredients laid out by each type."

"Impressive."

"Okay, let's get started on the sugar cookies first. They'll need longer to cool so we can ice and decorate them."

Clara gave him a salute. "Roger."

He pulled the measuring spoons from a drawer and narrowed his eyes, deciding which to use.

"Come on, let's get baking," she said, tossing a sprinkle of sugar at him.

His eyes popped open. Brent turned toward the bag of flour behind him and reached inside. He grabbed a handful and tossed it back at her. It was about time this kitchen had a little mess in it. He reached for Clara's hand and spun her around to the music. She let out a delighted scream. He wrapped his arms around her and pulled her in close. Brent ran a hand along her cheek, then twirled her again and leaned her backward. Her hair cascaded behind her. He dipped his head and kissed her on the lips with a mood that matched his enthusiasm. When he pulled back, they were both out of breath. His heart was racing. They locked eyes.

He stood her back up and let out a long exhale. Brent looked around his kitchen, and he felt his chest grow warm. He couldn't think of anything in the world he'd rather be doing at the moment than this. He looked at her again.

Clara gazed back at him, her eyes drifting to his mouth. Her cheeks were pink.

He leaned in closer, lowering his head, ready to meet her lips again.

Instead, she stuck out her thumb and wiped the tip of his nose. "Got some sugar there."

He laughed. The tender moment was not what he'd expected, but it was just as sweet.

As the two of them baked cookies side by side, Brent thought about the last time he'd felt this happy. It had probably been a year ago, when he and Clara had first begun to date, before the deployment. He thought back to how simple things were back then—before the realities of military life reared their ugly head into their new relationship.

Brent wondered again about the toll the deployment had taken on them as a couple. He knew Clara was uncomfortable talking about it. He knew she hadn't accepted being a part of military life yet. He also knew that when all of that was taken out of the equation, they were a perfect match.

He wanted this feeling to last forever. He breathed in the scents of the kitchen, rich and creamy, like butterscotch. The smell of burning dust from the unused oven lingered in the air. It reminded him of that time of year when the weather would turn cold, and he would switch on his heater for the first time of the season. That welcome smoky scent that signaled the return of the comforting chill of winter.

He watched Clara at the sink, washing out a mixing

bowl. His house looked the way he wanted it to—after months of renovations and a year away from it. His kitchen smelled better than anything he could dream up. And Clara, his fiancée, was right here—and happy. What more could he ask for? Maybe some of his hard work had paid off after all. When the two of them were together like this, everything was exactly as it should be.

The notes of "Blue Christmas" sounded from Clara's phone, interrupting his thoughts. It was sitting on top of the counter, but she didn't hear it between the music and the running water. Brent stole a quick glance at the screen. It showed an incoming call from Matthew. A picture of a man with dark hair and a strong jaw stared back at him. He looked like a model for a toothpaste ad, taunting Brent with his flawless smile.

Brent clenched his fists, and his stomach hardened. Why was *he* calling? Brent forced himself to remain calm. He supposed it was only reasonable that they kept in touch, especially since they'd worked so closely together over the past year. His jaw tightened at the reminder.

Clara used to fill him in on everything that went on at work; the things she was learning, the skills she was developing. Working with her ex was an unfortunate requirement of the job, but one that he'd accepted. She'd assured him it was never an issue, that they'd always remained professional. Still, he hated it.

The call went unanswered, but a few seconds later, a text appeared on the screen.

> Hey, Clar, just checking in to see how you're doing.

Brent's blood boiled. Why did Matthew need to see how *his* fiancée was doing? He wondered if it was a professional call or a personal one. The use of the familiar "Clar" would suggest the latter.

From their conversations over the past year, Brent had gotten the impression that Clara was no longer sure that hotel management was what she wanted to do for the long term. Maybe she had changed her mind about that and was keeping Matthew around for his industry connections. Was there still a friendship there? Was there still a personal connection?

After all, Matthew had been there beside her throughout the past year. Brent may as well have been a million miles away.

CHAPTER TWENTY-TWO
CLARA

"Tell me what we're doing with all these cookies again."

Clara was exhausted in the best way possible. She and Brent had been baking for hours, and she had completely lost track of time. It always did seem to fly by when she was with him.

"Operation Cookie Drop," he said.

"Sounds top secret." She raised her eyebrows. "Are you sure I'm allowed to know about this?"

He laughed. "It's something the military spouses coordinate each year on base."

She flinched. There was something about the words "military spouse" that still made her body tighten up.

Brent didn't seem to notice. "But since you'll be one of those soon, I think you can be privy."

She ignored the sour taste in her mouth.

He began placing the dozens of cookies they'd made into round tins. "After we pack these up, we'll bring them over to the squadron."

Clara helped him. "And what do we do with them there?"

"Well, the spouses in the squadron, along with other volunteers from the community, get together to package them up and deliver them to the airmen living in the dorms."

"The dorms? Why?"

"The dorms are, for the most part, occupied by young, single airmen. Many of these folks are new to the military and may not be used to being away from home. Some may be alone for Christmas for the first time ever. It's a way of spreading a little cheer to those who may be missing having their family around for the holidays."

"That's nice." Clara let out a sigh of satisfaction. She cast a glance around Brent's kitchen. The scents of vanilla, ginger, and cinnamon filled the air. It smelled like Christmas. She couldn't imagine not having a beautiful kitchen to bake cookies in, and she *certainly* couldn't imagine not having your loved ones nearby to spend Christmas with. Clara thought about how Brent had spent last Christmas without his family and his home. She couldn't imagine how lonely it must have been for him. She wished she could have been there for him during that time—actually been there.

She shook off any feeling of regret and decided to instead focus on the task at hand. Bringing holiday cheer to others, especially the troops, was an effort she wanted to be a part of, military spouse or not.

CLARA WAS SURPRISED to see so many people when they arrived on base. The entire operation was set up inside an airplane hangar. Brent began unloading their cookies. She spotted Janie, who beckoned her over immediately.

"Hey, Clara, over here. Grab an apron."

She joined the assembly line of folding tables and greeted Janie with an insecure wave. "I'm not sure what to do." She tied on an apron and smoothed it down. She stayed along the outside edge of the table and folded her arms, hesitant to get too involved.

"It's simple," Janie said. "Take a plate, fill it with each type of cookie from this platter. Wrap it up in the cellophane and tie on a pretty ribbon. Easy!" She motioned toward the two ladies beside her. "This is Laura, and this is Ava. They'll help you out with anything you need to know. I gotta go manage the incoming loads. Good to see you here." Janie pulled out her phone and drew Clara in close. She snapped a selfie of the four of them before Clara even realized what had happened. Then she bounced off.

Janie always seemed to be busy, and was so upbeat and full of enthusiasm. She wasn't exactly what came to Clara's mind when she thought of a military spouse. Although she still wasn't exactly sure what she *did* think being a military spouse would be like, she usually imagined something more depressing—a rather boring and lonely existence. A life that required you to sacrifice your own ambitions for the greater good. To submit your life to the career of your husband and the United States government.

She tossed a polite smile to Laura and Ava, both about her age and dressed in matching aprons with the squadron logo across the front. "It's nice to meet you both." Clara shifted her glance to the cookies in front of her. She didn't really want to engage in small talk with these ladies, as nice as they seemed. With any luck, they would leave her to wrap cookies in peace.

"Are you new to the squadron?" Laura turned to her with a bubbly grin.

Clara sighed to herself. Clearly luck was not on her side

today. "Sort of. I guess I'm new to—well, to all of this." She made an awkward gesture at the hangar, wondering how obvious it was that she wasn't used to this kind of scene. She just wanted to blend in, but it was evident by the looks on Laura and Ava's faces that a new person quickly drew interest.

She moved in closer, reluctantly resigning herself to a conversation. "I'm Clara. I'm Brent's—" She paused. Laura and Ava looked at her, waiting for her to continue. "Fiancée." She bit her lip, feeling guilty for even saying it out loud. She was still uncomfortable with this fact, or lie—depending on how you looked at it, and felt even more awful saying it around other military spouses.

Laura gave her a wide-mouthed smile. She had long blonde hair and wore a thick pair of glasses over her green eyes. "Well, congratulations, and welcome. You won't find a friendlier bunch of spouses to welcome you into the group."

"Are these all spouses?"

"Most of them," Laura said. "Wives—and husbands—of the service members on this base. But people come from all over to help us with our efforts. This community is really supportive. It's fun to watch people pull together—military and civilian—especially during the holidays."

"Which ones are your husbands?" Clara asked, nodding over to the group of guys loading boxes in the corner.

"Oh, Jeff's right over there." Laura pointed out her husband standing by Brent. She threw a careful glance toward Ava. "But Stephen is deployed."

Ava's bronzed cheekbones fell. She nodded. "This is going to be our first Christmas apart." Her dark hair was pulled into a ponytail that sat on top of her head, the curls spiraling to her slumped shoulders. She looked down at the table and stopped wrapping cookies.

"I'm sorry," Clara said. It came out sounding more emotionless than she had meant it to, but she didn't know what else to say.

Ava nodded. She took in a cleansing breath. "It's okay. I understand why he can't be with us. But my kids are young, so it's especially hard for them right now."

Clara tilted her head as she looked Ava in her almond-shaped eyes for the first time. "I'm sorry," she said again and really meant it. She did feel sorry for Ava—for her, her husband, and her kids. She felt bad for *all* the families who weren't together for the holidays. She grimaced as she thought about her selfish reaction to the news of Brent's deployment. She hadn't cared or even thought about the sacrifices of military families. She had thought only about herself and about not getting to spend Christmas with him.

Ava looked back at her and wrinkled her nose. "It's okay; it's part of our life, and I wouldn't change it for the world."

Clara crossed her arms in front of her and narrowed her eyes. "Really? But isn't it so hard?"

"Sure it is." She shrugged. "But it's worth it too."

"What do you mean?"

Ava set down a cookie and turned to her. "Our husbands don't just have a job, in the normal sense of the word. The Air Force has a mission, and we—you—are a vital part of it."

Clara tried to hide the massive eye roll happening inside her brain. She doubted it was as easy to see the big picture as Ava made it all seem. It couldn't possibly be that simple. She appreciated the sentiment, though, and nodded as if she understood the other woman perfectly.

Clara knew she probably shouldn't continue to pry, but

she couldn't seem to stop herself either. She was becoming increasingly curious about Ava's take on things.

"But to be without your husband on Christmas—I can't imagine." She lowered her head to study Ava's expression, hoping it would draw out her true feelings on the matter.

Ava gave a wry smile. "Well, it's not what either of us would choose, that's for sure. But what my husband and I *can* choose is how to make the most of our time apart."

"Hmm," she replied, unconvinced.

Ava cleared the cookies from the space in front of her, settling in for a deep discussion. She turned her body toward Clara so they were face to face. "Sometimes a couple can connect in a new way by enduring the hard separation together. When he's gone, you kind of get to know each other in a completely different way than when he's home."

Laura nodded in agreement as she continued to wrap cookies. "It's true. A long separation can certainly make you stronger as a couple."

Clara raised her eyebrows.

Laura shrugged. "I've experienced it myself."

Clara pressed her lips into a tight line. She thought about her grandmother and how she had said something similar about special connections that develop from a separation like this. She hadn't really believed her at the time and still didn't, if she was being honest. She realized a special connection with Brent was what she desperately needed.

For a second, she thought she felt a sharp pang of envy in her gut. She wasn't sure where it had come from. Clara knew she'd been feeling guilty about having skipped over the last year, but this was different. That connection was something she wanted, something she should have. It was almost as if she felt cheated out of the experience.

She shook it off, returning to the conversation. Sure, she admired these women for their positive perspectives on things. Still, she wondered how much of it was authentic. Maybe they had all simply drunk the Kool-Aid, and their job was to recruit new unsuspecting spouses into their club. Or perhaps this was the stuff they told themselves to feel better about their life choices. Either way, Clara still had her doubts.

She decided to dig a little deeper, careful not to appear judgmental. She tried to keep her line of questioning casual. She didn't want to come across as intrusive, but she wanted to know more—so much more. The desire surprised her.

"So how do you take care of the kids and the house, everything, all on your own? Especially when you're always living in a new place, without your family around. That has to be tough."

"Well, it is," Ava said. "In fact, anything that's going to break or go wrong *will* happen right after he leaves for his deployment. The kids get sick, the car breaks down, the air conditioning stops working." She looked over at Laura with a smile.

Laura dissolved into giggles as she grabbed a tray from behind her. "They call it the Murphy's law of deployments and I've seen enough of them to know this tends to be true. Every. Single. Time."

The two women laughed.

Clara thought that sounded awful and wondered how Laura and Ava kept their humor through it all. "Wow, you two have really gone through some stuff."

"Sure. We all have," Laura said. "And sometimes life's

circumstances are more challenging than other times, no matter how you spin it. But it's not like we're single parents either. Although our husbands may be gone a lot, they're still *there*, and the support goes both ways."

Clara shrugged. "I guess that makes sense."

Laura continued. "Besides, once you get to the other side of a long deployment, there's no better feeling."

Clara shook her head, not understanding.

Laura let out a long breath, and her shoulders rolled back. "There's a confidence, a feeling of independence, that is gained by going through it. You learn in these times that you can do more on your own than you may have realized. That doesn't mean that you *want* to or that it's better that way. But just knowing that you *can* is really an important part of life."

Laura glanced at some of the other spouses in the room. She raised her chin. "They call us dependents, but the truth is, we are actually incredibly *independent*, more so than most. And we have the battle scars to prove it."

Ava smiled as she waved to someone across the room. She turned back to Clara with a grin as if she were letting her in on a secret. "But at the same time, we are never truly on our own. I have always found military spouses to be the most supportive group of women I've ever had the pleasure to know. They will drop everything to help another in a pinch."

Clara let out a scoff before she could stop herself and hoped they didn't notice. She didn't want to insult them—it was just that she was usually skeptical of that sort of thing. Maybe it was because she'd had the same best friend since kindergarten. She'd always had someone—the same someone—by her side to do life with. She never needed to branch out for friendships much beyond that. Clara didn't really trust other women the way she did Lily. She couldn't imagine forming these types of bonds at her age. She certainly couldn't imagine doing it over and over again, with all new people, every few years.

This sisterhood of spouses thing sounded nice enough—for these ladies. But the truth was, Clara thought these women all seemed a little too good to be true.

"Wow, you guys are so positive about everything. Where's the bitterness? The resentment? Don't military spouses ever complain?"

Ava let out a cackle. "Oh, yeah, we do," she said.

She and Laura exchanged a knowing smile.

"Some of us more than others," Laura added. "We have so many different personalities in this group."

Ava pointed across the room to where a thin woman with a frown was wiping down tables. "Take Allison, for example. She will criticize just about anything. She's probably whining right now about how the cookies are too crumbly, or the hangar is too cold, or that the people around her are too annoying. But she still shows up to this stuff even though she doesn't have to. I suspect she loves it all; she'll just never admit it. I wouldn't exactly call her *delightful* to be around, but still, she's truly a caring and nurturing person. But don't tell her that, or she'll make fun of you."

Clara stifled a laugh.

Ava pointed out another woman with short, silvering hair. "Then there's Charlotte, our very own Pollyanna, who sees only the good in everyone and everything. You'll never hear her complain, no matter how many canceled plans or changed orders she puts up with. We suspect it's all just to torture Allison."

Laura and Clara both laughed.

Ava pointed out another woman across the room with perfect waves falling down her back. "And that's Meg. She always manages to make the ugliest base housing look like a page out of a lifestyle magazine. She's potentially a genius with a bunch of degrees but insists on catching up on celebrity gossip when she's with the group. She can be rather mysterious, though. One of these days, we're going to find out she's been working for the CIA—probably from her perfectly styled patio."

Laura and Clara were both doubled over in laughter. Ava was on a roll now, and Clara couldn't wait to hear more. "Go on," she said.

Ava pointed to a young lady who couldn't be any older than twenty-five. "That's Abigail. She cracks me up. She's a ton of fun and finds the humor in most things this Air Force life throws at us. She's still new to it, though. We'll see if she's still laughing a few deployments and several cross-country moves later."

Clara wiped away a tear from laughter herself. She recognized Abigail as the easily amused newlywed from the party the other night.

She loved how Ava had a way of making each one of these unique ladies sound interesting in the most lovable way. She could tell that Ava truly *did* like these women despite all their different personalities. Talking with Laura and Ava felt natural. It felt like she was having a conversation with Lily.

Laura gave Clara a wink. "The truth is, we have *a lot* of fun together. I know military life seems sort of sad at times, from movies and books, and it can be. But it's also a really active community to be a part of. Sure, it can be hard moving every few years and having to start over with friendships. But like anything else in life, the more you put into it, the more you get out of it. If you invest your time into making connections at each duty station, you'll be rewarded with friendships that will last a lifetime."

Ava nodded. "It's true. I love this lifestyle. I love the purpose, the community, *and* the opportunities. I've lived all over the country, and we're hoping our next assignment will take us overseas. How many people get to do that?"

Clara was thoughtful. Maybe these women weren't simple cookie-cutter wives after all. Perhaps these women were a lot more complex than she'd realized. Perhaps they were all normal, flawed, diverse individuals—just like anyone else. Just like her.

"What about your careers? Did you have to leave that all behind when you got married?"

Ava looked her in the eye. "You'd be surprised what many of these military spouses do. We have doctors, pilots, authors, artists . . . you name it. Some spouses start their own businesses, and some are stay-at-home moms like me. I love that I get to do that right now."

"Really?"

"Yeah, of course. Sure, we may have additional challenges when it comes to maintaining a career, but we're not confined to any one lifestyle."

Laura nodded in agreement. "She's right. And the truth is, not only in the military but everywhere—life is about sacrifices. You constantly have to prioritize different things at different phases in life. When you view these choices less as a sacrifice and more as an opportunity—you realize you're not so restricted after all. In fact, you may find that you have more freedom than you realized."

Clara thought about the hotel and her future there. She

wasn't sure anymore if hotel management was really her dream. Maybe it was a profession she sort of fell into, the next logical step in her career. She wondered what she would do if she could choose anything for her life. Maybe there was more out there for her to explore.

Perhaps Clara had more freedom in her career than she realized. Perhaps she always had; it was just up to her to decide how to use it. What if marrying into the military wasn't such a sacrifice? What if it was instead, like life in general, full of endless opportunities?

"Don't get me wrong," Ava added. "This life *is* hard. And there *are* sacrifices involved. Being a military spouse takes a certain strength. It takes resilience, patience, flexibility, courage. There are *a lot* of challenges, and not everyone is up for signing on to that. Not everyone enjoys it. It just doesn't work for some people for many different reasons."

Clara nodded, her eyes unblinking.

"But in my experience, it has been extremely rewarding," she added.

"Same here," Laura agreed.

Clara let out a long breath that sounded like a whistle. She'd learned more about this lifestyle from this one conversation than she had known about it her entire life.

She watched the other spouses who were boxing, wrapping, and working together. Seeing all the smiling faces, she felt the return of that all-too-familiar feeling of overwhelming guilt. These families all made sacrifices for their country—why couldn't she? Why did *she* think she was entitled to skip right over it when so many others had to go through it?

She was inspired by Ava and Laura, by all the spouses in the squadron. Perhaps being a military spouse wasn't what she'd imagined it to be at all.

Perhaps she was beginning to understand what this lifestyle looked like from another perspective, the real perspective.

For the first time, Clara suddenly felt something she had never thought she ever would—a yearning to be part of this incredible community.

CHAPTER TWENTY-THREE
BRENT

The snow fell into heavy heaps as Brent woke up just after sunrise on December 23. Everything was planned to perfection for their Christmas drive out to the country. Sure, Clara had been acting off lately—at times like a totally different person—but this day was going to be exactly what they needed to get their relationship to where it should be. He could feel it.

If only the weather would cooperate. He paced back and forth and threw a quick glance out the window. From the looks of things, his entire plan might implode. He forced himself to stand still, glued to the window. He rubbed an eyebrow, willing the heavily falling snow to stop.

His gaze flitted around the wintry scene, and his worry quickly gave way to awe. His shoulders rolled back, and his face relaxed. As Brent stared out at his property, he was struck by the beauty of the view in front of him. The bare trees were completely frosted in white. A bulky blanket of snow covered the ground; the massive snowflakes that fell from the sky, adding a fluffy thickness to it at a surprisingly quick rate.

The morning sun was covered by a gray overcast that gave a silvery hue to everything underneath it. He felt as if he had woken up in Narnia. The silence was eerie, and the stillness was stunning, except for the rapidly falling snow. For a moment, Brent felt as if he were the only living creature on Earth. It seemed like the everyday world had suddenly stopped so nature could put on a spectacular show.

He would have loved to marvel at the scene outside his window for hours. Not today, though. Today was crucial, and it needed to go perfectly. Brent grabbed his notebook. He had every detail planned out. He would pick up Clara, and they would drive to the other side of the river—over a covered bridge—to the rural Vermont countryside. They would meander through the scenic back roads that would take them through picturesque villages filled with old-fashioned charm. They would bundle up together in a horse-drawn sleigh for a cozy ride, surrounded by the sounds of jingle bells and the scents of maple syrup. He realized it was a bit early for sugaring season, but still, the thought of boiled sap coming from the tiny sugar shacks only added to the Norman Rockwell idea he had for their day.

To top it off, he'd made reservations at a historic inn for a candlelight dinner. The entire experience would be a blissful day of holiday romance that Clara wouldn't be able to resist despite *her* reservations.

Brent knew his real agenda, though—to talk about their future. He feared she still wasn't comfortable with their engagement, and he wanted to see where they stood now that he'd been home for a few weeks. He needed to know what she was thinking so he could make a plan for their future—so he could fix what needed to be fixed.

Returning to the window for one last look, he continued

to watch the snow falling. It looked as if it was just getting started, with plenty more to come. It appeared as if someone had cut open a pillow with an endless supply of feathers; the flakes floating softly down. The ground appeared fluffy and pure, not a blade of grass to be seen. It would have been beautiful if only it hadn't been so disappointing.

Still, waking up to the sight of a fresh snowfall, Brent couldn't help but feel a sense of renewal for the day to come. It was like a blank canvas, a new start—even if only for the present day. The world—and all its troubles—was now completely covered in white. Today needed to be a fresh start for them. He needed to get things back to where they were before this messy deployment scarred everything.

Brent glanced at his watch and pulled himself away from the window. He needed to get moving if he was going to salvage this day. He had to get to Cranberry Pines, to Clara's house, before the roads got worse. With any luck, by the time he got there, the snowfall would be slowing down, and they could get on the road with a timely departure.

He hurried out the door and hopped into his truck. He hated the feeling that was growing stronger inside him—the realization that he had no idea what this day was going to bring. Some people, like Dave, would call that the excitement of endless opportunities. To him, it was torture.

BRENT DROVE into town with caution. He squinted through the windshield as his wipers worked to keep up with the falling snow. He slowed his truck, turned onto Main Street, and let out a gasp. He'd seen this town plenty of times, but never before like this, completely covered in white. Main Street was nearly deserted. The sky was a dark gray despite the morning hour, and the street lamps were illuminated, giving a lustrous sheen to the snow. The ground appeared to be covered in millions of tiny diamonds.

Shops and cafés, all decorated in matching garlands and wreaths, lined the street. Brent passed a white church with a towering steeple. The red doors had matching wreaths hanging side by side. It was a quintessential New England town, and he had to admit that the snow only contributed to the perfect scene. Sure, it was messing with his plans, but despite the circumstances, he took a moment to appreciate the charm.

Brent turned off the main road in search of somewhere to park. He looked up to see a red-brick building with paper snowflakes hanging in the windows. Behind it stood the biggest sledding hill he had ever seen. Kids of all ages raced up the hill and flew down on sleds, saucers, and inflatable tubes. He was careful, pulling into a parking spot at the end of the street.

A high-pitched tone screamed from his phone. It was a weather alert.

Route 4 Closed.

Brent let out a laugh and threw his hands in the air. Canceled. There went all his planning. So much for their romantic day. So much for them talking about their future. He rubbed his temples in frustration, trying to figure out how to recover this date.

He trudged through the snow to Clara's townhouse, still not knowing what the new plan would be. It felt as if his feet were weighed down with the knowledge that the fate of their relationship stood on his shoulders.

Clara answered the door before he could even ring the

bell. She was holding up her phone with the road-closure alert displayed.

"I have good news." She gave him a playful smile. "The roads are closed."

"Why is that good news?"

"Because it's a snow day, and I say we go sledding."

"Sledding?"

Clara nodded, a huge grin on her face.

"Let's give it a little more time," he said. "They may open back up."

"There's no better place to go sledding than Cranberry Pines." She pulled him over to the edge of her front porch and pointed to the sledding hill down the street. "See?"

"Yeah, I saw that coming in. Looks like those kids are having a ball."

It did look like they were having fun, Brent had to admit, but they were also *kids*. The two of them had important things to talk about today. He wasn't sure going sledding was the best way to spend their time.

"It's *so* much fun, and I know the very best spot to go," Clara said.

He lowered his brows. "I don't know." He opened his mouth to speak again, then closed it, unsure what to say.

"Come on, lets go off plan for once." She looked up at him with her big blue eyes, full of excitement.

Brent ran a hand through his hair and snorted in amusement. He couldn't resist Clara's enthusiasm. Maybe he couldn't control the weather. Maybe his perfect plans had once again been scrapped. But as he looked at Clara's eager smile, he only cared about one thing at that moment—making her happy.

He shrugged. "Okay. Let's go sledding."

She squealed, grabbed Brent by the hand, and quickly

pulled him inside her house. She threw on her coat and mittens. He noticed two fully inflated snow tubes waiting for them in her entryway.

He laughed. "It looks as if you've made some plans of your own."

"Come on," she said, motioning for him to follow.

He picked up the tubes and followed her out the front door. They began a slow, heavy walk through the snow-covered town. She led him across the street and down to the next block. He would follow her anywhere.

"Where are we going?" he asked as they walked past the big sledding hill with all the kids.

"You'll see."

Clara continued to lead him a couple more blocks down a narrow road. Finally, they reached a steep hill that sat empty and deserted. The fresh mountain of snow was completely untouched. It looked like an enormous scoop of mashed potatoes.

Brent looked up. "What's this?"

"This is the hill only the true locals know about."

He squinted to get a better look. He couldn't help but appreciate the purity of the glistening hill. He was surprised by the beauty of *everything*: the snow-covered hill, the peacefulness of the town, the look on her face. There was that feeling again. The one he'd had in his kitchen when they were baking. The one he had on the dance floor at the party. It wasn't one he was used to. Brent was usually too busy making plans, looking ahead to the next thing to appreciate it. Sometimes, it was nice, though, to simply enjoy being exactly where he was.

He looked at Clara, holding her tube with a delighted expression. He clutched his hand to his chest and squeezed his eyes shut as he took in a deep breath of air. Then, he released it all. He let go and surrendered to a plan that wasn't his—it was better.

"First ones here," Brent yelled, pumping his fist. He gave her a high five. "Let's go!"

Clara laughed. "Well, you've changed your tune. What happened to all that stick-to-the-plan mentality?"

He shrugged. "I guess it *does* look pretty fun." He looked her in the eye. "Or maybe you bring something out in me." He wasn't sure why he had said that or what it even meant. The only thing he knew was that it was true.

Brent looked up at the massive hill. "Are we going all the way up to the top?" he asked. "This hill is much bigger than the one the kids were going down."

"We sure are. This is a hill you *only* take from the top." Clara looked at him with a sideways glance. "Why, you scared?"

"Yes," he answered immediately with a smile.

"Trust me, it'll be worth the effort," she said. She reached for his hand.

He looked into her eyes and held her gaze. "The best things usually are."

The two of them made the slow climb to the top of the hill, taking turns being in the lead. When they reached the summit, they were both panting, and the view from the top suddenly took away any remaining breath Brent had left in him. He took a long look around. He could see off in the distance, in all directions. Snow covered everything. He could see the town below with its white church steeple and tiny houses with smoke rising from their chimneys. Clara was right. It *had* been worth the climb.

Brent arranged their tubes into position and gave her a wink. "Are you ready for this?"

Her eyes widened as she glanced down the hill. Her

brow furrowed. He could see the sudden hesitation on her face.

"Who's scared now?" he asked, giving her a playful nudge.

She bit her lower lip. "I don't know. This looks pretty steep, now that we're up here," she said. "Why don't you go first, and I'll watch?"

"Not a chance," Brent said with a smile. "Come on, we'll do it together." He sidled his tube next to hers and held out his gloved hand. He urged her with his eyes to take a chance with him. "You scared?"

"Yes."

"Trust me," he said. "It'll be quite a ride. But we'll do it together." Brent wasn't talking about sledding down a hill, and they both knew it. He was talking about joining him on the adventure of a lifetime.

He knew Clara was hesitant, and rightfully so. He knew that by marrying him, she would be taking a huge plunge into the unknown. Air Force life was not unlike speeding down a massive mountain with nothing under-neath you but an inflatable tube. They would have no idea what to expect, where they would end up, or whether they'd even make it through safely. But with a committed partner by his side, he knew the whole experience could be an amazing ride.

Clara let out a long breath of foggy air. "I hope you're right," she replied, seeming to know what he meant. She placed her mittened hand into his and gripped it tightly.

They exchanged a long glance. The world around them stood still and serene. He could see her entire body relax. He understood the feeling. Her hand in his was all the assurance he needed that everything would be okay.

Clara nodded at him, letting him know she was ready.

"Okay, let's go." He squeezed her hand tighter as he pushed off.

They flew down the hill, their tubes spinning. They grasped tightly to each other's hands. The rush of cold air and the adrenaline of racing down the hill made Brent feel completely out of control. At the same time, the feeling of Clara beside him made him feel completely secure. Her screams of exhilaration and his hearty laughter filled the air.

When they reached the bottom, she was still laughing. Brent watched her for a moment and said nothing while he caught his breath. Her eyes twinkled.

He finally spoke. "So . . . was it worth it?"

She nodded at him, looking deep into his eyes from underneath her long eyelashes wet with snowflakes.

He scooted closer, a sudden urge to kiss her overwhelming all his other senses. Still sitting in his tube, Brent moved toward her. He leaned over as far as he could, but before he realized what was happening, he lost his balance and tipped over just before he reached her. He landed face-first in a fluffy pile of snow.

Clara howled with laughter.

Brent wiped the snow from his face and popped up quickly. "Want to go again?"

"Definitely," she said.

They immediately headed up the hill—this time running.

Clara no longer seemed scared. Even so, she held on to his hand tightly each time they raced down the mountain. He liked that it was still thrilling enough for her to want that comfort. She seemed to be having a blast, and he was happier than he had thought possible. Who cared if they didn't get to do any of the things he'd planned or talk about the things he'd wanted to talk about? Instead, they were simply having fun. Maybe that was what they needed more than anything.

On their fourth climb up the hill, they both began to run out of steam. Clara suddenly dropped to the ground right in front of him. She let out a small scream of pain.

Brent rushed to her side. "Clara, are you okay?"

She let out a small moan. "I wasn't watching my footing, and I twisted my ankle." She sat on the ground, holding her foot, her knee up to her chin.

He could tell she was in pain. He crouched down and lifted the bottom of her pant leg to look. When he removed her boot, he noticed her ankle begin to swell instantly.

"It's probably only a sprain, but we'll take a better look at it once we get back to the house."

"I feel so stupid," she said. "Who gets hurt from sledding?" She tried to stand, but crumpled to the ground as soon as she put weight on her foot.

Brent scooped her up in his arms.

Clara laughed. "Are you going to carry me all the way back to the house?"

"I sure am," he said.

She looked into his eyes and held his gaze with heavy eyelids. "My hero."

He melted.

BRENT BROUGHT Clara home and carried her into the living room. He placed her down gently on the couch, then took some time to build a fire.

Once the fire roared, he sat next to her on the sofa and placed her foot in his lap. He took her boot off again, along with her sock. After a few moments of silent inspection, he said, "Looks like it's just twisted. You should be able to walk on it soon."

"How do you know so much about ankle injuries? I thought you were a pilot, not a doctor."

He shrugged. "The Air Force always gives us basic first-aid training before a deployment, in case someone gets injured when we don't have a medic around."

"Ah," she said. "Have you ever been injured?"

His heart skipped a beat. He said nothing, refusing to react the way he had the other night. He only rubbed her ankle.

She pinched her forehead. "I mean . . ." She let out a breath. "I mean, I know you were injured. But do you want to talk about it?"

He didn't know what to say. The truth was, he *did* want to talk about it with her. The way they used to talk about it. The way they had talked about it when it happened. When Brent was deployed, he felt he could talk to her about anything. Now, every time it came up, Clara retreated. Or worse, got agitated. He was tired of constantly upsetting her by bringing up old memories.

He was thoughtful about what to say next. He scratched his neck. "Well, I can tell you that you were the best nurse a man could have asked for. Even from thousands of miles away."

She seemed surprised.

"What? Have I never told you that?"

She didn't say anything in return. She only smiled at him, her face warmed by the glow of the fireplace.

Brent began to wonder if he *had* told Clara enough about what she had meant to him over the past year. An unsettled feeling crept over him. He needed to work up the courage for the conversation, the one he knew they still needed to have. As much as she didn't want to talk about these things, they would have to discuss the deployment at some point. He needed to explain to her how much that time had meant to him so she could understand its importance. No, that time they spent apart wasn't just important, it was *everything*. He needed her to understand that.

Even more, Brent needed to know what was in store for their future—if they even still had one. His military career wasn't going anywhere any time soon. Unfortunately, neither were the hardships that came with it. There would be more deployments. There would be more last-minute missions, and canceled plans, and all kinds of challenges that would separate them from time to time. If she wasn't willing to sign on to this lifestyle, it was better he knew the truth now before it was too late.

On the other hand, he didn't want anything to interrupt the perfect day they were having. Brent let out his breath in a calm release. It *had* been a great day. He couldn't deny it. He thought about what Dave had said about Christmas surprises. Maybe it was true. Maybe the best moments in life aren't planned.

It was a nice thought, but certainly not one you could hang a future on.

CHAPTER TWENTY-FOUR
CLARA

Clara sat close to Brent, cozy and warm by the fire. The day had been nothing short of amazing. Undoubtedly magical.

She'd had the best time sledding with him. She knew it was more than just fun that she was having with him, though. When Brent had carried her home, she felt taken care of in a way she never had before. It was different from the way she'd felt with Matthew. With him, it had been more about dependence, helplessness. With Brent, it felt as if she was cherished.

Sitting beside him in front of the fire, her heart glowed with pure happiness. Maybe this Christmas magic thing *was* happening. Maybe she was truly beginning to fall for him. The relief she felt from this tiny admission gave her the reassurance that this whole situation would have a simple ending after all.

Brent got up and walked to the kitchen, leaving her alone with her thoughts. Clara bit down on her lower lip. Even with things working themselves out, as much as she tried to avoid the thought, she knew there was something she still needed to do. As difficult as it was going to be, she needed to be honest with him and explain what was going on.

The last thing on Earth she wanted to do was ruin this perfect day, but she knew it was finally time. She couldn't put it off any longer. She needed to tell him the truth if they were to enter into a lifetime commitment together. Clara thought about how she'd explain her wish in a way that would make any sense to him.

Brent returned to the living room carrying two steaming mugs with a thick layer of cream on the top. "Hot toddy?"

"Oh, those look wonderful," she said, carefully taking one from him. "What are they?" She took a sip. The sweet warmth of the beverage filled her entire body.

"Hot buttered rum. The perfect après sled beverage."

"Wow, you just whipped those up?"

He shrugged as if it was no big deal.

"Brent?" she said, carefully holding her drink with both hands. "There's something I need to tell you."

"Sure." He smiled, setting down his drink. "What is it?"

She looked into his dreamy brown eyes. He seemed so happy, making her feel awful about what she was about to say. She cleared her throat. "Brent, last year, when we found out you were being deployed . . ."

He nodded, waiting for her to continue.

"Well, there's something I haven't told you."

"Okay."

"Something that would maybe explain some of my behavior lately."

She noticed him stiffen. He sat on the chair across from her and placed his elbows on his knees. He leaned forward with his full attention.

"It's time I finally told you the truth."

Brent let out a puff of air. "I agree. It's definitely time we had this conversation."

She nodded.

"Look, Clara, I know you don't like talking about this past year, but—"

The room went dark, and Clara gasped. Everything was ominously quiet. Brent and Clara looked at each other through the darkness, realizing the same thing: The power had gone out. Neither of them moved. The soft glow of the fire illuminated his face. His eyebrows were drawn together.

"Go on," he said. "No more interruptions."

Brent looked nervous, as if he knew the weight behind the admission she was about to make. But how could he? He couldn't possibly be expecting anything like what she was about to say. Brent got up from his chair and came to sit beside her on the sofa. He took her hand in his and waited for her to continue.

He was right. She needed to get this over with. Perhaps the darkness would make it easier. She turned her head to look at him and realized she had nothing to fear. With him by her side, Clara couldn't imagine feeling any safer than she did at that moment. It was now or never.

She tried again. "Brent, I know this sounds crazy, but I made a wish—"

The table buzzed beside her.

She clenched her fists and shook them in the air. "What now?" She reached for her phone so she could shut it off completely. When she glanced at it, she saw a text from the Darlington front desk.

EMERGENCY! WE NEED YOU
HERE NOW!

Clara sat up straight. She had never received a text like

this from work before. This was serious. Her heart raced as she imagined all the possible problems that could be waiting for her.

She looked over at Brent with wide eyes and shook her head, not quite able to believe the unfortunate timing. "Brent, I can't believe this, but I have to go to the Darlington."

He said nothing at first, his brown eyes wide and unblinking. Eventually, he nodded in disappointed understanding.

Clara sat motionless for a moment beside him on the couch. The truth was, she didn't want to go. She actually *wanted* to have this conversation, as difficult as it may be. Twisted ankle aside, it would take every ounce of willpower she had to get up off the sofa and leave him. Still, she knew she needed to go to the hotel.

She reluctantly turned away from him, sadly realizing their perfect day was over whether she liked it or not. Clara threw the blanket off her lap and set down her drink. She looked at Brent and shook her head in apology. She didn't say anything. She didn't know what to say other than sorry. But she had already said that word too many times over the past few weeks. After a while, she felt as if her apologies were just as fake as the rest of her. She threw on her heavy coat and pushed through the pain of her twisted ankle to get her boots on.

Clara looked over at Brent through the darkness, the warm glow of the fire reflecting off his handsome face. She gave him a defeated shrug. He looked back at her with a weak attempt at a smile and an understanding nod of acknowledgment that she had to leave.

"Come on, I'll take you over there," he said.

She gave him one last look of longing, wishing she could

stay there with him forever. Clara wished she didn't have to leave, that she could take the time to finally tell him everything and work through the complicated situation she'd put them both through.

But what Clara was quickly realizing was that what she wished for was never as simple as it seemed.

CHAPTER TWENTY-FIVE
CLARA

"The snow has knocked out all the power!" Lucy was in a full panic when Clara arrived at the hotel. "Nobody has heat, the restaurant can't cook, there aren't enough flashlights . . ."

"Relax, Lucy. Calm down, and let's figure this out." Clara had just walked through the door and was trying to assess the situation. The usual dignified calm of the luxury hotel was missing, replaced with dark chaos. The eerie sound of silence from inside the Darlington was accompanied only by the loud whistle of the wind outside.

Clara stared at the hotel lobby, now completely dark, and immediately felt a shiver. She pulled her coat tighter and took a deep breath as she realized the uncomfortable truth: She was in charge.

She gathered her thoughts to form a plan as she pulled her hair back into a ponytail. There was so much she still didn't know about the hotel. She needed to think about what she *did* know. As much as she hated to admit it, when it came to this type of situation, it wasn't much.

Surely the Darlington had dealt with a power outage

before. How would Matthew have handled it? *Come on, Clara, think.* This was her responsibility now.

She looked out the window at the blizzard-like conditions she'd emerged from. She was grateful for the snow chains Brent had on his truck that allowed him to drop her off at the front door. There was no sign of the caramel-colored afternoon that usually loomed over Cranberry Pines at this time of day. Instead, the sky was a heavy black, punctuated only by the whirl of white wind. Clara imagined the inside of her brain looked much the same. She shook her head as she observed the weather. It was evident the power was not going to be restored any time soon.

As unforgiving as it was outside, things inside weren't much better. Clara scanned the lobby to find guests huddled in front of the hotel's only fireplace. As more people started piling in around it, she realized it wasn't going to keep everyone warm enough for long. She closed her eyes and drew in a shaky breath. She was in over her head. Why did she ever think she could be the general manager anyway?

Suddenly, the answer popped in her mind—generators. Clara may not have known much about the operations of the hotel, but she *did* know that the Darlington must have generators for a time like this—at least, she hoped so.

She looked at Lucy. "Call for maintenance. We need to get the backup generators working."

Lucy shook her head. "They already tried that."

"What?"

"They failed."

"How could the backup generators fail? What's the purpose of them, if not to work in times like these?"

Lucy shrugged.

Clara rubbed her hands together for warmth. The obvious question hung between them: *What do we do now?*

Clara was at a complete loss. She was only a sales manager. Her expertise was attracting new clients and booking room blocks. She knew how to entertain clients, set up their meeting rooms, and market the event space. What did she know about handling a massive power outage?

Clara looked toward the front desk. Staff were slowly beginning to file in behind it. They huddled together, looking as confused about what to do as Clara felt. She gave them all an apologetic smile. They looked back at her with blank stares, waiting for her direction.

Clara felt the panic rising in her chest. She could feel the heavy pull of tears beginning to form. No, she would not give in to the fear. Not this time. She would not even allow herself to cry. She would not run off to collect herself. She was the general manager of the Darlington Hotel, and she had much more important things to do than to get emotional. Despite her insecurity and her inexperience, she needed to keep an air of authority.

She glanced at the fireplace again. There seemed to be an argument brewing. A small group of women were bickering. It appeared they'd been helping themselves to the free wine that had been set out at the bar to keep the guests happy. They were edging each other out with their elbows, all vying for a spot near the warmth. The volume of their voices intensified.

Lucy turned toward her with a sympathetic tilt of her head. The fear must have been written all over Clara's face. Her voice was soft, a hint of defeat lying underneath. "Do you want me to call Matthew?"

Clara nodded as if in a daze as she tried to assess the situation. Everything around her was going wrong. Guests were starting to come out of their rooms, seeking any source of heat they could find. They all seemed to be growing more concerned and angrier by the minute. Meanwhile, the air felt as if it was getting colder by the second. She was surrounded by total darkness, except for a couple flashlights held by the staff. The Darlington lobby—normally warm and bustling with life—appeared now to be in the dead of winter.

She knew nobody around her could truly understand what the real problem was—what *her* problem was. For all they knew, she had spent the past year training with Matthew for exactly this situation.

Clara looked at the floor, the shame making her head too heavy to hold up. She had let so many people down over the past few weeks. She was constantly screwing up, and things only continued to get worse each day.

She didn't want to be in charge anymore. She didn't want to be in this situation anymore at all. She just wanted to snap her fingers and have everything around her disappear. Clara couldn't see how she was going to get herself out of this mess. She closed her eyes and blew out her breath with a sad realization: She simply couldn't do this.

She thought about her history with the hotel. She'd loved coming there ever since she was a child. There was something magical about the Darlington—especially at this time of year. Splurging on an overnight stay at the hotel was a special holiday tradition for locals and tourists alike.

Clara thought about the qualities of the hotel that she loved the most. Years of sales pitches loomed in the back of her mind as she thought about the Darlington's stately rooms that provided beautiful, upscale amenities. The expansive views of the town green—frosted in a thick layer of white this time of year. The on-site restaurant, offering fine dining on its heated front porch facing the sights of Main Street. She would tell her clients that indulging in a cocktail in the ritzy lounge or partaking in the restaurant's famous hot-cocoa service were special experiences that only added to the town's undeniable charm during the holidays. All of it was true. It was all a part of what made the place so special.

Yes, the Darlington had a reputation to uphold, an experience to deliver. And right now, she was the one responsible for doing it. She was suddenly overcome with a sense of pride for her hotel. It wasn't only because she was the general manager. No, Clara realized at that moment that she played a minor role in something far more grand. Everyone who worked there did too. They were part of the traditions of that hotel, of Cranberry Pines. Together, they all contributed to something bigger than each of them could individually. Whether she liked it or not, Clara was a part of the legacy of this hotel. What she did here today mattered. It would define, in some small way, the hotel's history.

Clara felt her phone buzz in her coat pocket. She took it out to see a text come in from Janie. It was a picture—the selfie she had taken with Laura and Ava at the squadron the other day. The four of them, all in their matching aprons, had huge smiles, aside from Clara, who appeared bewildered. She looked at the picture and couldn't help but smile now.

Her thoughts suddenly turned to those military spouses she had met the other day. She thought about everything she'd learned from them. When things went wrong during a deployment, which they inevitably would, they simply handled it. On their own. These ladies were so incredibly independent because they had to be. They had no choice but to be the ones responsible for fixing things and solving problems. Even if they didn't want to.

And in the end—once they got to the other side—they were left with a feeling of accomplishment, a sense of independence, and confidence in knowing they could handle the next thing that would come their way.

She took a deep breath and slowly exhaled. *She* could do it too. She could get control of this. What other choice did she have?

"No!" she yelled to Lucy before she could pick up the phone. "Do *not* call Matthew."

"Really? Are you sure?"

"I'm sure."

She realized that in the midst of total darkness, it was easy to feel overwhelmed. What she needed now was to push through the fear of the unknown and get to the other side of things. There would always be light at the end of a dark tunnel. Sometimes, one simply didn't know how to get to it or how long it might be before they would see it.

Clara understood at that moment that she had no other choice but to get through this as best she could. A huge smile spread across her face as the realization hit her like a ton of bricks. She really *could* handle this. She didn't simply tell herself it; she believed it. For the first time in her life, Clara seemed to realize something about herself that she'd never truly known: She could do enormously hard things. She didn't need to try to avoid them all the time. Sometimes, the best way to deal with a challenge was to face the struggle head-on—whether you wanted to or not.

The realization was so simple, but also seemed so massive.

Clara shook off her insecurity with a poised nod. "Okay, everybody, let's get to work."

An attitude of confidence began to quickly replace the panic. Clara rallied the staff behind the desk. She thought about Brent, with his checklists and his constant well-thought-out plans. She had always thought that approach to life seemed like more work than it was worth. When it came to solving problems, her approach had always been to hope they'd go away. She laughed now at the absurdity of that philosophy.

Maybe snapping her fingers—or making a wish—wasn't actually the best way to tackle a tough situation. Magic may be easy, but nothing could replace hard work.

She looked at the staff, all knowledgeable in their individual departments, and for the first time wondered what *she* was actually capable of. Did she really have what it took to lead this hotel out of darkness? Well, the time had come to find out. She needed to come up with a plan. Then, she needed to see it through. Clara made a quick checklist in her head of the most pressing problems and quickly reviewed everything she'd learned by working with the staff over the past few weeks. They all looked back at her, ready to receive her direction.

"Maintenance, I need you in conference room A in ten minutes so we can talk about the plan for getting the generators working. First, bring all the flashlights you can find from the utility closet so we can see what tools we have to work with. I need someone to find the manufacturer's manual for the generators so we can start working on the problem."

The three maintenance men all nodded and headed off in the appropriate direction.

"Food and beverage, we're going to put all the perishables in ice chests for now. Let's salvage what we can from the restaurant. First, though, bring out all the snacks and sodas we have and put them out in the lobby. Cheese plates, veggies, fruit, deli meats . . . anything we have. These guests are going to need something to distract them from the cold." She nodded toward the fireplace. "Oh, and let's pull back the wine for now."

The chef gave a salute and hurried off toward the kitchen. The bartender nodded and headed to the lounge.

"Lucy, I need you to get all the housekeeping staff downstairs immediately. We are going to deliver every single one of our blankets and extra bedding to all occupied guest rooms. We should also bring everyone some candles while we're at it."

Lucy nodded. "You got it, boss."

"Let's go, team," Clara said with an enthusiastic clap. "The Darlington is known for its exceptional service, and this is no time to let up."

As the staff scattered, left alone behind the check-in desk, Clara wondered if she could actually pull this off. She had no idea how long the power would be out. She had no idea how everything would turn out. She had no idea if anything would work out at all. She was in the midst of total darkness, both literally and figuratively. But deep down, Clara knew there was light on the other side. She could do it.

She just needed to deal with one problem at a time— just like those military spouses.

CHAPTER TWENTY-SIX
CLARA

The Darlington Hotel was once again warm and full of light. Clara smiled as the backup generators buzzed, having restored the lobby to a state of grandeur and brilliance. She sat by the fire alone, a warm cup of coffee in her hand. The guests were happy to be back in their rooms or in the restaurant. She looked around at the decorations, fully illuminated again. The sounds of the lobby Christmas music playing made her take in a slow, easy breath.

She tipped her head back as she sank deeper into her chair. She was exhausted, but she felt great. The hotel had power again, and the staff had everything back under control. She had really done it. She had got them through the crisis.

This was what real accomplishment felt like, she realized now. It wasn't something she had ever felt with Matthew helping her get a job, or by telling her what she wanted to hear, or by making things happen for her. Clara wondered why she'd wasted so much of her life running from the hardest things in life. The most rewarding things.

Enjoying her coffee, she took a moment to think about

her career and reconsidered whether working for the Darlington was really what she wanted. Was it possible that by Matthew giving her opportunity after opportunity, it had become too easy for her to stay and take them?

It seemed like she was stuck in a career that he had carved out for her more than one she'd set out to get for herself. Maybe what she really needed was to branch out on her own. Maybe she needed to independently make her career what she wanted it to be instead of doing what Matthew had encouraged her to do.

She thought again about what Ava and Laura had said—that military spouses' lives and careers didn't have to fit into the traditional mold. Each of them was capable of making the choices that best suited them and their families. These families were giving so much of their lives for this country's freedom. Didn't they deserve the freedom to have choices in their lives? Of course they did. And if they could do it, then she certainly could too.

A cold rush of air hit Clara, interrupting her thoughts, as the doors to the Darlington swung open. A bundled-up man appeared in the lobby, breathless and panting. Taking off his hat and shaking the snow out of his hair, he looked around the lobby until he caught her eye. Matthew.

He spotted her immediately and hurried over. He stopped in front of the fire to warm his hands, then turned to her with a nod. "I heard the power was out here and figured you'd need me."

"I appreciate you coming but—"

"Don't worry, I'll take care of things." He looked straight over Clara's head, scanning the lobby. "It looks like the power's back on, but I'm sure there's a mess of problems waiting for me." He quickly turned to head in the direction of the desk.

"Matthew, I don't need your help."

He stopped mid-stride and turned around. "What's that?"

"I took care of it." She continued sipping her coffee calmly by the fire.

He looked at her underneath a skeptical brow. "*You* handled all this?"

"Yes," she replied, a relaxed smile on her face.

Matthew let out a slight laugh. He appeared to be taking another look around the lobby. All was calm, all was bright, and she could tell he seemed surprised. No, he was shocked. Clara knew he'd been expecting a disaster. He came over anticipating chaos; her complete reliance on him. He'd been prepared to see customers complaining, employees panicking, and her completely helpless. Matthew had come in here thinking he'd be the hero who was going to rescue her. He was definitely used to doing that.

"Matthew, I don't need your help anymore," she said. Saying the words out loud felt as if a boulder was lifted from her shoulders. "In fact, I never really did. I just thought I did."

He just looked at her, confusion in his eyes.

"But you were right," Clara continued.

He raised his eyebrows at her. "Oh, yeah, about what exactly?"

"That I do need experience in the operations side of running a hotel before I become a general manager."

"Well, I thought I'd given you that—"

She lifted her hand to interrupt. "But I want to get that on my own. I'm going to leave the Darlington."

He narrowed his eyes at her. "Oh, to go where?"

"Another property, maybe. Or another career entirely—who knows?"

"And do what?"

"Anything I want," she said. "I'm capable of it, after all."

Matthew seemed to be processing what she was telling him. He looked at her with interest, as if he was trying to gauge whether she was serious or not. Finally, he let out a resigned huff of air and walked back over to her by the fire and sat down. He crossed his leg over his knee and sat back in his chair. He didn't say anything for a while. He looked around again at the lobby, assessing the situation. He looked directly at her, a sincere smile beginning to replace the suspicion as he blew a stream of air through his lips. Finally, he spoke.

"Well, Clara, I have to admit, I am impressed. You've certainly surprised me here. Everything looks like it's completely under control."

She sipped on her coffee, a surge of excitement hidden behind a calm smile.

Matthew's gaze continued to linger on her eyes as if he was deep in thought.

She looked away.

"You know, I've been thinking about us lately." He smiled.

Her eyes shot open. "Us?"

He uncrossed his legs and leaned forward in his chair. "Yeah. I mean, maybe we should give things another try. What do you think?"

Clara nearly spit out her coffee. She thought about how many times she had heard those words from him over the years. How every time she would believe them—because she wanted to believe them—only to end up hurt again.

Wasn't it just like him to choose a moment like now to

throw this at her? Right when everything was beginning to feel under control. Just when she knew exactly what she wanted in life—and *who* she wanted.

Clara wondered why she had wasted so much time with him over the years. She could see he wasn't good for her, that he never had been. Matthew seemed to look down on her in a way she'd never truly noticed before. Or perhaps she had, but didn't want to acknowledge it. Why had she spent so much of her time chasing after his approval anyway?

She supposed the honest answer was that she hadn't believed enough in her own abilities. She had always felt she needed Matthew in order to accomplish anything big. The simplest answer, though, was that the relationship was easy. Matthew was there, day in and day out. It had been too easy to stay in a relationship with him and too difficult to get out of one.

It was more complicated than that, though. When they first met, Matthew had been a great boyfriend. Attentive and kind, he genuinely seemed to want to impress her and to please her. That was until he'd had her for a while. Several years and many breakups later, Clara supposed he started taking her for granted. Maybe she had made the relationship too easy on him by always going along with whatever he'd wanted her to do.

Perhaps having to work hard for something, especially a relationship, made someone appreciate it more. Maybe enduring hardship for what you really wanted was a necessary part of life. Perhaps without that, you can never know how much you value it. It made sense after all. Look at Brent; he had put a ton of work into their relationship over the past year, and he seemed to be more in love with her than Matthew had ever been. Yes, Brent did seem to adore her, didn't he? She smiled just thinking about it.

Well, this time was different. It was the easiest decision Clara would ever have to make.

"Definitely not, Matthew."

"Oh." He looked as if he'd been punched in the gut.

She let out a sigh. "It's time I move on from you—for good."

He seemed slightly stunned, slowly beginning to drop his eyes to his lap. He appeared to be hurt. Clara suddenly realized this could be the first time she'd ever been the one to hurt *him*. The first time she'd ever had any sense of control in the relationship at all. In a moment of pity, she took him gently by the hand. If there was anyone who could understand how this felt, it was her.

She softened. "The truth is, Matthew, that I'm in a relationship now that makes me happier than ever."

He scoffed. "Oh, you mean the guy who hasn't been around at all. The *Top Gun* pilot who took off and left you for an entire year. That guy? Meanwhile, I've been the one here for you, day in and day out."

Clara paused, finally looking at him through entirely different eyes than she ever had before. "Matthew, this is goodbye for us." She paused again, giving his hand a squeeze. "But I do appreciate everything you've done for me. Really."

It was true. Clara was grateful for the many opportunities Matthew had given her over the years. She realized, though, that that wasn't the same thing as being in love. She was truly beginning to understand love in a completely different way. It was what she felt for Brent. She closed her eyes and thought of him. She glowed with excitement. Yes, she was, without a doubt, falling in love with Brent.

Her eyes popped wide open. She needed to tell Brent everything. She needed to explain to him why, up until now, she hadn't been able to understand how he could have been so sure about their relationship. She couldn't understand why he'd been ready to make a lifelong commitment to her already. She couldn't understand how his feelings were so much stronger than hers. But now, she understood perfectly—because she now understood what real love was.

It wasn't necessarily easy, that was for sure. Sometimes, it didn't show up the way you had planned. Sometimes, it required more patience and understanding than you thought you were capable of. At times, it was just plain hard. But it was *always* worth it.

The realization took her by surprise as she finally understood the reality of her feelings. It hadn't been Christmas magic that she'd needed to fall in love. No magic was needed for her to realize her feelings for Brent.

It hadn't mattered whether she figured it out over Christmas, over a deployment, or over a cup of coffee. Clara knew without a doubt that she was actually in love with Brent.

"Goodbye, Matthew," she said one last time.

He looked to the floor and shook his head, seeming to wallow in the rejection. After a moment, he looked up and nodded in understanding. They both stood, and he reached toward her for a final hug. Clara let him hold her for a moment. She smiled and let all her breath out of her lungs with explosive relief. A heaviness left her that she hadn't realized she'd been carrying around for many years. It felt so good to finally let go of that part of her life.

CHAPTER TWENTY-SEVEN
BRENT

The cold wind whipped Brent in the face as he made his way to the Darlington through the heavy snow. He'd been forced to park his truck back at Clara's house and walk over since the city streets were covered in a thick layer of ice. He wasn't going to let her do this alone, not when he could be there to support her. She had been *his* constant source of support over the past year. He still didn't know if she understood how important that had been—and still was—to him. All he knew was that it was time he tried to repay the favor.

As he made the difficult trek over to the Darlington, Brent thought back to the first time he had met Clara there. She'd seemed so confident at her job, so knowledgeable about the hotel. He knew she could manage this. He knew she had the good judgment and sharp leadership skills to be successful. Still, he felt bad that she had to leave so abruptly.

Clara had been trying to tell him something important for weeks. He knew they still needed to have a long talk about their future. Right now, though, Brent had no plan for what he would do once he got to the hotel. He didn't know if there was anything he really *could* do to help her. He wasn't even sure she'd want his help. All he knew was that he wanted to be there. He realized he couldn't always be present physically. But when he could, he was going to show up for her.

Brent finally arrived at the Darlington, out of breath with exhaustion and chilled to the bone. He entered through the lobby doors, hit with a welcome wave of warmth. He immediately spotted Clara sitting by the fire in the corner of the lobby.

His muscles tightened. She was talking to *him*—Matthew. A deep jealousy came over Brent as he glared at the two of them through narrowed eyes. He knew Matthew had been her boss for years. He knew they used to date. He knew they had a long history together. What he didn't know was why he was there with her now.

Brent moved closer to them, standing out of view behind the Christmas tree. He watched as Clara talked to Matthew, a peaceful smile on her face. He leaned closer, trying to make out what she was saying, but Christmas music was coming from the speaker right beside his ear. Brent frowned. He moved around the backside of the tree to get a better viewing position.

Clara reached for Matthew's hand and held it, telling him how much she appreciated everything he'd done for her. Brent's heart plummeted to the floor. He suddenly felt sick to his stomach.

He watched Matthew take her in his arms for a long embrace. Struck with a startling realization, Brent felt his world fall apart.

Clara was still in love with Matthew. It all made sense

now. That explained why she had been so distant since he'd returned home. It explained why all the memories from the past year had been so much more important to him than they were to her. It certainly explained why she hadn't accepted his proposal with more enthusiasm. Of course. She had probably been growing closer to Matthew the entire time he had been away.

With Brent deployed, she'd probably felt sorry for him and didn't want to break his heart while he was overseas. Then, he'd proposed so publicly she couldn't have possibly turned him down in front of everyone. No wonder she'd been acting so strange about everything.

This whole time, Brent thought they were just going through an adjustment period after some time apart. Now, he knew the hard truth. She was in love with Matthew, not him. It made sense. What Clara wanted was someone who could actually be there for her every day.

And perhaps it was what she really deserved. Brent felt as if time had stopped completely. All the color drained from his face. He nodded his head in sudden under-standing.

That must have been what she'd been trying to tell him —but couldn't. Each time she'd tried, it was obvious she had been expecting a difficult conversation. Clara had tried to tell him for weeks—they just kept getting interrupted. He felt like an idiot, having dragged on this relationship that she'd been trying to get out of since he'd been back.

He thought about the past year and what it had meant to him. He thought they'd been growing so close as a couple. He thought they had truly fallen in love in such a special way. How could he have been so blind? How could he have been so stupid?

His heart sank. He shook his head. After all the work he

had put into their relationship, Brent finally realized that when it came to love, his plans didn't matter. No matter what he did or how hard he worked, the heart was more powerful than anything within his control.

Heartbroken, Brent slowly backed out of the Darlington Hotel.

CHAPTER TWENTY-EIGHT
CLARA

It was Christmas Eve and already afternoon by the time Clara managed to get on the road. Her stomach was filled with butterflies as she was finally able to make her way over to Brent's house. She'd been forced to wait for hours while the roads were being cleared from yesterday's storm. She had tried to call him all morning, but he hadn't answered his phone, his battery likely dead from the power outage.

As soon as the roads opened, Clara couldn't wait to get going—to get to Brent. She arrived at his house just as the bright afternoon sun lit up the perfectly unclouded sky. After yesterday's storm, the clarity of the blue sky seemed like a metaphor for what was going on in her mind. Clara took a slow, deep breath and savored the feel of the frosty air filling her lungs. Her feelings for Brent, now clear to her, brought her a happiness she had never quite experienced before. She was overcome with a surprising exhilaration over her newly discovered emotions.

Clara smiled, appreciating the significance of the day. She felt that same excited anticipation that the day before Christmas had always brought her ever since she was a child. Full of possibilities, Christmas Eve had always served as an exciting prequel to a day she knew would bring her joy, gifts, and hope for the new year. The waiting was brutal at times, but the excitement of the next day was assured. It described exactly what she was feeling at the moment. She was on the verge of something wonderful—a fresh start and a bright future with Brent.

She still didn't know how she was going to explain the complexities of the entire wish situation to him. She needed to find a way, though—and quick. This was a conversation she would not avoid any longer. It was time she finally told him the truth about everything. She needed to come clean about her year—or lack of it—so they could truly be on the same page. It was the only way they could move forward.

The simple truth was that she loved him, and she knew with all her heart that he was worth going through all the hardships of a long deployment. Clara only wished she had realized it sooner.

It was more than that, though. Clara understood that she *wanted* to go through it. She wished she could have really gotten to know him, slowly, the way he got to know her. She knew this deployment would have made them stronger as individuals and as a couple—like Ava and Laura had said. Like Grams had said. Clara just wished she hadn't robbed herself of the whole experience.

It was such a dumb wish anyway—a simple solution to a complicated problem. She thought about everything that wish had deprived her and deprived Brent of. The regret she felt for skipping over the year was only made worse by the hurt it had caused him. She needed to talk to him.

Clara approached Brent's house, her legs shaking with nervous anticipation.

An unexpected greeting with a southern accent took her by surprise. "Hey, Clara."

She turned to find Brent's friend sitting on a rocking chair on the front porch. "Oh, hi, Will. Where's Brent?" she asked quickly.

Will shook his head. "Apparently, he volunteered for a mission. It looks like he just left."

"A mission?"

Will shrugged.

"When will he be back?"

"I can't really talk about it—operational security and all that." He frowned. "But I don't think he's going to be back anytime soon."

Clara recalled the Christmas Eve mission Brent had been discussing with his commander at the party. She specifically remembered his commander telling him that he wouldn't be assigned to it since he'd recently returned from a deployment. She knew she hadn't misunderstood that. Surely, nothing had changed. Besides, would he really leave without telling her? Something wasn't right here.

She bit her lower lip. "What do you mean—he volunteered?"

Will shrugged. "He must have. His name showed up on the roster for it late last night."

Clara felt her stomach tighten. Her heart raced as her brain tried to understand what Will was telling her. "But why would he do that?"

"That's exactly what I was wondering myself. When I saw his name on the flight plan, I came by to check on him. I figured something must be wrong. I mean, I couldn't imagine what would make him *volunteer* to fly at Christmas after waiting so long to spend the holidays with you."

Clara was silent, staring ahead in a fog of disbelief.

"But when I got here, he was already gone." Will looked at her sideways. "Is everything okay with you two?"

A sickness overtook her stomach as the realization came together in her mind. Her legs gave way to a slight wobble, and she had to hold on to the porch rail to keep herself upright. She shook her head, looking at the ground, not quite able to accept what Will was telling her.

She was too late. She had waited too long to tell Brent the truth—to tell him how she really felt. Now, he was gone.

Clara felt the sharp sting of tears forming, and her lower lip quivered. How could she possibly have messed this up any worse? She finally understood her real feelings for him, but it made no difference now. She was too late.

Will stood up and held out an envelope. "I found this on the doorstep. It's for you." He handed it to Clara and gave her a sympathetic pat on the shoulder. "Well, I've gotta run, but I hope everything works out between you two." He gave her one last look of sympathy before turning to leave. "Merry Christmas."

Will left, leaving her standing on Brent's front porch alone, holding the red envelope with her name on it. Her entire body shook with fear. She sat down on the rocking chair and opened the envelope slowly, terrified to read the contents.

Dear Clara, I'm sorry we won't be spending Christmas together after all, but duty calls. I'm also sorry for everything I put you through over the past year; I really thought we could make it work. I understand now, though, that this entire situation was too much to ask of you. It wasn't fair to you, and you deserve more. You'll never know how much the past year meant to me. Being your boyfriend, even from afar, was the greatest year of my life. In fact, I'd do it all over again if I could. I'm sorry that I ultimately couldn't give you what you needed. I wish you all the best in life.

Love always, Brent.

The excitement of Christmas Eve and all its anticipation instantly vanished before her as she understood the sad truth—Christmas would not be coming for her. Clara dropped her face into her hands, clutching the note, and began to cry.

She had ruined everything. She had wanted everything to be so easy and fast—so simple. In the process, she had completely lost sight of what really mattered. She had deprived them both of what they needed most in their new relationship—time.

All they'd really needed was time to grow together as a couple. That was exactly what the deployment would have given them. Clara's grandmother had been right when she had told her not to deprive herself of what could be a blessing in disguise. It *would* have been a blessing, more than Clara could have even imagined—if only she hadn't been so impatient. If only she would have had the strength and the courage to endure it.

All this time, she thought that spending one Christmas together was all they needed. That if they could just be together—instead of thousands of miles apart—for Christmas, everything would work out. Clara realized it wasn't physical proximity they had needed. No, it was something more than that. It was the shared experiences, the common stories, and the memories. *That's* what really made Christmas—or life for that matter—special with someone.

Wait a minute, that was it! That was the answer to her security question.

She pulled out her phone and typed in the word *memories*.

Suddenly, she was in. There, in front of her, sat an endless digital montage of the past year. There were photos from Lily's wedding, videos of Clara and her grandmother planting their spring garden, links from several of the events she'd held at the Darlington. It was all there. An entire year she possessed absolutely no memory of. Sprinkled throughout the pictures were messages from friends. Happy birthdays around the time she turned another year older and, more recently, sincere messages of support. Some were from friends she hadn't spoken to in ages. They were all encouraging and uplifting, though underlined with a hint of sympathy.

Thinking of you during this difficult time

Wishing you comfort and strength

Sending you hugs

Did all these people really care that she'd been going through a stressful long-distance relationship? Perhaps they had heard that Brent had been injured. It was clear she'd been the only one left in the dark about it all.

Clara gritted her teeth, kicking herself for all the mistakes she had made. She wished she had known then what she knew now. If only she could go back in time and do everything differently.

She thought about what Brent had said in the letter: *I would do it all over again.* Was that true? Would he really be willing to do a yearlong deployment all over again, to be with her?

She stood up from the rocking chair and wiped the tears from her eyes. She clutched the letter to her chest. Maybe that was it. They would do it all over again! Except this time, they would do it together. He wouldn't endure another long deployment alone. No, this time she would be right by his side through it all.

Clara realized she needed to set things right, once and for all. If that enchanted ornament could make her skip a year—well, then it could probably work in reverse, right? She was going to fix this, and she knew exactly what she needed to do.

CHAPTER TWENTY-NINE
CLARA

Clara's bones shivered with nerves as she reached her grandmother's house just as the clear blue sky was beginning to give way to the night. She wished desperately that her grandmother was there instead of on the other side of an ocean. She needed to tell her about the wish she had made. She needed to tell her about the engagement. She needed to unload all the stress and embarrassment of the past few weeks. She needed so much from her: her advice, her comfort, and her help. She could do that later, though. Right now, she needed to get her hands on that magical ornament.

As Clara pulled into the driveway, she immediately noticed the uncharacteristic darkness. Not a single candle in a window, not a decoration on the house. It made sense that Grams wouldn't decorate if she wasn't spending the holidays there and didn't have her annual party to think about. Still, something didn't feel right about the scene in front of her. It was Christmas Eve, after all.

Clara pulled out her house key and slid it into the lock. No dogs barked.

"Hi, Clara," came a voice from behind her.

She turned around and recognized Mrs. Roberts, her grandmother's neighbor. She wore a long black coat and held her yellow labrador on a leash.

"Oh, hi, Mrs. Roberts. Merry Christmas. Do you know when my grandmother will be back?"

The older lady seemed not to hear her question. "I'm taking Max out for a quick walk, and then I'd be happy to come over and help with anything you need to do around the house."

"Oh, I'm just here to grab something."

Mrs. Roberts nodded. "Okay, then." She pulled back on Max's leash, who was ready to go. "Like I told your folks, I'm here to help with anything. I know they hadn't finished taking care of all her affairs yet. Your grandmother's voice-mail message is still the same as she left it over the summer." She tsked. "So sad."

"Excuse me?"

"They've been so busy taking care of things around here lately. I'm glad they were able to take a little break to travel for the holidays."

Clara swallowed the lump that was forming in her throat. "My grandmother? Grams. She's in Paris with them." Her eyes were wide with terror, waiting for her to answer. "Right?"

Mrs. Roberts looked back at her, a sympathetic tilt of the head. "Oh, Clara, I'm so sorry. I know Christmas must be especially hard for you. Your grandmother was a special lady."

Was? Clara became sickened with shock as she tried to make sense of what was going on. "What do you mean?" she asked, her voice a shaky whisper.

Mrs. Roberts shook her head, clearly puzzled by Clara's

confusion. "You poor dear. I know it's been six months already, but I'm sure it's still hard to accept."

Clara's eyes widened in disbelief. "You mean, she—" She couldn't continue, the words too awful to say out loud.

Those messages on her social media account. *Thinking of you during this difficult time, wishing you comfort and strength, sending you hugs.*

Mrs. Roberts shook her head. "It was a surprise to us all. She had always been so healthy. It goes to show, you never know how much time you have left. We never could have imagined that summertime trip to Paris would be her last one." She shook her head and clicked her tongue.

Clara stared ahead in utter astonishment.

Mrs. Roberts turned her attention back to Max as he began to pull her in the direction he wanted to go. "Well, let me know if you need help going through her things. I know it can be a lot of work. I'll be around. Merry Christmas, dear." Mrs. Roberts and Max left her standing alone in shock on her grandmother's front porch.

Clara's head started spinning as she grasped the reality of the crushing situation. Grams had died. She held an arm against her stomach and leaned over, hardly able to stand.

Grams wasn't in Paris with her parents. She was gone. It was why she hadn't been able to get her help through any of this—help she badly needed. She would never get her grandmother's help on anything ever again. She would never *see* Grams again. There would be no more Christmases at her house. No more cocoa by the fire, no more cozy fireside chats. Clara had missed her grandmother's last months of life.

What had she done? Clara dropped to her knees on her grandmother's porch and burst into tears. How could she have been so stupid as to make that wish? How could she have deprived herself of all that precious time with the person she loved more than anyone in the world? How could she have been so short-sighted as to skip right over an entire year of her life? She felt as if she were swimming in an enormous sea of regret, fighting the current of her choices. Her thoughts whirled around in her head. Her hands clutched her throat.

With time being so valuable, especially with loved ones, Clara couldn't believe she had squandered so much of hers the way she did. And for what? It had all been to simply avoid an unwanted experience. One that didn't cooperate with her desired timeline. And just look at what it cost her.

Clara sat on the front steps, her entire body heaving as she sobbed. She had no control over the tears that poured out and no control over her violent shaking. She had no control of anything anymore.

She had lost Grams. And she had lost Brent. She felt like she had the previous night at the Darlington—when she had just wanted to snap her fingers and disappear.

But she couldn't do that. No, she needed to do something harder than that—she needed to fix this. Suddenly, Clara decided to stop crying and set things right, once and for all. She needed to push through despite the crushing darkness. She needed to roll up her sleeves and take care of what needed to be done. She needed to undo that wish.

Clara got up from the porch steps with a determined nod, wiping her coat sleeve against her eyes. She turned the key in the lock to let herself in and headed straight through the darkness of the empty house and up to the attic. She found the box of Christmas decorations right away and dug through it.

Her eyes grew big. Sparkling like the brilliant Christmas star leading her in the right direction, the ornament appeared before her eyes. She opened it, stared at the pocket watch, and shook her head. She looked at the photo of her grandparents and spoke aloud to it.

"I should have been here to spend that last Christmas with you, Grams."

Her eyes landed on something else in the box. It appeared to be an old stack of weathered letters tied up in a red bow. She wasn't sure why they were in there with the Christmas decorations, but her gut told her she needed to look at them.

Clara carefully untied the ribbon and sifted through the letters. They were written decades ago by her grandparents. The latest one was dated November 1967. That was one month before that photo was taken. One month before the Christmas they met and fell in love.

They had known each other before that Christmas? From the bundle of letters in her hand, it appeared they had been writing to each other for months before that fateful holiday. Clara unfolded the letter that sat on the top of the stack and read.

My dearest Phyllis, I'll be finally coming home soon, just in time for Christmas. I can't wait to see you in person after all this time. The letters we have written each other over the past year have provided me with a comfort that my words could never explain. I am so grateful for that serendipitous note you sent on a whim to boost the spirits of some lonely soldier you'd never met. From that first correspondence, I knew there was something special about you. Now, after all these months of writing to each other, I feel as though I've known you my entire life. I can't wait to get home and spend the holidays together. My Christmas wish will soon come true.

Love, Frank

She thought again about what her grandmother had told her about that first Christmas with her grandfather. Clara had always assumed it had been so easy, some enchanted force that brought them together one evening. Evidently, it hadn't been that simple at all. Clara had known that her grandfather had just returned from war before they spent that first Christmas together. What she had *not* known was that they had written each other dozens of letters over that time, truly getting to know each other. That one holiday—that magical Christmas—was the culmination of months and months of communication. Of connection. She finally understood the real magic that was involved in her grandparents' love. It was the same one that had brought her and Brent together.

The simple truth was that there was no magic fix when it came to falling in love. It took time. It took hard work. It took patience.

She read the inscription on the ornament again. It was the same one she had read the other day, only now, she saw it in a whole new light.

Time is precious when love is new,

A Christmas wish will soon come true.

She read the first line again. *Time is precious when love is new.* Clara finally understood what it meant. Time is precious, and time together—shared experiences—is what makes it so valuable. She thought again about everything that wish had deprived her of. *I have to make this right.* Clara squeezed the ornament in her hand tightly, exactly as she had before. Mustering every ounce of faith in Christmas magic she could, Clara wished for what she now wanted more than anything in the world.

She wished she could have been around to spend the past year with Grams. She wished she could have been at Lily's wedding. She wished she had taken the time to get the experience she needed to achieve her career goals. Most importantly, she wished she had gone through that yearlong deployment with Brent. She needed to do the hard stuff and not take the easy way out—for herself, for Brent, and for their relationship. Clara closed her eyes and wished she had never made that wish at all.

The room instantly went black, leaving her once again, completely in the dark.

CHAPTER THIRTY

CLARA

Clara awoke to the sound of "Jingle Bells" coming from her phone. Startled out of a deep sleep, she rolled over to check it.

It was just a text, although a long one. Clara read it sleepily, her eyes still blurry from one of the best nights of sleep in a long time.

Good morning, sweetheart, sorry I fell asleep on you last night. I know this deployment will be hard, but I'm here for you. Also, I told your parents about Brent, and they decided they're coming home for Christmas. They said they can always take their cruise next year, but that they want to be home to support you right now. So it looks like we'll all be together this Christmas!

At the end was Gram's signature emoji, the one she ended every text with—the adorable hug emoji with the smiley face and splayed-out hands.

Clara blinked her eyes several times to make sure she

was seeing it correctly. Yes, this was undeniably from Grams. Her grandmother had sent her this message!

It took a minute for her thoughts to fully catch up. She sat up with a start. Her phone was playing "Jingle Bells" again! It wasn't playing "Blue Christmas." If she never changed her ringtone, then that meant . . .

Clara's eyes widened. Brent had never left.

Her heart raced as she rubbed the sleep out of her eyes to look at the date on her home screen. It was December 5, the day he was scheduled to leave for his deployment. She quickly tapped on the calendar app, her eyes going straight for the year. There, staring back at her, was the most beautiful sight she had ever seen.

It was the year she had met Brent. It was the year he had told her he was going to deploy. It was the year she had made that stupid wish. It was the year she had wanted to see.

Relief flooded Clara's entire body. She closed her eyes and said a sincere prayer of gratitude. She was back where she needed to be.

Her eyes widened as she saw the time on her phone. She should have been on base already. She needed to get there immediately. Clara was *not* going to let Brent leave without seeing her. She only hoped she wouldn't be too late.

CHAPTER THIRTY-ONE
BRENT

The jet engines roared. Brent paced back and forth, watching for the bus that would bring any last-minute guests out to the flight line.

He shifted his weight from one foot to the other, picked up his cap, and tugged at the top of his hair. The morning sky was gray and dreary. The heavy clouds overhead felt like a thick, somber blanket, weighing him down in a holding pattern of uncertainty. He longed to see a break in the clouds, just a sliver of sunlight peeking in. A glimmer of hope.

"Hey, man, are you waiting for someone?"

A thick southern accent interrupted his thoughts. Brent turned around to find another airman in a tan-colored flight suit identical to his. It was the uniform they'd be wearing for their desert deployment. He didn't recognize the guy.

Brent gave him a wry smile. "Yeah, but I don't think she's coming."

The airman gave him a nod of understanding. "I'm Will. I'm new to the squadron, and it looks like we'll be crewmates and roommates on this deployment."

"Nice to meet you, I'm Brent." He shook Will's hand, then turned back around for another look out to the flight line.

"So who are you waiting for?"

Brent sighed. "I guess it doesn't matter. It doesn't look like she's coming."

Will folded his arms across his chest and turned his gaze in the same direction. He bowed his head. "I'm sorry, dude. I know goodbyes can be rough. I just kissed my wife and daughters goodbye for a year. I can't believe it—my youngest is a baby. She'll be a toddler when I return."

Brent turned back to Will with a simple nod, a small gesture of solidarity. "I know this life can be hard on relationships."

Will raised his chin to the sky. Then he turned to Brent and gave him a compassionate slap on the back of his shoulder. "It'll all work out—if it's meant to. I'll see you on board." He walked off toward the plane, leaving Brent alone with his thoughts.

He supposed Will was right. It was fate that would determine whether things worked out between him and Clara. There wasn't anything he could do about it himself, whether he liked it or not. Brent could make checklists and plans until he was blue in the face, but at the end of the day, there were forces bigger than him that needed to work in their favor. From the way things looked, they wouldn't be working out at all.

She really hadn't come. Brent supposed he shouldn't have been too surprised. He knew she had been freaked out by his bombshell news last night. He knew she had been uncomfortable with the whole idea of a long-distance relationship. Still, he sincerely believed they could have made it work. He only wished she had thought so too. He shook his head in resignation.

Brent shuffled to the C-17 and loaded the last of his deployment gear onto the aircraft. He turned around to take one more look for any late arrivals. It was finally time to accept that Clara wasn't coming. He knew the separations of military life weren't for everyone. Brent stared off into the distance at nothing in particular, then gave a half-hearted shrug. She just wasn't willing to go through this. Unfortunately for him, it was outside of his control.

CHAPTER THIRTY-TWO
CLARA

Clara's heart raced as she arrived at the base and frantically hurried to the security office. She was desperate to get out to the flight line. She needed to get there, to see Brent before he left.

"Please, my name is right there on the list," she pleaded to the security officer. "I'm running late, and I have to get out there—now."

"Well, ma'am, there's a little bit of paperwork we need you to—"

"Airman Peck!" Clara recognized the same old stodgy Senior Airman immediately. She ran over to him with a look of desperation. "Please, I need to get out there immediately. You remember me, don't you?"

He looked at her sideways. "No, ma'am, I sure don't."

"I'm a friend of Major McNally's, and I have to see him before he leaves." Clara looked up at him, pleading with her eyes.

Airman Peck turned toward the security desk, looking for confirmation. The guy only nodded. He looked back at her and softened a bit. He let out a long sigh. "Well, okay. Come on."

Clara grabbed him by the shoulders and gave him a kiss on the cheek. "Thank you." She hurried ahead of him to the bus that would take her out to the flight line.

He followed behind, working hard to keep up with her fast pace.

They boarded the empty bus. Where was everyone else? Was she too late? Had she missed it completely?

"To the flight line. Now!" she said to the driver.

The driver turned to look at Airman Peck, who only shrugged his shoulders. "Go ahead, I guess," he said. "Let's get her out there."

Clara watched out the window as the bus started to move. She closed her eyes and said a prayer that she wouldn't be too late. She couldn't bear the thought of Brent leaving, thinking she never showed up. She needed to see him before he left. There was so much she needed to tell him.

She stiffened, her brain suddenly slammed with a new thought. What exactly *would* she tell him when she saw him? Clara had been ready to tell him the truth yesterday, about everything. She couldn't exactly do that now since they were back to the previous year. There was no wish to even tell him about. She hadn't skipped anything yet. In fact, she wouldn't be skipping anything at all. The whole messy ordeal had never even happened.

She certainly didn't want to tell him about her newly discovered feelings for him. Not yet, anyway. She didn't want to freak him out since they had just started dating. Clara laughed, feeling relieved to be back on a timeline that made sense to her. Besides, she wanted him to fall in love with her the right way—slowly.

No, all she needed to tell him now was that she was willing to do the hard work. To be in this relationship with him. The rest would work itself out in its own time.

Airman Peck tapped away at his tablet. "It looks like you're going to be okay, ma'am, the plane—"

"Look!"

As they approached the flight line, they both looked up to see a gray plane taking off into the foggy sky. Clara's heart sank. She was too late. She had missed him.

The bus came to a stop, and Clara immediately rushed off. Her eyes looked painfully at the sad sky and the departing plane as she stood at the bottom of the steps. She watched as it lifted higher into the sky, leaving her alone on the cold ground. She wrapped her arms around herself and dropped her chin to her chest. All the emotions of the past few weeks—or perhaps the past year—spilled out of her like a burst dam. She covered her face with her hands and leaned forward as she wept into them.

Airman Peck watched her from the top of the bus stairs. "Ma'am, are you okay?"

She looked up at him through her tears. "I never got to tell him," Clara cried.

He said nothing; he just stared at her with a stunned look.

"I never got to tell him that he's worth the wait." Clara paced back and forth, wringing out her hands as she thought about all the things she'd realized over the past few weeks.

She was no longer talking to Airman Peck. She was addressing her thoughts more to the sky—and to the plane that had left. "I didn't get to tell him that we would get through this year together. I didn't get to tell him that this deployment could be a blessing for us. That it could bring us closer together in a way I could have never understood initially. And I never got to tell him that I'd be honored to be a part of something as important as serving our country, even in the smallest of ways."

Well, Clara supposed there *had been* more she needed to tell him. It didn't matter now, though. She had been too late for any of it.

Airman Peck continued to stare at her. A hint of a smile crept in as his gaze fell behind her.

She turned around to see what he was looking at. Her eyes widened, and her jaw dropped. There, in a sand-colored flight suit, looking exactly the way he'd looked last year, was Brent. Another C-17 stood behind him, where several airmen were loading equipment.

A heavy weight immediately disappeared from her shoulders. She pressed her palms to her eyes and wiped the tears so that she could see more clearly. She stared at Brent. She hadn't missed him. She hadn't been too late.

He looked at her. His eyes sparkled, and his left dimple was exaggerated.

"Did you hear all that?" she asked.

He nodded and walked closer. "I was afraid you weren't going to come out and see me off." He shook his head. "I wasn't sure how I was going to deal with that. It wasn't part of my plan."

Relief flooded her as she smiled back. "Well, sometimes surprises can work out even better than our plans."

Brent smiled, coming even closer until he was right in front of her. "I couldn't agree with you more. Speaking of surprises, I have one for you, but you'll have to wait for Christmas morning to get it."

Clara closed her eyes in gratitude, thinking about the blue star she knew would be waiting for her. "I can't wait."

She stood on her tiptoes to hug him, then stopped to reconsider. "Actually, on second thought, some things are worth the wait."

Pulling her in close, he gazed into her eyes.

She ran a hand along his cheek. "Brent, I want to be here for you, no matter what you go through out there. I'm here to support you. Okay?"

He smiled back. "And I'll be here to support you too." He moved a piece of hair out of her face. "Speaking of . . . What are your big plans for the next year?"

Clara was quick to answer. She knew exactly what her priorities were going to be. "I'm going to spend a lot of time with my Grams—she won't be around forever, you know. I'm going to help Lily plan a beautiful wedding. And I'm going to quit my job at the Darlington and start something new."

Brent raised his eyebrows. "Really?"

She nodded.

"Wow. You seem to have it all figured out already."

She flinched, suddenly hit with a strange feeling. It was more like a realization of a concept she hadn't felt much of lately—reality. Sure, her magical experience had given her a glimpse into a future that *could* have been. But would it unfold that way now that she was back in the real world?

Clara bit her lip as she realized she knew the truth; she had no idea what was actually in store for her year ahead or for her future in general. How could she? How could anybody know what the next year would bring? She closed her eyes and felt that same feeling of intense fear she had when Brent had first told her about the deployment. What would happen? Would it all work out? Could she actually do this?

No, she wouldn't let these thoughts hold her back this

time. She was an entirely different person now. Clara knew things about herself that she didn't then. She knew she was capable of handling whatever life threw at her. She knew that time and patience were vital for life and love to flourish. And she knew that sometimes you simply needed to be brave and take a chance, even if there were no guarantees.

She shrugged in reply. "Actually, the only thing I really do know about the next year is that I'm going to make a lot of memories—with you."

Brent smiled and pulled her close to him.

She pressed herself against his chest, her heart pounding with excitement.

The gray sky suddenly gave way as a bright ray of sun sliced through the clouds. A light snow began to gently fall around them. The sound of jet engines roared in the background. It was the most comforting sound in the world.

Brent leaned down and pressed his lips to her mouth. She melted into him, and it felt like magic. Clara had the distinct feeling that this Christmas would be their best one ever, even though they'd be apart.

With the year they had in store for them, she knew one thing was certain—the real magic was just getting started.

The End

ACKNOWLEDGMENTS

First and foremost, my deepest appreciation goes to all the readers who picked up my debut novel. Thank you for embarking on this exciting journey with me.

I would also like to express my sincere gratitude to Jenny Hale, the founder and director of Harpeth Road Press, for believing in this story and taking a chance on a brand-new author. I will always be grateful to have you as a mentor and for having Harpeth Road as my publisher.

Many thanks to my incredible editors at Harpeth Road —Charlotte Fry, Donna Hillyer, Becky Philpott, Lara Simpson, and Lauren Finger. Thank you for giving me the tools and insights I needed to polish up this story. I have become a better writer thanks to your experience and talent. Special thanks to Vanessa Mendozzi, for your creative vision in designing a beautiful cover that draws readers into my book.

My heartfelt thanks to my mom, dad, and sister, who have been my constant source of support long before this book came into existence. A special thank you to my three wonderful daughters. To my oldest, for showing me the magic that can happen when we try new things—you are an inspiration. To my middle daughter, for always being by my side—you are my very own cheerleader. And to my youngest, for stoking my creativity with your imagination—I owe the title of this book to you.

Finally, to my incredible husband. Thank you for

believing in me. Your continuous encouragement and support were essential in making this book a reality, but it was your enduring love that inspired it.

Above all, thanks be to God for the seeds He sows and the gifts He gives.

AUTHOR LETTER

Hello!

Thank you so much for picking up my novel, *Wishing for Christmas*. I hope this story surrounds you with the magic of the season and leaves you feeling warm and uplifted.

If you'd like to know when my next book is out, you can sign up for new Harpeth Road release alerts for my novels here:

www.harpethroad.com/caroline-stowe-newsletter-signup

I won't share your information with anyone else, and I'll only email you when I have news or when new books are released.

If you enjoyed *Wishing for Christmas*, I'd be so grateful if you'd write a review online. Feedback from readers helps persuade others to pick up my book for the first time. It's one of the biggest gifts you could give me.

With love,
　　Caroline